You can find them online at:
ChristinaLaurenBooks.com
Facebook.com/ChristinaLaurenBooks
@ChristinaLauren

ROOMIES

CHRISTINA
LAUREN

piatkus

PIATKUS

First published in the US in 2017 by Gallery Books,
an imprint of Simon & Schuster, Inc.
First published in Great Britain in 2017 by Piatkus

1 3 5 7 9 10 8 6 4 2

A CIP catalogue record for this book
is available from the British Library.

TPB ISBN 978-0-349-41754-7

Printed and bound in Great Britain by
Clays Ltd, St Ives plc

Papers used by Piatkus are from well-managed forests
and other responsible sources.

MIX
Paper from
responsible sources
FSC® C104740

Piatkus
An imprint of
Little, Brown Book Group
Carmelite House
50 Victoria Embankment
London EC4Y 0DZ

An Hachette UK Company
www.hachette.co.uk

www.littlebrown.co.uk

ROOMIES

one

According to family legend, I was born on the floor of a taxi.

I'm the youngest of six, and apparently Mom went from "I have a bit of a cramp, but let me finish making lunch" to "Hello, Holland Lina Bakker" in the span of about forty minutes.

It's always the first thing I think about when I climb into a cab. I note how I have to shimmy with effort across the tacky seat, how there are millions of neglected fingerprints and unidentifiable smudges clouding the windows and Plexiglas barrier—and how the floor of a cab is a *really* terrible place for a baby to meet the world.

I slam the taxi door behind me to block out the howling Brooklyn wind. "Fiftieth Street station, Manhattan."

The driver's eyes meet mine in the rearview mirror and I can imagine what he's thinking: *You want to take a cab t*

*subway in Manhattan? Lady, you could take the C train all the
way there for three bucks.*

"Eighth Ave. and Forty-Ninth Street," I add, ignoring the
clawing flush of awareness that I am absurd. Instead of taking
the cab all the way home, I'm having the driver take me from
Park Slope to a subway stop in Hell's Kitchen, roughly two
blocks from my building. It's not that I'm particularly safety
minded and don't want this cabbie to know where I live.

It's that it's Monday, approximately eleven thirty, and Jack
will be there.

At least, he should be. Since I first saw him busking at the
Fiftieth Street station nearly six months ago, he's been there
every Monday night, along with Wednesday and Thursday
mornings before work, and Friday at lunchtime. Tuesday he's
gone, and I've never seen him there on the weekend.

Mondays are my favorite, though, because there's an intensity in the way he crouches over his guitar, cradling it, seducing
it. Music that seems to have been trapped inside all weekend
long is freed, broken only by the occasional metallic tumble of
pocket change dropped into the open guitar case at his feet, or
the roar of an approaching train.

I don't know what he does in the hours he's not there. I'm
also fairly certain his name isn't Jack, but I needed to call him
something other than "the busker," and giving him a name
made my obsession seem less pathetic.

Sort of.

The cabbie is quiet; he isn't even listening to talk radio or
any of the other cacophonous car-filler every New Yorker gets
used to. I blink away from my phone and the Instagram feed

full of books and makeup tutorials, to the mess of sleet and slush on the roads. My cocktail buzz doesn't seem to be evaporating as quickly as I'd hoped, and by the time we pull up to the curb and I pay the fare, I still have its giddy effervescence simmering in my blood.

I've never come to see Jack while drunk before, and it's either a terrible or a fantastic idea. I guess we're about to find out which.

Hitting the bottom of the stairs, I catch him tuning his guitar and stop a few feet away, studying him. With his head bowed, and in the beam of the streetlight shooting down the stairs, his light brown hair seems almost silver.

He's suitably scruffy for our generation, but he looks clean, so I like to think he has a nice apartment and a regular, well-paying job, and does this because he loves it. He has the type of hair I can't resist, neat and trimmed along the sides but wild and untamed on top. It looks soft, too, shiny under the lights and the kind of hair you want to curl a fist around. I don't know what color his eyes are because he never looks up at anyone while he plays, but I like to imagine they're brown or dark green, a color deep enough to get lost in.

I've never seen him arrive or leave, because I always walk past him, drop a dollar bill in his case, and keep moving. Then, covertly from the platform, I look over—as do many of us—to where he sits on his stool near the base of the stairs, his fingers flying up and down the neck of the instrument. His left hand pulls out the notes as if it's as simple as breathing.

Breathing. As an aspiring writer, it's my least favorite cliché, but it's the only one that suits. I've never seen someone's fingers move like that, as if he doesn't even have to think about it. In some ways, it seems like he gives the guitar an actual human voice.

He looks up as I drop a bill into his case, squinting at me, and gives me a quiet "Thanks very much."

He's never done that before—looked up when someone dropped money in his case—and I'm caught completely off guard when our eyes meet.

Green, his are green. And he doesn't immediately look away. The hold of his gaze is mesmerizing.

So instead of saying, "Yeah," or "Sure"—or nothing at all, like any other New Yorker would—I blurt, "Iloveyourmusicsomuch." A string of words breathlessly said as one.

I'm gifted with the humblest flicker of a smile, and my tipsy brain nearly shorts out. He does this thing where he chews on his bottom lip for a second before saying, "Do you reckon so? Well, you're very kind. I love to play it."

His accent is heavily Irish, and the sound of it makes my fingers tingle.

"What's your name?"

Three mortifying seconds pass before he answers with a surprised grin. "Calvin. And yours?"

This is a conversation. Holy shit, I'm having a conversation with the stranger I've had a crush on for months.

"Holland," I say. "Like the province in the Netherlands. Everyone thinks it's synonymous with the Netherlands, but it's not."

Oof.

Tonight, I've concluded two things about gin: it tastes like pinecones and is clearly the devil's sauce.

Calvin smiles up at me, saying cheekily, "Holland. A province *and* a scholar," before he adds something quietly under his breath that I don't quite make out. I can't tell if the amused light in his eyes is because I'm an entertaining idiot, or because there's a person directly behind me doing something awesome.

Having not been on a date in what feels like a millennium, I also don't know where a conversation should go after this, so I bolt, practically sprinting the twenty feet to the platform. When I come to a halt, I dig in my purse with the practiced urgency of a woman who is used to pretending she has something critical she must obtain immediately.

The word he whispered—*lovely*—registers about thirty seconds too late.

He meant my name, I'm sure. I'm not saying that in a false-modesty kind of way. My best friend, Lulu, and I agree that, objectively, we're middle-of-the-pack women in Manhattan—which is pretty great as soon as we leave New York. But Jack—Calvin—gets ogled by every manner of man and woman passing through the station—from the Madison Avenue trustafarians slumming it on the subway to the scrappy students from Bay Ridge; honestly, he could have his pick of bed partners if he ever took the time to look up at our faces.

To confirm my theory, a quick glance in my compact mirror reveals the clownish bleed of my mascara below my eyes and a particularly ghoulish lack of color in the bottom half of my face. I reach up and attempt to smooth the tangle of brown strands that every other moment of my life are straight and lifeless, but have presently escaped the confines of my ponytail and defy gravity around my head.

Lovely, at present, I am not.

Calvin's music returns, and it fills the quiet station in this echoing, haunting way that actually makes me feel even drunker than I thought I was. Why did I come here tonight? Why did I speak to him? Now I have to realign all these things in my brain, like his name not being Jack and his eyes having a defined color. The knowledge that he is Irish just about makes me feel crazy enough to go climb on his lap.

Ugh. Crushes are the worst, but in hindsight a crush from afar seems so much easier than this. I should stick to making up stories in my head and watching from a distance like a reasonable creeper. Now I've broken the fourth wall and if he's as friendly as his eyes tell me he is, he may notice me when I drop money in his case the next time, and I will be forced to interact smoothly or run in the opposite direction. I may be middle-of-the-pack when my mouth is closed, but as soon as I start talking to men, Lulu calls me Appalland, for how appallingly unappealing I become. Obviously, she's not wrong. And now I'm sweating under my pink wool coat, my face is melting, and I'm hit with an almost uncontrollable urge to hike my tights up to my armpits because they have slowly crept down beneath my skirt and are starting to feel like form-fitting harem pants.

I should really go for it and just shimmy them up my waist, because other than one comatose gentleman sleeping on a nearby bench, it's just me and Calvin down here, and he's not paying attention to me anymore.

But then the sleeping gentleman rises, zombielike, and takes one shuffling step toward me. Subway stations are awful when they're empty like this. They're caves for the leches, the harassers, the flashers. It isn't that late—not even midnight on a Monday—but I've clearly just missed a train.

I move to my left, farther down the platform, and pull out my phone to look busy. Alas, I should know that drunk and persistent men are often not swayed by the industrious presence of an iPhone, and the zombie comes closer.

I don't know if it's the tiny spike of fear in my chest or a draft passing through the station, but I'm hit with the cloying, briny smell of mucus; the sour rot of spilled soda sitting for months at the bottom of a trash bin.

He lifts a hand, pointing. "You have my phone."

Turning, I give him a wide berth as I circle back toward the stairs and Calvin. My thumb hovers over Robert's phone number.

He follows. "*You*. Come here. You have my phone."

Without bothering to look up, I say as calmly as possible, "Get the hell away from me."

I push Robert's name and hold the phone to my ear. It rings hollowly, one ring for every five of my pounding heartbeats.

Calvin's music swells, aggressively now. Does he not see this person following me around the station? I have the absurd thought that it really is remarkable how deeply he gets in the zone while playing.

The man starts this shuffling, lurching run in my direction and the notes tearing out of Calvin's guitar become a soundtrack for the lunatic chasing me down the platform.

My tights keep me from running with any amount of speed or grace, but his clunky run speeds up, turns more fluid with confidence.

Through the phone, I hear the tinny sound of Robert answering. *"Hey, Buttercup."*

"Holy crap, Robert. I'm at the—"

The man reaches out, his hand wrapping around the sleeve of my coat, jerking my phone away from my ear.

"Robert!"

"Holls?" Robert yells. *"Honey, where are you?"*

I grapple, trying to hold on because I have the sickening sense that I'm off balance. Dread sends a cold, sobering rush along my skin: the man is not helping me stay upright—he's *shoving* me.

In the distance, I hear a deep shout: "Hey!"

My phone skitters along the concrete. *"Holland?"*

It happens so fast—and I guess things like this always happen fast; if they happened slowly I'd like to think I'd do something, *anything*—but one second I'm on the nubby yellow warning line, and the next I'm falling onto the tracks.

two

've never been inside an ambulance before, and it's just as mortifying to snort awake in front of two sober professionals as I'd imagine it would be. A female paramedic with a permanent furrow etched into her forehead stares down at me, expression severe. Monitors beep. When I look around, my head becomes a rocket ship, counting down to some manner of combustive event. My arm is sore—no, not just sore, *screaming*. A glance down tells me it's already restrained in a sling.

With the distant roar of an oncoming train, I remember being pushed onto the tracks.

Someone pushed me onto the subway tracks!

My heart begins doing a chaotic version of kung fu in my chest and the panicked tempo is echoed by the various machines surrounding me. I sit up, struggling against the monumental wave of nausea, and croak, "Did you catch him?"

"Whoa, whoa." With concern in her eyes, the paramedic—

her name tag reads Rossi—gently urges me back down. "You're okay." She nods at me with confidence. "You're okay."

And then she presses a card into my hand.

National Suicide Prevention Lifeline
1-800-273-8255

I flip it over, wondering if the other side says,

Who to call when a drunk dude
pushes you onto the tracks

Unfortunately, it does not.

I look back up at her, feeling my face heat in indignation. "I didn't *jump*."

Rossi nods. "It's okay, Ms. Bakker." She misreads my mystified expression and adds, "We got your name from your purse, which we recovered just off the platform."

"He didn't take my purse?"

She presses her lips into a frown and I look around for backup. There are actually two paramedics here—the other is a scruffy Paramedic of the Month calendar-model type who is diligently charting something from where he stands just outside the ambulance. His name tag reads Gonzales. Beyond, a cop car is parked at the curb, and a pair of officers chat amiably near the open driver's-side door. I can't help but feel this isn't the smoothest way to intervene in a potential suicide situation: I've just pig-snorted, my skirt is awkwardly bunched near my hips, the crotch of my tights is somewhere south of the equator, and my shirt is unbuttoned to make room for the adhesive cardiac monitors. A suicidal individual might suffer a touch of humiliation here.

Scooching my skirt down with as much grace as I can manage, I repeat, "I didn't jump."

Gonzales looks up from his paperwork and leans against the ambulance door. "We found you there, sweetie."

I screw my eyes closed, growling at his condescension. This still doesn't add up. "Two paramedics just happened to be wandering through the subway right after I fell onto the tracks?"

He gives me a tiny flicker of a smile. "Anonymous caller. Said there was someone on the tracks. Didn't mention anyone pushing her. Nine times out of ten it's an attempt."

Anonymous caller.

CALVIN.

I see movement just outside the ambulance, at the curb. It's dark out, but it's definitely him, holy shit, and I see him just as he stands. Calvin meets my eyes for the briefest pulse before startling and jerking his face away. Without another look back, he turns to walk down Eighth Avenue.

"Hey!" I point. "Wait. Talk to *him*."

Gonzales and Rossi slowly turn.

Rossi makes no move to stand, and I stab my finger forward again. "*That* guy."

"*He* pushed you?" Gonzales asks.

"No, I think he's the one who called."

Rossi shakes her head; her wince is less sympathetic, more pitying. "That guy walked up after we arrived on scene, said he didn't know anything."

"He lied." I struggle to sit up farther. "Calvin!"

He doesn't stop. If anything, he speeds up, ducking behind a taxicab before jogging across the street.

"He was there," I tell them, bewildered. *Jesus, how much did I drink?* "It was me, that busker—Calvin—and a drunk man. The drunk guy was going for my phone, and shoved me off the platform."

Gonzales tilts his head, gesturing to the cops. "In that case, you should file a police report."

I can't help it—the rudeness just flies out of me: "You *think*?"

I'm given another flicker of a smile; no doubt it's because I don't look the part of a ballsy back-talker with my saggy tights and unbuttoned shirt with pink polka dots.

"Holland, we suspect your arm is broken." Gonzales climbs inside and adjusts a strap on my sling. "And you may have a concussion. Our priority now is getting you down to Mount Sinai West. Is there anyone who can meet you there?"

"Yeah." I need to call Robert and Jeff—my uncles. I look up at Gonzales, remembering how my phone was in my hand one moment, and I was being flung onto the tracks the next. "Did you also find my phone?"

He winces and looks up at Rossi, who gives me her first—apologetic—grin. "I hope you have their number memorized." She lifts up a Ziploc bag holding the shattered remains of my beloved device.

- - - -

Once my head is checked (no concussion) and my right arm is casted (fractured ulna), I file a police report from my hospital bed. It's only when I'm speaking to the two intensely intimidating officers that I register that I was avoiding making eye contact with the man grabbing me. I didn't get a good look at his face, though I can quite accurately describe his smell.

The cops exchange a look before the taller one asks me, "The guy got close enough to grab your jacket, yell at you, and shove you over onto the tracks, but you didn't see his face?"

I want to scream, *Obviously you have never been a woman running away from a creepy dude before!*, but instead let them move on. I can tell from their expressions that my lack of a physical description dissolves the credibility of my *I-didn't-jump* story, and in the wake of this mild humiliation I decide it would seem even more suspicious if I knew the name of the busker at the subway and he still failed to stick around to help me out. So I don't bother to mention Calvin by name, either, and they jot down my generic details with only the vaguest display of investment.

After they leave, I lie back, staring up at the blank gray ceiling. What a crazy night. I lift my good arm, squinting at my watch.

Morning.

Holy shit, it's nearly three. How long was I down there?

Above the dull throb that painkillers don't seem to dim, I keep seeing Calvin standing up from where he'd been waiting at the curb. It means something that he was still there when I came to, doesn't it? But if he was the anonymous caller—and I assume he must have been because we all know the zombie didn't have a phone—why didn't Calvin tell the police that someone pushed me? And why lie and tell them he wasn't a witness?

The telltale rushing click of dress shoes on linoleum crescendoes from the hallway, and I sit up, knowing what's coming.

Robert bursts past the curtain, followed more smoothly by Jeff.

"What. The. *Fuuuuuuuck.*" Robert stretches the last word into about seventeen syllables, and takes my face in his hands, leaning in, examining me. "Do you realize how freaked out we've been?"

"Sorry." I wince, feeling my chin wobble for the first time. "My phone got knocked out of my hand."

Seeing my family's panic makes the shock set in, and I start shaking wildly. Emotion rises like a salty tide in my chest. Robert leans in, pressing his lips to my cheek. Jeff steps closer, too, resting a gentle hand on my knee.

Although he isn't related to me by blood, I've known Uncle Robert my entire life; he met my mother's younger brother Jeff several years before I was born.

Uncle Jeff is the calm one; it's the midwesterner in him. He is steady, and rational, and deliberate. He is, you may have guessed, in finance. Robert, by contrast, is motion and sound. He was born in Ghana, and moved here when he was eighteen to attend the Curtis Institute of Music in Philadelphia. Jeff tells me that Robert had ten job offers when he finished, but he chose the position of youngest-ever concertmaster of the Des Moines Symphony because the two of them fell in love at first sight the weekend Robert was in town interviewing.

My uncles left Des Moines when I was sixteen and headed to Manhattan. By that point, Robert had been promoted out of the ensemble to become the conductor of the symphony. Moving off-Broadway, even as a musical director, was a big step down for him in pay and classical prestige, but musical theater is where Robert's heart beats, and—maybe more importantly for them—it's long been much easier for a dude to be happily married to a dude in New York than in Iowa. They have thrived here, and two years ago, Robert sat down and composed what would soon become the most popular production on Broadway, *It Possessed Him*.

Unwilling to live away from them for long, I came to Columbia for my MFA in creative writing, but have basically stalled out. Being a baby graduate with an MFA in New York makes me a mediocre guppy in an enormous school of brilliant fish. Without an idea for the Great American Novel or any aptitude for journalism, I was virtually unemployable.

Robert, my savior, got me a job in theater.

My official title is archivist—admittedly a strange role for a twenty-five-year-old with zero Broadway experience—and given that we already have a million photos of the production for the program, I'm keenly aware that this job was created solely as a favor to my uncle. Once or twice a week I'll walk around, randomly taking pictures of sets, costumes, and backstage antics for the press agency to use on social media. Four nights a week, I work front of the house selling *It Possessed Him* T-shirts.

But unfortunately, I can't imagine dealing with the wild bustle of intermission or holding my gigantic camera with only one good arm, and it punches an additional gust of guilt deep into my belly.

I am so useless.

I pull one of the pillows out from under my head and let loose a few screams into it.

"What's going on, Buttercup?" Robert pulls the pillow away. "Do you need more medicine?"

"I need more *purpose.*"

He laughs to dismiss this, bending to kiss my forehead. Jeff's gentle hand slips into one of mine in quiet solidarity. But Jeff—sweet, sensible, number-crunching Jeff—has found a love for throwing clay in the past year. At least he has the passion for pottery pushing him forward through the tedium of a Wall Street workday. I have nothing but my love for books other people have written, and the anticipation of seeing Calvin play guitar a few days a week at the Fiftieth Street station. After tonight's stunt, I'm not even sure I'll feel that anymore. The next time I see him, I'll be less inclined to swoon, and more inclined to get up in his face and ask why he allowed me to be thrown under the proverbial bus. Or train, as it were.

Maybe I'll go back to Des Moines while this fracture heals and take some time to think about what I really want to do with my degrees, because when it comes to liberal arts, one useless degree plus another useless degree equals zero jobs.

I look up at my uncles. "Did you call Mom and Dad?"

Jeff nods. "They asked if they should come out."

I laugh despite my dark mood. I'm sure that without even seeing the extent of my injuries, Jeff told them not to worry. My parents hate the urban bluster of New York so much that even if I were broken in half, in traction, it would still be better for everyone if they stayed in Iowa. Certainly it would be less stressful for me.

Finally, Jeff eases down on the mattress next to me and glances up at Robert.

I notice that Jeff licks his lips before he asks something difficult. I wonder whether he knows he does it. "So, what happened, Hollsy?"

"You mean, why did I end up on the C line tracks?"

Robert gives me a knowing look. "Yes. And since I'm confident the little suicide intervention advice we were just given in the waiting room was unnecessary, maybe you can tell us how you fell."

"A guy cornered me. He wanted my phone and when I got too close to the tracks, he shoved me over."

Robert's jaw drops. "That's what was happening when you called?"

Jeff's cheeks go brilliant red. "Did you file a—"

"Police report? Yeah," I tell him. "But he was wearing a hoodie, and you know how making eye contact with crazies only encourages them, so I couldn't say much other than that he was white, probably in his thirties, bearded, and drunk."

Jeff laughs dryly. "Sounds like most of Brooklyn on a Friday night."

I turn my eyes to Robert. "A train had just left, so there weren't any other witnesses."

"Not even Jack?" Both uncles know about my subway crush.

I shake my head. "His name is Calvin." Answering the

question that forms in their eyes, I say, "I'd had a couple cock-tails and asked him."

Robert grins down at me. "Liquid courage."

"Liquid idiocy."

His eyes narrow. "But you're telling me Calvin didn't see anything?"

"That's what he told the paramedics, but I think he was the one who called them."

Robert slides a sturdy arm around me, helping me up. "Well, you've been cleared to leave." He kisses the side of my head and utters six perfect words: "You're coming home with us tonight."

three

'm lucky enough to live alone in Manhattan—an absurd rarity, and owed entirely to the generosity of my uncles. Robert, for the job, of course, and Jeff because he makes a crap ton of money and pays a pretty big chunk of my rent. But as much as I love living in my little apartment, I'll admit I'm glad to not be there tonight. Going home with a broken arm to my small but lovely space would only remind me that I am a useless, phoneless, privileged heap of bones who is so pitiful she let a drunk dude harass her and push her off a subway platform. Being at Jeff and Robert's is cushy, but at least here I can scrounge up minimal value: after some sleep, I am the board game companion Jeff wishes he would find in Robert. I am the absurd singer-along Robert always wants in his company. And even with one arm, I am the cook that neither of them will ever be.

Jeff takes Tuesday off to make sure I'm okay, and when

we're all up and moving, around noon, I whip up a decent eggs Benedict for the three of us. Even with only one good arm I manage a better outcome than either of them would have. Robert fell in love with the dish sometime back in the nineties, and as soon as I was competent with a blender and frying pan he informed me that it needed to be my specialty because there is *Hollandaise* sauce on it. "Get it? Get it?" he always adds.

Jeff and I still groan every time.

The afternoon rolls by with the three of us curled up on the enormous couch, watching *Brigadoon* and *An American in Paris*. Robert told me to take the night off, and he doesn't need to be at work until around five today anyway. I know I won't see Calvin tonight, so I'm trying—and failing—to banish him from my thoughts. The memory of my first glimpse of his face and voice is blurred by a cocktail of feelings: First, there's disappointment. He was my happy place . . . why was I compelled to venture outside my predictable routine and ruin it by speaking?

Next, there's anger and confusion. Why didn't he tell the paramedics the truth? Why did he run away?

And finally, there's attraction . . . I still really, *really* want to make out with him.

- - - -

With a hammering heart, I jog down the stairs into the station the next morning, bag tight to my hip as I nudge past the slower-moving commuters. At the bottom, I pull up short, always unprepared for the sound of Calvin tearing through more up-tempo, elaborate pieces. Most days, he's strictly classical guitar. But for whatever reason, on Wednesdays he seems to favor flamenco, chamamé, and calypso.

The crowd is thick at 8:45. It smells like dirty steel and spilled soda, coffee and the pastry the guy next to me is unself-consciously shoving in his mouth. I expected to feel at least some emotional turbulence when returning to the scene of my near death, but other than wanting some answers from Calvin, I don't. I've been here so many times that the banality of my memories still overrides the trauma. It still just feels . . . *ooh, busker* and *meh, subway.*

I take the last few seconds to rally before Calvin comes into view. I'm generally not one for confrontation, but I know I'll never stop overthinking what happened Monday night if I don't at least say *something.* His feet appear first—black boots, turned-up cuffs—then his guitar case and legs—a rip in the knee of his jeans—hips, torso, chest, neck, face.

A traffic jam of emotions always clogs up my throat when I see his expression, and how transported he becomes when he plays, even in the chaos of the station. I push them down, digging for the memory that *he left me shouting like a crazy person in the back of an ambulance.*

He looks up right as I move in front of him. The shock of eye contact makes my heart roll over and I wince; my righteous indignation has deserted me. His eyes drop to my cast, and then return directly to the strings of his guitar. Beneath the shadow of his stubble, I can see a flush climb over his cheeks.

This acknowledgment buoys me. I open my mouth to say something just as an E train shrieks to a stop on the platform only a dozen yards away, and I'm quickly swallowed in the sea of people pouring out of it. Breathless, I look back through the crowd, only to catch Calvin packing up his guitar and jogging up the stairs.

Reluctantly, I move deeper into the station, nestled in the herd of commuters. It's notable that he looked up, right? He doesn't usually do that. It's almost like he was waiting for me to appear.

The C train pulls into the station, too, and we all take a few steps closer to the tracks, closer to each other, ready to jockey for a spot inside.

And so begins my completely unnecessary ritual.

- - - -

Robert is waiting for me in front of the Levin-Gladstone Theater when I approach. It's probably more accurate to say that he's waiting for the coffee I bring every Wednesday through Sunday. When I hand it over, I catch a flash of the telltale logo on the cup, and am sure Robert does, too. Madman Espresso is ten blocks away. If Robert realizes that I take the train every morning to an out-of-the-way coffee shop because I want to see Calvin, he doesn't mention it.

He probably should. I need my ass kicked.

The wind blows Robert's red scarf up and around his black wool coat, like a wild flag waving in the middle of the gray steel view along Forty-Seventh Street. I smile up at him, letting him have this quiet moment of transition.

Work is stressful for him lately: *It Possessed Him* has

taken off in a really insane way in the past nine months, and all shows are sold out for the foreseeable future. But our lead actor, Luis Genova, only signed on for a ten-month run, which comes to an end in a month. At that point, screen legend Ramón Martín will take over, and with his intense Hollywood fame comes even more intense pressure on Robert to make sure the orchestra lifts Ramón into the Broadway stratosphere. If Robert wants to walk around outside a little and drink his coffee to procrastinate, I'm game. I'm not going to make him go into that building any sooner than he wants to.

He takes a sip, studying me. "How'd you sleep last night?"

"Painkillers and emotional exhaustion ensured that I fell like a brick into bed."

Robert nods at this, eyes narrowed. "And how was your morning?"

He's working up to something. I squint suspiciously back at him. "It was fine."

"After what happened on Monday night," he says, and lifts his cup, "you still went to see him at the station today?"

Damn it. I should have known he was onto me.

Maybe I will make him go inside. I pull open the heavy side-entrance door and bat my lashes in his direction. "I don't know what you mean."

Robert follows me into the cool shadows of the theater. Even with the sounds of people working behind the scenes and onstage, it's quiet compared to the electric atmosphere of show time. "You go get me coffee at Madman every workday."

"I like their coffee."

"As much as I love that you bring me caffeine every morning, you and I both have perfectly functional coffeemakers in our apartments. You're taking the subway ten blocks and back every morning for fancy espresso. You think I don't see what you're doing?"

I groan, turning to move deeper inside, toward the stairs leading to the second-floor offices. "I know. I'm a mess."

Robert holds the stairwell door open, looking incredulous. "You still like him even after he left the paramedics thinking you were a jumper?"

"In my defense, I went there this morning in an attempt to confront him."

"And?"

I growl into another sip. "And I didn't say anything."

"I understand what it's like to have a crush," he says. "But do you think you should put him so squarely in your daily routine?"

As we ascend, I poke his side with my undamaged left elbow. "Says the guy who moved from Philly to Des Moines because he fell in lust with the waiter serving him a rib eye."

"Fair point."

"And if you don't approve, then point me in the direction of someone better." I spread my hands, looking around us. "Manhattan—particularly musical theater—is a beast for single women. Calvin was a safe but fun little diversion. I never planned on getting nearly murdered in front of him, let alone actually speaking to him."

We emerge from the stairwell, and Robert follows me into his office. It's a tiny room along a hallway with four identically tiny rooms, and is in constant disarray, with sheet music everywhere and paintings, photos, and notes on Post-its lining every inch of wall. Robert's computer is, I think, one generation older than the desktop I took to college six years ago.

He pokes at the keyboard to wake up his screen. "Well, I notice that Evan in strings is always looking at you."

I do a quick mental file through his strings section. All that comes to mind is his lead violinist, Seth, and Seth is not attracted to the ladies. Even if he were, Robert wouldn't let me date him even over his dead body; despite being invaluable to the production, Seth has a knack for throwing tantrums and stirring up drama within the ensemble. He is the only person I've ever seen make Robert truly angry.

"Which one's Evan?"

Twirling a finger over his close-cropped hair, he says, "Long hair. Viola?"

Ah, now I know who he means. Evan is sexy in a Tarzan kind of way, but . . . the rest of him might be a little *too* wild. "Yeah, Bobert," I say, holding up my hands, "but the fingernails on his bow hand . . ."

"What are you talking about?" Robert laughs.

"How can you not see this? It's like he's plucking his strings with a shark tooth." I shrug. "He just seems oddly carnivorous. I don't think I could overlook it."

"Carnivorous? You devoured your lamb chop last Wednesday. It was feral."

He's right. I did. "I cook great lamb, what do you want from me?"

From the doorway comes the sneering groan of my boss. "What the *fuck* are you even talking about?"

With a grin I answer, "Lamb," just as Uncle Robert answers, "Man claws," and Brian's frown turns radioactive.

In an effort to keep nepotism at the minimum I don't actually report to Uncle Robert but to the stage manager, the brilliant yet douchey Brian, who I'm convinced has odd collections of things at home, like a hoarder's cave with every single back issue of *National Geographic*, or butterflies pinned to dusty boards.

"Super-cute family bonding." Brian turns to sashay away, calling over his shoulder, "Holland. Stagehand meeting. *Now.*"

With a last zany smile thrown to Robert, I follow Brian downstairs to the stage and the weekly meeting awaiting us.

- - - -

The stagehand team consists of twenty people. Brian oversees all the details—blocking, cues, props, scenery, and ensuring that Robert's job runs smoothly—which means that he likes to claim credit for the current cult fever over *Possessed*. But the real heroes are the ones behind the curtain responding to his barked orders: the people Brian pleasantly refers to as his minions.

Don't get me wrong—Brian's job is a beast, and he is very good at what he does; the production runs smoothly, the sets are stunning and noted in nearly every one of the raving reviews the production receives. The actors hit their cues and the lighting is absolutely perfect. It's just that Brian also happens to be a power demon with a rampant petty side. Case in point, just now a text arrives on my phone:

> I see that your incapacitated, so I'm not quite
> sure how you plan to handle job duties this week.

Brian's inability to get the *your/you're* distinction correct makes something itch deep inside my brain. And he's texting me about this—while sitting a mere three feet away—not only to avoid direct confrontation (at which he is terrible) but also to give a clear message to the stagehand currently speaking that he doesn't care what she has to say.

He might be a dick, but unfortunately, he's also right. I can barely hold my phone with my right hand peeking out of the sling, I have no idea how I'll maneuver my camera. It takes some time, but I manage to type a reply with my left.

> Other than front of the house, are there things
> I can help with for the next couple weeks?

It pains me to hit send on such a vulnerable text, it really does. Even though my tiny archivist salary is comprised of money from nearly every department, Brian feels the most put-out for even having to deal with me on a regular basis. I already know this job is a gift—I don't need his gleeful reminders of that fact every time we interact.

While the stagehand continues to update us on the progress in painting the new drop-down forest, Brian ignores her and types, sneering down at his phone.

> Looks like you're uncle needs more help than I do.

It takes me a minute to understand his meaning, but when I do, it's accompanied by an almost comically timed, deafening cymbal crash coming from the orchestra pit.

The entire group assembled for the meeting onstage stands from their seats and peers down as the aforementioned lead violinist, Seth, shoves clear of the percussion section, shoulders past Robert, and begins to storm up the center aisle.

I glance down at Seth's chair; he left his violin just sitting there. I can't stop staring at it—I've heard from Robert that Seth's violin cost upward of *forty thousand dollars*, and he just plopped it on his chair before leaving in a huff. From the second position, Lisa Stern leans over, gingerly picking it up. I'm sure she'll return it to him later; no doubt Seth assumes she will, too. What a dick.

He has tantrums all the time, but for some reason, the stillness in the theater that follows *this* outburst feels profound.

My stomach drops.

Seth has three long "duets" with the lead, and those segments are the heart of the soundtrack. Seth's violin is more than part of the orchestra ensemble; although he doesn't appear onstage, he's truly one of the lead cast members and has even been featured on our primary merchandise, and in mainstream media. We can't have a single performance without those solos.

What transpired must have been major, because Robert's calm voice carries through the entire theater: "Let me be clear, Seth. You know what it means if you walk out today: Ramón Martín begins in a month, and you won't be joining him."

"Fuck you, Bob." Seth jerks his arms into his jacket, and doesn't look back as he yells, "I'm done."

four

My new phone vibrates just as the credits roll on my third consecutive *Vampire Diaries* episode of the night. I wouldn't normally be mainlining addicting teen dramas on a work night, but Robert balked when he caught me awkwardly trying to fold Luis Genova T-shirts and kicked me out after the Wednesday matinee, thereby exacerbating my guilt spiral. I can't go to yoga, I can't try to write, I can't go have a drink because of these painkillers. I can't even focus on reading without the intrusive worry about what Robert is going to do without Seth leading the orchestra.

My phone vibrates again and I cross the room to where it's charging on the kitchen counter, next to the laptop I haven't touched in weeks. I'm wholly expecting it to be my brother Davis calling to ensure I'm not out venturing the mean streets of Manhattan with only one arm to protect myself, but am pleasantly surprised to see Lulu's smiling face light up the screen instead.

"Hello, there." I open the fridge, scanning the contents.

"How's my little invalid?" Judging by the sound of voices and clanking silverware coming from the other end of the line, Lulu is at Blue Hill, where she is—like many in Manhattan—an actress waiting tables while awaiting her big break.

I tuck the phone between my chin and shoulder, and with my good arm pull a casserole dish out of the fridge and set it on the counter. "I'm home. Robert said I looked like a three-legged puppy at a dog show and told me to go home for a few days."

"What a monster," she says with a laugh.

"Are you at work?"

"Yeah. Actually . . . hang on." A few moments of muffled silence pass and then she returns, the background quieter now. "I had an early shift, so I'm leaving soon."

"You're off tonight?" I stop with my plate of cold lasagna just shy of the microwave, outlook suddenly brighter. "Come over and I'll make you dinner. I'll only need one of your hands."

"I have a better idea. I got a two-for-one on the cover to see this ridiculous band, and Gene can't go. Come with me!"

I know this story well: Lulu found tickets to a venue on Groupon and couldn't pass them up because they were *such a good deal*. Most of the time, I love her impulsivity and obsession with random adventures. But it's cold tonight and going out requires changing out of my pajamas—which means putting on actual clothes that I'd have to wrestle my way into.

"This is a pass for me, Lu." I pop my food into the microwave while she whimpers into the line.

The sound is so pathetic, it chips away at my resolve and I don't even have to say anything—she knows it. "Come on, Holland! The band is called Loose Springsteen! How amazing is that?"

I growl.

"Don't make me go to Jersey by myself."

"A cover band in *Jersey?*" I say. "You really aren't sweetening the deal here."

"You'd rather stay home in your pajamas eating leftovers than have the night of your life with me?"

I snort. "You might be overselling it just a bit."

She whimpers again, and I break.

- - - -

Lulu was absolutely overselling it. Hole in the Hall is a . . . *bar?* That's really the nicest thing I can say about it.

The subway station lets out just across the street from a nondescript brick building and Lulu giddily dances down the sidewalk. The neighborhood is a mixture of business and residential, but at least half the surrounding buildings look vacant. Opposite the bar is an empty Korean restaurant, with shuttered windows and a sign hanging crookedly near the doorway. Next door is a converted house with neon letters that spell *House of Hookah*; the once-bright tubes are now dark and dusty against the tin roof. It's not exactly a mystery why Hole in the Hall would need to seduce potential new clientele with Groupon deals.

Lulu turns to perform her dance backward, luring me

across the shiny wet street. "This is promising, at least," she says brightly as we join a small crowd of people lined up near the door.

The opening notes of Journey's "Don't Stop Believin'" can be heard through the brick walls, and each time the door opens the music rushes out, as if escaping. I have to admit it feels good to get dressed and leave my worries to languish in the apartment for a few hours. Leggings and a dressy top weren't too much work, and Lulu and her two good arms helped me blow-dry my long hair. For the first time in a couple of days, I don't look and feel like a troll doll. This night might not be so bad after all.

When it's finally our turn to enter, Lulu brandishes her two-for-one coupon like a badge and shimmies through the line.

Unsurprisingly, it's pretty no-frills inside. The walls are lined with old video games, and carved-up tables stand in clusters surrounding the bar. The decor is a questionable mix of Harley-Davidson, taxidermy, and Old West paraphernalia. A stripper pole stands proudly on a platform at one end, and a stage at the other. The lighting is dim and dusty, and combined with a makeshift fog machine, it makes the band members little more than backlit figures moving around onstage.

Settling at a table, Lulu flags down a waitress and we order drinks that materialize almost disturbingly quickly, like they were poured hours ago and left to grow stale behind the bar.

Lulu studies her cocktail, charmingly titled Adios Motherfucker. With a tiny why-the-fuck-not shrug, she takes a swallow, wincing as it goes down. "Tastes like 7Up."

I am mesmerized by the blinking neon ice cube in her glass. "I worry your drink is going to give someone a seizure."

She takes another sip and her straw blooms with fluorescent blue alcohol. "Actually, it tastes like sparkling water."

"See, that's the house-made moonshine killing your taste buds."

She ignores this and turns her brown eyes on me. "Is the cast a giant pain in the ass? I've never broken a bone." She grins. "Well . . . none of my own, *ifyouknowwhatImean*."

I laugh, looking down at my purple cast peeking out of the black sling. "It could be worse. The camera's a bit unruly and I can't fold shirts very well yet, but I mean . . . I could be dead?"

She nods at this, taking another sip of her drink—which is already half-gone.

"I mean," I say, "let's be honest, I only need one hand to take people's money during intermission, so it's not that bad."

"I hear you're great one-handed." She slaps a beat on the table and makes a rim-shot noise.

"The best." I wink. "What about you, any auditions?"

Lulu shakes her head with a little pout and then does a shoulder shimmy to the beat of the music. She might waitress to make ends meet, but she's dreamed of being an actress since she was old enough to know it was a possibility. We met in grad school, where she was studying theater and I was writing. She's told me on several occasions that she should become my muse, and I can write script after script for her. This should tell you a lot about our dynamic, which—despite this Jersey sidequest—is generally more entertaining than tedious.

She's been in a few low-budget commercials (she played

an accident-prone chicken in an insurance commercial, and I have several gifs of this performance I like to occasionally text her out of the blue), attended almost every acting class offered in New York, and (as a favor to me) was given a small part in one of Robert's shows. It didn't last long—because, as Robert put it, "Lulu is good at playing Lulu and only Lulu"—but as long as she draws breath, she will believe that her big break is just around the corner.

"No auditions this week." She watches the stage while taking another neon pull from her drink. I gingerly sip my watered-down Diet Coke. "Crowds haven't died down since the holidays, so we're all taking on extra hours." Nodding toward the musicians, she says, "I feel like I'm being visually assaulted by the crotch of that guy's outfit, but this band? They don't completely suck."

I follow her gaze to where the lead singer has moved to stand under a single bright spotlight. His acid-washed jeans are so tight I can see every lump he has to offer. A few more hours in those pants and I'm confident he can kiss his child-fathering years goodbye. The band shifts from the closing notes of Def Leppard's "Pour Some Sugar on Me" into a cover of Great White's "Rock Me"—I have my older brother Thomas's addiction to hair metal to thank for this knowledge—and a brave (or drunk) group of women gravitate to the edge of the stage, dancing to the bluesy opening chords.

And why not? I sway a little in my seat, drawn in by the way the guitar player drags out each note, like a maddening seduction, his head bent low in concentration. Loose Springsteen might be a cheesy cover band—and most of them are wearing at least one dangly earring and/or an article of clothing covered in animal print—but Lulu is right: they aren't half bad. With a little polish I could see them playing in a bigger club somewhere, or in an eighties revival off-off-Broadway.

The singer falls back and the guitarist moves into a circle of smoky light, beginning his requisite solo. There's a surprisingly loud reaction from the women up front . . . and there's something familiar about the way he holds the guitar, the way his fingers glide up the neck, the way his hair falls forward . . .

Oh, holy . . .

He lifts his chin, and even with his eyes in shadow and half his face turned away, I know.

"That's him," I say, pointing. I sit up straighter, pulling my phone out. I'm still on enough painkillers to not entirely trust my eyes right now. I zoom in, snapping a blurry picture.

"Who?"

I stare down at the screen and recognize the cut of his jaw, his full mouth. "Calvin. The dude from the subway."

"*Shut* up." She squints, leaning in. "That's *him*?" There's a moment of silence where I know she's looking him over, seeing exactly what I've seen almost every day for the last six months. "Damn. Okay." She turns to me, brows pointed skyward. "He's hot."

"I told you!" We both look back over to him. He's playing high on the neck, screaming out the notes on his guitar, and unlike the meditative lean of his posture at the station, here he's completely playing to the audience. "What is he doing here?" What if he sees me? "Oh my God. Is he going to think I followed him?"

"Come on, how would you possibly know he's the guitarist for Loose Springsteen? You're not exactly a member of their fan club." Lulu lets out a happy cackle. "As if they *have* a fan club."

She's right, of course, but even now, the way I can't take my eyes off him, I *feel* like a stalker. I already know so much about his schedule—I saw him just this morning, after all—and I know even more now. Is this the kind of thing he does when he's not busking? Good Lord. Maybe this is why there's such a fire to his playing at the station; he has to physically force this music out of his head.

The song ends and the lead singer slips his mic into the stand, muttering that they're taking a break before smashing his bottle of Rolling Rock to his lips and triumphantly draining it.

I'm out of my chair before I know what I'm doing. People shuffle back to their seats to refuel on bad beer, and the lights go up just enough that I see Calvin disappear into the shadows and reappear a moment later at the opposite side of the bar.

Whereas the rest of the band is a veritable cover spread of 1980s fashion don'ts, Calvin is in a black T-shirt, with the hem tucked lazily into the front of his dark jeans. He's wearing his black boots, too, and the left one is presently propped on the brass rail near his feet. The bartender places a dark beer in front of him and he lifts it, staring ahead.

I'm not sure how to approach him, and he still hasn't seen me standing a few feet away. Saying his name somehow feels sincerely weird, so I square my shoulders and slide onto the barstool beside him.

Only once I'm seated do I register that there were about

ten other women working up the nerve to do the same thing, coming at him from all angles. He turns slowly, like this happens at every set break and he's never sure what manner of companion he's going to end up with.

But when our eyes meet, he startles, face immediately relaxing into a genuine smile. "Hey, it's the girl from the Netherlands."

And I can't help it. Incredulity makes it burst out of me: "'Hey'?"

Calvin's smile turns a little sympathetic, like he gets it, and waves to the bartender, who immediately approaches. "Whatever she wants," he tells the older man.

I hesitate. I didn't come over here to have a drink with him. I came here to scratch that tickle of curiosity in my head that's been plaguing me for the past few days . . . and maybe tell him off a little. But his inherent easiness is disorienting. I expected him to be shy, or stiff. Instead he's nothing but relaxed, smiling charisma.

The bartender taps an impatient finger against the bar.

I apologize under my breath before ordering, "Club soda with lime, please."

"A real wild child you are," Calvin teases.

I meet his eyes, giving him a forced grin. "I'm on painkillers." I nod to the cast. "Broken arm."

He grimaces playfully. "Right."

The question is so much easier to ask than I'd expected: "So why didn't you tell them what you saw? They told my family I *jumped*."

He nods a few times, swallowing his sip of beer before

speaking. "I'm sorry. I am. But I didn't think the police would believe my version."

Pre-subway-platform-dive Holland would be losing her mind right now at the way his accent moves every word to the front of his mouth, and *think* comes out as *tink*—a tiny coin dropped into a cup.

Okay, Holland of today is losing her mind a little, too, but she's at least trying to keep her cool.

"Well," I say, "they didn't believe my version, either. They handed me a couple of self-help pamphlets and probably aren't even looking for the guy who did it."

Calvin turns, meeting my eyes. "Look. Being in the station, I see . . ." He shakes his head. "I see people do terrible shite all the time and then report it themselves. Crime fetish, or somethin'. That's all I could think about in that moment. Your bum ran off, and I was more concerned with getting you safe than stopping him."

As he talks, he reaches into the front pocket of his jeans for a tube of ChapStick, absently pulling off the cap and running the balm quickly over his lips. The move is so distracting that I don't realize I'm staring at his mouth until the bartender loudly deposits a tumbler of sparkling water and limes on a napkin in front of me. Calvin slips the tube back into his pocket as he nods in thanks.

My brain shuffles through memories of Monday night, and I have to admit that what he's said makes sense—even if it doesn't explain why he lied to the EMTs. But does that matter? It was embarrassing to be handed the suicide prevention card, yeah, but in reality, Calvin called 911, and stayed to make sure

I was okay. Now what feels remarkable isn't that he fled after I was safely awake in the ambulance, it's that he stayed that long to begin with.

Calvin holds out his hand. "Apology accepted?"

I take it, and grow a little breathless knowing that he plays his guitar with the fingers he currently has wrapped around mine. A hot pulse works its way down my spine. "Yeah. Apology accepted."

Releasing me, he stares at the cast for a few seconds. "I see you've got no names written on there."

I follow his attention down. "Names?"

"It's required when you choose a little-girl color, love. You *beg* your mates to mark it all up."

Oh. Something turns over inside me at his playful smile, exposing my vulnerable underbelly. I realize now that a significant fraction of my brain was hoping he wouldn't be so amiable when he saw me, that he would be defensive and sharp, so I'd have a good reason to tuck my crush away.

"I'm still traumatized by the gore of my friend's sweaty, smelly, graffitied cast in fourth grade." I grin over at him. "I'm trying to keep this one pristine."

The band begins to reconvene on the stage, and Calvin glances over his shoulder before draining his beer.

He stands, and then grins down at me. I'm overcome by his exultant smile. "Well, if you change your mind and want it dirtied up, you know where to find me."

five

Luis Genova is a magical human, and I don't say that lightly. When I read reviews of him as Theo in my uncle's show that say he was "born for the stage," I feel sorry for whatever uncreative journalist wrote it because it's not a profound statement; it's akin to declaring that a bird is born to fly.

One night, very early after the production launched and received its first standing ovation, the cast and crew went out to celebrate at the Palm. I was, as I am now, not even an official stagehand and barely worth anyone's notice, and at the time Luis didn't yet know my relation to Robert. That night, Luis made the rounds of the entire private room, shaking hands and giving thanks. When he was several people away from me, the air shifted, became charged somehow. There were four of us minions standing together, snacking, trying to stave off self-consciousness, and we all turned and watched him approach as if we were being compelled.

I explained it to Lulu later, describing it almost like if a UFO had landed and deployed some magical brain magnets. We all *had* to turn and watch him. None of us could continue babbling about how good the calamari was or whether we'd have a Dark and Stormy or a gin and tonic next when Luis Genova was walking toward us. When he reached for my hand and thanked me for all my hard work, he looked me right in the eye and my inane brain lost all capacity for language.

Blinking, I shook his hand, giving him a numb "Okay" before he moved on to thank the person beside me.

Well played, Holland.

It's not that he's tall, or particularly good-looking or muscular. He's just . . . present. The light prays at the altar of his cheekbones. His hair hits his jaw in a smooth black sheet and he tucks it behind his ear, revealing eyes that crinkle into that smile. Lord, his smile.

His smile, which is right here, not ten feet from me.

"Holland, for the love of God, stop *gawking*."

I startle, turning at the sound of Brian's voice. Unfortunately, Luis and Robert—who had been having what appeared to be a lovely conversation and which I would have been happy to witness for a good ten minutes longer—also turn to see what's happening. Everyone nearby looks at me, their smiles tilting from confused to sympathetic.

Poor fangirl, busted for ogling.

Story of my life, I guess.

My neck heats and I push through the assembled cast and deeper backstage, apologizing under my breath. Admittedly, I get to see Luis a lot, but never standing still like that, so close, and my opportunities are dwindling. He has created a nation of adoring followers, and in only a month, he's leaving us.

I'm not even a Broadway junkie, and I'm heartbroken. No wonder Twitter is flipping out. No wonder Robert is a stress monster about making sure Ramón nails it when he takes over.

I find a quiet place to sit in the shadows and watch Luis and Robert walk onstage, hugging briefly before Robert waves Lisa up from the pit. She joins them, lifting her violin to her chin and following Robert's lead before she begins playing. Again and again they practice, blending their two "voices"; Luis has only a handful of performances remaining, but I can see he wants to make them impactful. His final show will be a star-studded event and covered by press that's already profiled the show a hundred times.

Unfortunately, even to my ear it's clear that Lisa is no match for Luis in sound or presence, and I have no idea what's going to come next. Seth is already gone. Luis is leaving soon. Ramón Martín is coming in with a blockbuster voice, and Lisa's hand is too soft to accompany him.

For the first time, I'm truly worried about my uncle.

- - - -

Robert finds me in his office later, absently punching holes in a blank sheet of paper. He looks a little dangerous: his dark eyes are bloodshot, his normally smiling mouth is a grim, pale line.

"Are you making a mess in here?" he asks. He takes his glasses off, folding them carefully on the desk.

Sheepishly, I sweep the small pile of punched-out circles into the recycling bin. "I can't believe anyone uses a single-hole punch anymore."

"No one does." He sits in the chair opposite me and bends, putting his head in his hands.

"You okay, Bobert?"

He says pretty much what I expect: "I don't know how I'm going to pair Ramón. He'll drown Lisa."

Robert's pianist, a man named Luther, is pretty wonderful. "Can Luther carry the solos?"

"On *piano*?"

I shrug. "Just spitballing here."

He appears to consider it, and then shakes his head. "The songs don't lend themselves to keys. The strings have a richness, a vibrancy that the piano can't mimic. It needs to stir something inside you. Luther is amazing, but we need a musician who demands your attention. Who makes you *feel*."

The idea seems to heat my blood, and I straighten. "Wait. Wait."

Robert looks up, confused.

I hold up my hand. "An idea is forming in my brain."

His expression clears in understanding. "No, Buttercup."

"He's exactly what you're describing," I insist. "You've never heard him, but trust me—he is."

"He plays guitar. Honey, I know you're enamored, but—"

"It's not that, I swear. And he's not just some busker hanging out on the street. He's *gifted*, Robert. Listening to him play is like watching Luis onstage. I *feel* the notes. I know I'm not . . ." I search for words, flushing. Trying to tell Robert how to do his job is dangerous; he may be my uncle, but he's been a brilliant musician for much longer.

"I'm not a trained musician like you are," I say carefully, "but I feel like classical guitar might work here. It's gentle, and soft, yes, but has the passion and—the vibrancy you mention? It has that. If we're changing the sound entirely by bringing in Ramón, why not change it this way, too? Have a guitar sing with Ramón, instead of a violin?"

Robert stares at me, speechless.

"Just come with me once." I grow dizzy from the awareness that I might be convincing him. "*Once.* That's all it will take. I know it."

– – – –

There's something almost comical about seeing the impeccable Robert Okai walk into a subway station the following Monday. As he descends into the shadows of the stairs, it occurs to me that since I've lived in New York, I've never ridden with him in anything other than a town car or a cab. He grew up in the dusty streets of western Africa, playing on the world's most battered violin and wearing nothing but a pair of shorts and sandals, but it's impossible to imagine him in any other state than he is today: wrapped in a long wool coat, blue cashmere scarf, black tailored pants, and polished shoes. It's safe to say I look slightly less polished in my purple cast and fuzzy pink cardigan.

But he isn't snobby; he dives right into the crowd. He isn't squeamish about the grime on the handrail or the puddle of filthy water at the bottom of the first flight of stairs. It's more that Robert gives off the sense that his humble beginnings could never deny who he was meant to become: an exceptionally talented maestro.

As for me, my heart is hammering wildly beneath my breastbone, and I have both fists wrapped around the strap of my bag to keep them from trembling. Not only is Robert coming with me to listen to Calvin play, but it will be obvious to Calvin that I've brought someone here specifically to *watch him play*, thereby making it apparent that I have watched him in the past, maybe *many times* in the past, and thought about how someone else should join me.

Also, I really don't want to be wrong about this. Robert's esteem means everything to me. If he doesn't agree about Calvin's talent, I know deep down it will tarnish something within me about Calvin in particular, and my own creative compass in general.

But my nerves may be wasted: other than the screech of the train or the occasional burst of an announcement audible on the stairs, the station is mostly silent. In the past several months, Calvin has been here every Monday night. Has he abruptly changed his routine in one week?

My stomach drops. Sometime, weeks ago, it stopped occurring to me that Calvin might eventually move on from the busking gig. It's one of those unintentionally selfish assumptions I'm always shocked to find myself making: I just imagined he would be here forever—or at least until I stopped wanting to see him every day. The prospect of never seeing him again sends a cold shiver of panic down my arms.

But as we turn the corner to go down the last flight, the iconic, seductive opening notes of "El Porompompero" drift up, and Robert pauses, his foot caught midair.

As always, the song begins slowly, flirtatiously, and Robert's pace picks up. Calvin's feet come into view—then legs, hips, and guitar, then torso and chest and neck and head—and the rhythm increases, the music taking off in an addicting swirl; Calvin alternately strums his guitar and gently slaps it like a drum.

I watch Robert as he listens. In any audience, Robert is a fascinating mix of wildly effusive praise and stern critique, and the only sign I have that he's mesmerized—for he's looking down at the floor, as if working out some complicated mental logic problem—is the tiny tap of his index finger in time with the music.

Moving my eyes up just the smallest bit, I catch the quickened rise and fall of his breath in his chest. For my part, I can barely breathe. We're here, watching Calvin together, and the enormity of the proposition—*Consider him for your production*—and the fact that he is indeed considering him hit me in a dizzy haze.

Desperate to contribute something, my emotional brain immediately sprints to shelter: *I could be saving Robert!*

My logical brain holds up a hand: *Don't get ahead of yourself, Holland.*

Calvin's eyes are closed, his head bent chin-to-chest. I watch him sway, lost to the music he's making. Would his posture change if he had any awareness that the composer of *It Possessed Him* was standing only four feet away?

Calvin usually takes a small break between pieces, tuning his guitar under the apparent impression that he's in a bubble. With a final flourish of fingers over strings, he stops, pauses, and then inhales, wearing an expression of bliss as he looks up.

But he's never in a bubble, and we're standing *right there*. His breath catches, and his eyes widen. He's not looking at me.

He knows exactly who Robert is.

six

Calvin sits up, jerking his guitar to stand on one thigh. "Mr. Okai." He swallows. "I didn't realize you were standing there."

"My niece tells me your name is Calvin."

Calvin looks between the two of us, working this out. Robert, with his smooth dark skin and meticulously short hair. Me: pale and freckled with a chaotic, weedy bun on top of my head.

Robert reaches out a hand, and Calvin immediately takes it, standing. "Yes. Calvin McLoughlin."

This makes my uncle laugh, and the boom of it eases the line of Calvin's shoulders. "That's a pretty Irish name for someone with such a good tan."

"My mam is Greek," he explains, and then looks back and forth between me and Robert again, as if asking a question of his own.

Robert tilts his head to me, releasing Calvin's hand and saying in turn, "I married her uncle."

Calvin smiles, quietly saying, "Ah."

I sense Robert straighten beside me, and Calvin mimics the posture. My heart turns into a snare drum: it is time to get down to it.

"I am the musical director down at the—"

"The Levin-Gladstone," Calvin interrupts. "I know. I've seen *It Possessed Him* seven times."

"*Seven?*" It's the first time I've spoken, and Calvin turns to me.

He lifts his chin in a nod. "I think you sold me a T-shirt."

I tink ye sold me a t-shairt.

I pull my surprised mouth closed to speak. "You didn't think to mention this before? On Wednesday night?"

"You saw each other Wednesday?" Robert asks.

We both ignore him. "I didn't put it together until now," Calvin says, in that easy way of his. "I knew I'd seen you before, I just figured it was at the station."

Robert redirects us. "So you know the production, then."

Calvin pales. "Of course I do."

"And, if you've seen it seven times," Robert continues, "I'm inclined to think you've heard that Luis Genova is leaving, soon to be replaced by Ramón Martín."

"I have." Calvin scratches his jaw. "And I've also heard that Seth Astorio hasn't played in four days. How's the search goin'?"

Robert pulls back, studying him. "It sounds like you're skeptical I can replace him."

"Of course I think you can replace him." He laughs. "*Seth* doesn't."

"You know Seth?" Robert asks slowly.

"We studied together."

My uncle pauses, and I watch as his eyes narrow. "Seth attended Juilliard."

Calvin lifts his chin with a cocky smile. "Aye. He did, in fact."

I move past Calvin and sit heavily down on his stool.

Juilliard.

Holy shit. Calvin attended *Juilliard*.

Robert doesn't beat around the bush any longer. "Would you like to come down to play for us tomorrow?"

A hysterical urge inside wants me to pipe up that Calvin is busy on Tuesdays. At least, he must be, because he doesn't ever do his regular gig of Juilliard-man-playing-for-change at the Fiftieth Street station then. I press my palm against my mouth to hold the words in.

"To play for *you*?" Calvin repeats, awestruck. "Ah, go on."

"I'm serious," Robert says with a tiny grin. "I'll see you tomorrow at noon."

- - - -

I'm still awake at four in the morning, sitting on my couch, leg jiggling.

Nothing helped me sleep.

Not chamomile, not whiskey, not my favorite pink vibrator, not PBS.

I stand, absently shoving the vibrator beneath a couch cushion, turning off the television, and taking my array of glassware one-handed to the kitchen sink.

If I'm nervous like this, then Calvin must be losing his mind. Unless he thinks he's only playing for the orchestra, which would be no big deal for someone from *Juilliard*. Of course Calvin would have no idea who else is coming today: At noon, he will play not only for Robert Okai—former conductor of the Des Moines Symphony and current musical director at the Levin-Gladstone Theater—but for two renowned Broadway producer brothers, Don and Richard Law, and the production director, Michael Asteroff, all of whom had planned to come meet with Robert anyway.

Because Calvin will play in the pit, Robert won't be able to keep his audition a secret. Brian and whoever has come early from the orchestra will also be there, in the shadows, listening.

At dinner last night, Robert and I strategized: I wanted Robert to simply offer Calvin the role if he performs as well as we expect him to. Robert is the composer, he's the musical director. Can't he pull rank?

But Robert disagreed. "Theater politics are delicate."

He would bring in Calvin without giving the others much information about him. A young guitarist, he would say. Someone Holland had heard play, and who transfixed him as well.

He would tell Michael that he wanted to brainstorm ways to incorporate the juxtaposition of Calvin's polish and scrape. He would see how Calvin performed in front of such an intimidating audience. And then he would wait for it to be someone else's idea that Calvin take over Seth's solos.

"Not mine," he said, and looked at me, "not yours. Trust me on this, Buttercup. It has to be Michael's idea."

But no matter what we say to anyone else, Robert, Jeff, and I know that the idea was mine.

I'm nearly desperate for it; the craving is so powerful I'm buzzy. If Michael agrees we can bring a guitarist in to take over the part Seth once played, I will have contributed something irreplaceable to this production. I'll no longer be on the sidelines, useless.

I will have silently earned my place.

- - - -

Robert meets me outside the theater at 11:45. Calvin is coming at noon.

My uncle catches my eye and grins before we turn, heading in the side door. It isn't crowded backstage, but it's not dead, either. Most of the cast start showing up around three for makeup and lighting, but the principals in the orchestra often come in earlier on Tuesdays, after a day off, to have lunch together, tune their instruments at a leisurely pace, meet with Robert.

At first, everyone is joking with one another; no one else feels the weight of this. It's not uncommon for Robert to bring in musicians to audition when one or another of our orchestra leaves. However, there aren't currently any guitarists in the ensemble. When word circulates that a guitarist is coming in to play, interest spikes: *Seth is gone. Luis is leaving. And now we're auditioning a guitarist?* I see people bending over their phones, texting. Soon the theater is full of cast, crew, and orchestra.

Brian is in a quiet tizzy, asking everyone within earshot who invited this new musician, what's happening, why didn't anyone update him sooner?

Robert doesn't get nervous—at least, not about things outside his control, like this. He was smart not to overpromise. And now he stands near the head of the pit, talking to Michael, both men feigning obliviousness while energy buzzes around them. The doors to the lobby open at twelve sharp, and Calvin walks in, his guitar case in his left hand, right hand tucked easily in the pocket of his jeans. A hush falls over the group, and it seems an eternity passes while we all watch him walk from the top of the aisle down to the pit.

Robert doesn't bother introducing him to everyone; Calvin is here for him, Michael, Don, and Richard. Anyone else is a bystander and it's up to them to listen in if they choose. From where I sit at the edge of the curtain, I can only barely make out Calvin's face. Even so, I can tell he feels the weight of eyes on him. He's a little hunched, smiling and nodding a lot. He pulls out his ChapStick twice.

I want to know how he got here, to this moment. How does one go from Ireland, to Juilliard, to busking and cover bands? People camp out in front of the theater for single tickets to *Possessed*; they pay insane prices on resale sites. How connected is he that he managed it seven times?

He shakes hands with Michael and Robert before turning to greet the quieter, more observant Don and Richard, and then is invited to sit down in a folding chair that has been placed right up front.

Calvin sits and then pulls his guitar out, quietly tuning the instrument. His smile is easy and infectious. Inside my chest, my heart jackhammers.

Looking up at Robert, he asks, "What would you like to hear?"

Robert pretends to think. I don't know what he's going to say right now, but I know him well enough to bet my life that he has an entire playlist already strategized.

"'Malagueña.'"

Smart. It's bright, and catchy—reminiscent of the energetic opening number of *Possessed* without being too on-the-nose. It also perfectly showcases Calvin's training, because it's a piece that requires precision, speed, and several changes in tempo.

With a little nod, Calvin bends, eyes closed, and strums the first, brilliant note.

I feel the collective intake of breath, the way bodies behind me in the shadows shift forward now to see, not only hear. I see the way Michael's eyebrows seem pinned high on his forehead, the way sullen Richard has released his arms from their omnipresent cross and tucked his hands more easily in his pockets, rocking back on his heels.

I see Calvin impress the entire fucking theater, and clap a hand over my mouth. Is it weird that in this second I see my street musician, Jack, up there and want to scream? Is it weird that I sense how much this means to him, even if I don't know anything else about him in the world?

I want to dance across the stage, I am so proud.

- - - -

In all, Calvin plays three and a half pieces for Robert and the other show executives. The half comes into play when, mid-"Blackbird," Michael stands and claps twice, saying, "I think we've heard enough."

No one responds as if this is at all abrupt—not even Calvin. I'm sure nearly everyone here was amazed he got to play as much as he did.

Calvin stands, gathering his guitar and case, shaking hands again, and leaving without a look back.

"Let's head upstairs to the room," Michael says, referring to the small boardroom-type space we have on the second floor, with a large round table and a random assortment of enormous and tiny chairs—some of which are so high they're nearly thrones, and some of which are so low, the people seated in them invariably feel like they need booster seats.

Robert turns, leading Don and Richard backstage. Brian follows. Michael greets a few cast members and then rounds out the back of the group, but pauses when he gets near me.

"You coming?" he asks.

I glance back over my shoulder on instinct.

"You." He leans in, blue eyes twinkling. "Holland."

He knows my name?

"I can, if you need photos?"

"Robert says you brought him to see Calvin play. I'd like to hear why you thought to mention him."

He gestures for me to follow, and my blood vibrates right up against my skin.

- - - -

I take a seat on the far end of the table in one of the thrones. I was actually hoping for one of the kid chairs—would have felt more at home there in this crowd—but instead I sat before really thinking. And Brian, who clearly wanted to be seated between Robert and Richard, ended up with the shortest of straws and looks like a scowling toddler across the table from me.

"Holland," he whisper-yells, looking around incredulously and then back to me. "Why on earth are you in here?"

"I invited her," Michael says breezily, waving away any concern. "So, Holland. Let's hear it. Who is this guy?"

"Um, well." My voice wavers a little and I sense Brian vibrating with irritation across the table. "He plays a few mornings a week at the Fiftieth Street station—"

"He's a *subway musician*?" Brian cuts in.

"Brian," Robert cautions, his voice low. "Just let her explain."

"I saw him one morning when I was headed to a doctor's appointment uptown," I say, "and even though I don't need to commute because I only live a few blocks—"

Robert clears his throat, an unspoken *Get to the point, Holland*.

"So," I say, cheeks heating, "I listen to him all the time. Everyone at the station watches him while they wait. He's so good, and I told Robert about him and, um." I press my hand to my forehead. I feel overheated under the pressure of their eyes on me. "I wanted Robert to hear him. Turns out he's Juilliard trained." I see Robert nod in my peripheral vision, encouraging. "He's amazing. Anyone can see that."

"He *is* amazing," Don says, "and I'm glad we were here for

it. It's always good to keep an eye out for talent, for whatever comes next."

Inside, I deflate because they don't seem to have clued in to the unspoken suggestion that we bring Calvin into *Possessed*, but I nod to Don—as if my agreement carries any weight. I don't meet Robert's eyes. I don't want to see my disappointment mirrored there.

Now that my bit has come and gone, the attention is turned away from me and back toward Robert and Brian.

Robert tells Don about the circumstances of Seth's departure, and Brian confirms the spectacle of it. Brian updates the Law brothers on the new set pieces that have been constructed to replace two that cracked in rehearsal a month ago. But through all of it, Michael is staring at the table, tracing his finger around a swirl in the wood over and over.

Questions are thrown out and answered, and I try to shrink as low as I can in my seat. I'm a lowly T-shirt seller, the unnecessary archivist; I'm not needed here. But because I chose a seat in the back of the room, it would be more disruptive to stand and leave than it would be to just sit here on my raised platform, listening in. Besides, no one seems all that concerned—or aware—of my continued presence.

Except Brian, who thinks it's a great time to text me.

> I don't need to remind u that u should not repeat any of there conversation outside of this room

Honestly, his grammar. I type a quick reply—Of course—before putting my phone facedown on the table.

"Do you think . . ." Michael begins during a lull in the conversation, and then laughs, shaking his head. "I think Holland might have had a smart instinct bringing him here today." He holds up his hands, and my breathing halts. "Hear me out: listening to you speak about Seth leaving, and given my concerns—which I know you share, Bob—about Lisa as a replacement . . ."

There is thunder in my chest. I look up and briefly catch Robert's eye.

"I think we should consider the guitarist to accompany Ramón in *Possessed* solo sections," Michael continues. "I'll be the first to admit it feels like a big departure, and of course I defer to you here, Bob, but it feels like it might be the perfect change."

I bite my lips to keep them from bowing upward, and blink down at the table.

At the other end of the room, Robert hums thoughtfully. "It's certainly an interesting idea."

"I do like him," Don agrees. "I'm not the musical strategist here, but do you think the soundtrack couldn't lend itself to a more rustic feel?"

"It would be unexpected," Michael says, grinning.

Richard nods, smiling. "I think it's a wild, *wonderful* suggestion. The music is sexy. That kid was *blindingly* sexy."

Every head turns to Robert.

"Bob," Michael says, leaning forward. "Does this ruin your vision? Would you consider it?"

A tiny grin—so brief I'm sure no one else would name it anything other than a wince—jumps across Robert's face, and then he reaches up, rubbing his hand over his mouth. "Guitar," he says, as if mulling it over. "A guitar . . ."

Robert looks at Michael, but his smile is only for me. "Holland does have good instincts. I think Calvin and Ramón could be brilliant."

Don raps the tabletop with his knuckles. "Let's give him a quick call."

At this, I stand to leave, but Robert gestures for me to sit back down. I can't tell whether he agrees that my leaving would be disruptive or he wants me to be able to enjoy this moment, but it's clearly only awkward for me at this point. I don't even have a notebook to pretend like I'm here writing down meeting minutes.

Robert reads out Calvin's cell phone number, and Michael types it into the phone sitting in the middle of the table. It rings twice, and my heart is absolutely lodged in my throat.

His voice comes through—scratchy and deep—as if he's been sleeping. "'lo?"

"Calvin, hi. Michael Asteroff. I'm here with Robert Okai and the Law brothers."

"*Oh.* Hi." There's some shuffling in the background, and although he left here only an hour ago, my pervy brain imagines him shirtless, sitting up in bed, the sheets falling to his hips.

Hopefully he's alone.

"Great work today," Michael says. "Truly superb."

Calvin pauses, and when he speaks, his voice shakes. "Thank you, sir."

"Look," Michael begins, "we're wondering what your schedule looks like for the next several months."

"*My* schedule?"

"More specifically, we're wondering whether we could interest you in a place in the orchestra here. With *It Possessed Him*."

The question is met with blistering silence.

Robert leans in toward the speakerphone. "We'd like you to take over Seth's parts."

"Honestly?"

Everyone but me laughs at this.

"Yeah." Michael grins. "*Honestly*."

"Aye, I'm flattered. I . . ." A pause. "I'm dyin' to say yes."

"So say yes!" Richard sings.

On the other end of the line, Calvin growls. "It's just that, ah . . ."

And, in this instant, I know.

I know.

I know.

I know why he's hesitating, because it's got to be the same reason he didn't want to get too involved with the police the night of my accident.

"I'm not exactly here legally, y'see."

The table falls silent. Michael and Robert look at each other, and Robert blows out a slow breath.

"I was here on a student visa, and ah, it expired, yeah? I couldn't find it in me to leave. This here, what you're offerin', it's my dream."

"How long ago did it expire?" Michael asks, nodding at

Robert like this might work. "Can we work on an extension, using this as an internship?"

Calvin pauses again, and I think I hear a dry laugh through the line. "It'd be four years now."

Robert groans, leaning back in his chair. It's not uncommon for foreigners to join the cast—it happens all the time. And artist visas are a dime a dozen in New York. But Jeff's best friend from grade school works in immigration, and I know from overhearing Jeff and Robert discuss other artists in the past that getting leniency for people who've been here for six months illegally is hard . . . so *four years?*

When no one replies, another laugh—this one decidedly sad—comes through the line. "But I sure do appreciate the offer."

seven

Michael hits the disconnect button and leans back, pressing the heels of his hands to his eyes. "Well, that's all right. We didn't even know about him until this morning. We should continue with violin auditions immediately."

The words are met with silence, and the Law brothers exchange a dubious look. I can tell that Robert and I aren't the only ones who are already invested in Calvin.

"There's got to be a way around this," Don says. "Some string to be pulled."

"Four years is a long time." Robert's voice is quiet and he meets my eyes, grimacing. "I'm not sure even with the connections we have that we can work around that."

"Jesus Christ." Brian bursts from his tiny chair, dropping his fists onto the table. "The answer is obvious, isn't it? Just have Holland marry the guy. They've been dating for months in her head, anyway. Two birds, one stone."

I let out a garbled sound of shock and immediately feel the way everyone turns to look at me.

Everyone except Robert, who slowly lowers his glasses down his nose, fixing a dark gaze on my boss. "Brian. If you're not going to be helpful, please feel free to step out."

Brian leans back in his seat, grinning snidely at me before looking to Robert. "If this is as dire as you say, if"—he sweeps his hands dramatically—"you are unable to find a suitable musician in all of *New York City*, then let us consider how every department can step up to help you hire your subway busker. I think we should hear what Holland thinks about the idea."

Robert doesn't give me a chance to reply—not that I'd have the faintest idea what to say. "Your tone is quickly passing insulting and moving into shocking territory." The room has gone still, each set of eyes following the conversation as if it is a tennis match. "I am not only the composer and musical director of this production, but I am also Holland's uncle. I'll suggest you tread carefully here."

Brian is an angry, splotchy red. Robert's lips have practically disappeared, they are so tight. Meanwhile, my head is spinning. I am far from Brian's favorite person, but does he really think that's a viable solution here?

"It was just a suggestion," he says, scrambling to triage the situation. "Everyone here knows you're the out-of-the-box thinker, Robert. I was trying to come up with an out-of-the-box solution."

Michael speaks up. "It's a bit more than out-of-the-box, Brian. It's also illegal."

If possible, the color of Brian's face deepens and he swings his gaze in my direction. Brian is petty, and at times completely unreasonable, but he hasn't always been *wrong* in his criticism of me. I don't belong here. Someone more deserving and qualified *should* have this job. My stomach turns over, sour.

Done with the conversation, Robert slips his glasses back on and looks at the others around the table. "Brian, you can head downstairs. The rest of us need to get back to finding a realistic solution. We're running out of time."

Seriously. What the fuck, Brian.

I throw a frozen dinner in my microwave and pace the ten-foot length of my living room, back and forth.

"What an asshole," I growl.

The microwave dings, but I ignore it, instead going to the fridge to grab a beer. I snap the top open and drink half of it before slamming the can down on the counter.

For the life of me, I can't get this afternoon out of my head.

I'd excused myself from the meeting once they finally broke for coffee, leaving them to go over the list of possible replacements on their own. Even without eavesdropping in the hallway, I knew they were all lukewarm on the alternatives, no matter how talented they may be. Seth is a douchebag, but his charisma is undisputed, and he and Luis seemed to move in perfect unison when they performed together. We need someone like that for Ramón Martín—whose voice is like rich honey—and given the fluency of his playing, I know that person is Calvin.

I pick up the beer again, finishing it and crumpling the can in my left hand. Returning to the fridge, I grab another, making a mental list of the present circumstances.

1. Ramón starts rehearsing in two weeks.
2. Lisa isn't even pushing to claim the lead violinist chair; in fact, she offered some names to Robert.
3. Robert brought Calvin in after listening to him play at the station for a mere three minutes. My uncle has a musical ear that goes beyond anything I've ever witnessed—and I spent a good part of my childhood in the symphony hall, watching him.
4. Without a doubt, we need Calvin.

How could Brian think I would do something like this?
I close my eyes, wondering at the ball of heat in my chest.
Would I?

- - - -

Sleep doesn't come easily.

By midnight I'm back to pacing the apartment.

By one I'm on my phone, frantically researching visa requirements and examples of immigration leniency. There aren't many.

By two my battery is almost dead. I decide I'm worrying over something completely beyond my control and spend the next hour going through my clothes and getting rid of things I haven't worn in years.

By three thirty I'm on my bedroom floor, tethered to my phone again, which is itself tethered to the outlet. Scouring theater gossip sites, I look for productions that have lost two major leads at once, hoping I'll identify a slew of shows that came back bigger and better than ever.

Spoiler alert: I don't.

By the time the sun starts to brighten the sky, and after zero hours of sleep, I feel a little crazy, but Brian's suggestion feels less so.

Empty hangers swing on the rod overhead as I stare at my closet ceiling. Exhausted and apparently beyond rational thought, I decide to make another list—this time of the pros and cons of marrying Calvin. This activity could probably be taken more seriously if I weren't also wearing an old bridesmaid dress and a pair of knockoff Valentino flip-flops from Chinatown last summer.

"Pro: he's gorgeous." I sit up, searching a discarded handbag for something to write on. "Let's start with that."

The back of an envelope works, and I add the first item to the Pro column.

Con: I don't know him.
Con: This idea is varying shades of illegal.

Oof. That's a big one. I swiftly move back to the pros.

Pro: Robert really wants Calvin, even if he'd never admit it.
Pro: I adore Robert more than life itself.

Pro: Calvin was made for this role. I know it.

Pro: Robert has done more for me than any single person. This could be my chance to repay him. When will I ever have this opportunity again?

Pro: I can't figure out another way to make this work.

There's something else inside me, urging me forward. Why on earth does it feel like I nearly want to leap without looking? I look over the list, knowing what's missing. Even in my head, my voice is a shameful whisper.

Pro: I sort of really want to do it.

Con: But would I feel pathetic? Having had a crush on him all this time?

I shouldn't rely on my own infatuated brain here; I need to bring in reinforcements. I can't call Robert and I definitely can't call Jeff. He'd skin me alive for even suggesting it. I won't even bother to call Lulu, because she already wants me to pole dance down at Private Eyes so that I can give her stories to help her *empathize* and *relate* in various auditions. Without even asking, I know I can put her in the Fuck Yeah, Marry Him column.

So I do what I always do in this situation: when I can't talk to Robert, I call my brother.

Older than me by nineteen months, Davis is a bank teller in Milwaukee by day, and a rugby fanatic by all other hours. Where Robert and Jeff are refinement and culture, Davis is mud and beer and cheese sticks. It would never occur to him to grow a beard to be trendy; he grew one in college, years before the hipsters did, purely because he was lazy.

I give him the courtesy of waiting a couple of hours, so I'm nearly frantic by the time I get him on the line at eight. "Did I wake you up?"

"Holls, most of us don't start work at three in the afternoon."

"Okay, good." I begin pacing my tiny kitchen. "I need your solid advice. Robert brought the busker in yesterday to play—"

"Jack?" Davis asks, and then snaps a bite of something crunchy. I'm assuming less apple-slices-for-breakfast and more Cheeto.

"His name is Calvin."

"Who is Calvin?"

"The busker."

"A different busker than Jack?"

"Oh my God, Davis!"

"What?"

I close my eyes, leaning my head back on my couch. Something is lumpy beneath me, and I reach down, finding my vibrator. Nice. Perfect moment to feel the full power of my singlehood. I shove it under the other couch cushion.

"Jack *is* Calvin," I explain. "I never knew his name, remember? It turns out it's Calvin."

"Oh, got it, got it." A bag crinkles on the other end of the line. "So where did Robert want him to play?"

I groan. "At the theater. Just listen, okay? I'm getting to all that." Davis has this way of distractedly carrying on conversations while he watches TV or plays on his phone that makes me want to spend my precious money to fly to Milwaukee and just slap him. "So, Calvin is the busker. We've learned that he's Irish. He went to *Juilliard*." I wait—no response to this from Davis, so I continue. "Robert brought him in yesterday to play, and he's amazing. Everyone wanted him to join the orchestra."

He mumbles, "Okay," and then laughs at something on the television.

I really need his full brain on this. Despite claiming to be a rugby brute, Davis is sharp as a blade. So I retaliate with force, using the nickname he despises. "*Dave.*"

"Ew. Gross, Holland."

"Turn off *The Bachelor*. Listen to me."

"I'm watching last night's John Oliver."

"But can you listen? Nasty Brian suggested I marry Calvin so he could join the show when Ramón Martín comes on."

The sound of the television disappears in the background, and Davis's voice returns, stronger. "He *what?*"

"Calvin isn't here legally," I explain, "and because it's going to be really hard to get him a visa, Brian blurted out in a meeting that I could marry him, just for the run of the show."

"You can*not*—"

"Davis," I say quietly, "just let me try to explain all sides, okay?"

I wonder whether this is a huge mistake. Davis is my buddy and in all ways a laid-back bro, but inside that round torso is a heart that beats wildly for his family with a type of loyalty that seems rare these days. How can I admit that I don't hate the prospect of marrying Calvin even a fraction as much as I should? I feel like I'm defending the idea of marrying a stranger for absolutely zero benefit to myself. At least in *Green Card* Andie MacDowell got the fucking greenhouse.

"Robert said no," I assure him. "He wouldn't even entertain the idea."

"*Good*," Davis cuts in, sharp.

"But—I made a list, Davis, of the pros and con—"

"Well, I mean, *absolutely* let's consider it if *you have a list.*"

"Will you shut up? I know it's crazy—I do—but you haven't heard Calvin play, and . . . it's unlike anything I've ever heard. I'm not even musical and I'm obsessed. He would be so good for the production."

"Holland, are you really considering this? You like him that much?"

Ughhhhhh.

"I'm attracted to him," I admit, "but it's not like I *know* him. This isn't about that."

"What is it, then? It's not like you're all that invested in *Possessed*. I always had the impression it was just a job for you."

I hesitate. "I want to do it for Robert. It feels like a chance for me to give back a little."

"Give back?" Davis repeats. "You *work* there. You don't owe them your virginity."

This makes me laugh. "Right. Unless they have a time turner and can go back to 2008 and Eric Mordito's basement, I think that ship has sailed."

It takes him a few seconds to compute and then, "Gross, Holls. *Mordito?* Eric and I shared a pottery wheel my sophomore year."

"It's possible you're missing the point," I say. "The only

reason I have a job is because of Robert. The show could fail without a new star. Robert's invested so much, he could ruin his reputation if this tanks. I can't let that happen."

After a few moments of silence, Davis asks, "Are you asking my blessing or my advice?"

I close my eyes, tilting my face to the ceiling. "Both?"

"Look, Hollsy," he says, gentler now, "I get it. I know you and Robert are super close, and I know you feel guilty sometimes about working there and living in the apartment. But this seems extreme to me, *really* extreme."

It's not until he's said those words that I understand what really draws me to this. It's unlike anything I would ever do. I am shit at taking risks; I'm bored to hell with my life already, and I'm only twenty-five. Maybe the reason I can't write about fictional life is because I haven't actually *lived*.

"I think that's why it's appealing. It feels like a crazy thing to do, and I need a little more crazy."

"Well, *this* is it!" he says, laughing. "My advice, of course, is don't do it." Davis pauses. "But I feel like you've already decided, haven't you?"

I can't even say it aloud.

Am I insane?

My older brother exhales slowly across the line. "Just make sure you're safe, okay? Check him out and get an attack dog or something before you go bull-in-a-china-shop your life, woman."

"And—"

"And don't worry: I won't tell Mom and Dad."

eight

No one in the history of the New York City transit system has ever taken so long to descend a set of stairs. At least that's the way it feels as I take them one by one, shoved side to side by the commuters rushing to get around me.

As you might have guessed, I'm stalling. Have the ceilings always been this particular shade of gray? I didn't know they were replacing the light bulbs in this station. How have I never noticed the texture in this paint—oh, that's not paint.

But then, like some preternatural tease, Calvin's music rises up, beckoning.

I reach the bottom landing and see him there, bent over his guitar, lost in the music. Every time I hear it, I become a bottle of carbonated water, lifted and shaken. Inside, everything grows too tight, as if pressurized.

The chaos of the late-morning commute is a little like

being in the middle of a giant ant farm, and people dart between us and on each side, swarms moving in every direction.

He hasn't seen me yet, and doesn't look up as he transitions from one musical piece into another. I cross to stand in front of him, blurting the first words that come to mind. "Do you want to have lunch?"

Even down here it sounds like I've shouted. My voice rises above the squealing cacophony of the trains.

Calvin looks up, and his notes trail off before he gives the strings a final, dramatic strum. "Lovely Holland. How are ya?" I'm rewarded with a smile that sprouts from one corner and grows across his full mouth. "Sorry. What did you say?"

I swallow, wishing I could reach up and wipe my gloved hand across my forehead. I'm sure I'm sweating. "I asked, do you want to have lunch?" I repeat, wondering a little if he's messing with me.

He hesitates, and his eyes dart around us before landing back on my face. "Lunch?"

Someone, quick: Pass me a remote control. I am going to slam my hand on the rewind button.

But instead, I nod. "Lunch. With me. Food. Middle of the day?"

Oh, Holland.

I imagine a horrified Lulu beside me. Her artfully thick brows rise. Her brown eyes roll. Imaginary Lulu drawls in that drawn-out way she has: *"Jesus Christ, Appalland."* And imaginary me turns to her, growling, *"You agreed with me about this, asshole."*

Calvin's laugh is this sweet but tentative thing, like he suspects I know about the visa but isn't sure what my endgame is.

"Sure." He blinks up at me. "Now? I could eat."

- - - -

By the time we reach the restaurant, even imaginary Lulu has abandoned me. When the hostess asks us the requisite "How many?" I react like this is my first adventure out with another person.

"Two. Yes. Two of us. Me and him. Can we sit far away from everyone? I mean, have a little privacy or . . . ?"

The hostess goes still with her hand floating just above the stack of menus.

I feel the gentle weight of Calvin's hand on my arm, and he clears his throat. "We'd like that booth in the corner, please." He drops his voice so only I can hear: "The lady requested *privacy*, did she?"

My face is on fire as we follow her to the table, sit down wordlessly, and bury our noses in our menus.

I take one look at the monstrous list of options and decide on the gnocchi. I'd probably rather have the spanakopita, or a salad, but the image of me indelicately collapsing giant hunks of greasy lettuce into my mouth—or worse, getting strips of spinach stuck in my teeth while I'm trying to casually propose to a stranger—makes a hysterical laugh bubble up in my throat.

It's then that I'm hit with the full weight of what I'm about to do. If Calvin says yes, I'll have to explain this somehow to my parents and the rest of my siblings . . .

Or hide it indefinitely. Davis tells me every chance he gets that I'm in over my head in New York, that I should move home and do something with my degree. With my *life*. My parents always admonish him, and remind him that I am essentially the baby in the family and haven't quite found my place in the world yet.

I don't think marrying a stranger is exactly how they meant for me to find it.

The other bit of awareness is that if Calvin says yes . . . we'll be married. Husband and wife. We'll have to live together . . . proximity, nakedness, my fantasies about him expanding into something barely manageable.

Calvin scratches his jaw, runs a finger thoughtfully up and down the skin just below his ear, up and down, up and down. I feel it on my own face, like we are neurologically linked somehow. I've been with my share of guys, of course, but my type has always been more the nerdy, clueless-about-appearance kind of guy. I've never dated someone in Calvin's stratosphere. Think me: turtleneck sweaters and sensible shoes. Think him: artfully layered shirts and jeans that he's poured into each morning. His casual sexiness is a leaf blower to the brush fire of my nerves.

If only I'd been more sensible today. I scoot in my seat, adjusting my skirt. It's this annoying cheap, slippery fabric, and against the vinyl bench it keeps sliding up my thighs, exposing my ass. I wore it because this morning I thought it looked cute and eccentric with mustard tights and boots, but Calvin is giving the menu exponentially more consideration than he's giving me. I suspect my efforts were wasted.

"Spanakopita or chopped salad?" he muses.

I laugh at how our brains ended up in the same place, but mine then veered into Eating Neatly territory. Guys just . . . never do that.

"I'm getting the gnocchi," I say.

Finally, he looks up at me and smiles. "That looks good, too."

We put in our orders, make small talk about the weather, and tourists, and our favorite part of *Possessed*, until a meaningful silence falls . . . and there's nothing else to do but dive right in.

I adjust my napkin on my lap. "I'm sure you think it's weird that I asked you to lunch."

"Not weird." He shrugs. "Nice. Unexpected."

"The music was amazing the other day. At the theater."

It's almost like something warms from inside him when I say this. "Thanks. I know this sounds trite, but what a bloody honor to be called in. To be offered that gig." He pauses, dipping his straw in and out of his water distractingly. "I assume you heard why I had to turn it down."

I nod, and for the next two breaths, he looks devastated. But then his posture loosens again, and his smile is back.

"It's . . . sort of why I wanted to see you today," I say. The bite of bread I've eaten settles into an uncomfortable glob in my stomach. "So. Calvin."

His eyes sparkle. "*So*. Holland."

Our food arrives and breaks the tension. Calvin bends, stabbing a bite of lettuce and neatly maneuvering it into his mouth. Teeth and chin: spotless. He looks up at me expectantly. "You were saying?"

I clear my throat. "Robert was so impressed by you."

He blushes, chewing and swallowing. "Yeah?"

"Yeah. They all were."

He bites back a smile. "That's lovely to hear."

"I'm thinking . . . I might have a solution."

He stills. "A solution? Do you have an in with the border patrol, then?"

"Ramón Martín is coming on in two weeks," I begin, and Calvin is nodding, "and has a ten-month run. I was thinking . . . that if you—if *we* . . ."

He continues to stare, unmoving. When I don't finish my sentence, his eyebrows slowly rise.

I swallow a gulp of air and push the words out in a rush: "I was thinking *thatwecouldgetmarried.*"

Calvin sits back, surprised.

I look at the other tables, a little unsettled. Is he going to find this not just bizarre but outright immoral?

He puts down his fork. "Aye, why not. It's only Holy Matrimony." He tilts his head back and laughs delightedly. "Surely you're only joking?"

Oh God. Someone flush me out of this room right now. "No, actually."

"*You,*" he says quietly, "want to marry *me?* For this?"

"Not indefinitely, but for a year or so. I mean, until your run is up and then . . . we can do whatever we want."

His eyebrows pull low as he works through this. "And Robert's okay with that?"

"Um . . ." I chew my lip.

Calvin's eyes widen. "He doesn't know you're asking me, does he?"

"Of course he doesn't." I wash down my anxiety with another gulp of water. "He'd try to stop me."

"Yeah, I imagine he would. I imagine he'd do a lot worse to me." He shakes his head, still wearing a dumbfounded grin. "I've never met anyone who loved my playing enough to want to put a ring on it."

I scramble to salvage my self-respect here. "Robert would never ask, but I know he wants you. I saw his face while you played." I don't know how to say this next part without sounding pathetic, so I just go for it. "Robert has been more like a father to me than an uncle. I was raised watching him conduct, watching him compose. Music is everything to him, and the reason I have the life I do is because he takes care of me. I want to do this for him."

Calvin finds this either heroic or pathetic. I can't tell from his expression which it is.

"And . . . I do love your music. I can see what it means to you, too."

Calvin bends, taking another bite. The entire time he chews and swallows, he studies me. "And you'd do this for me?"

"I mean," I hedge, mortified, "unless you're a violent criminal."

Wincing, he picks up his water, draining it in a few gulps, and my stomach bottoms out.

"I did steal a pack of gum once," he says at length. "Age ten. Though no one was hurt."

I let out a shaky laugh. "I think I can overlook that."

He nods, licking his lips before touching his napkin there. "You're serious."

The moment seems to be slowing down, warping a little into a surreal bubble. "I think so?"

This makes him smile, and I notice how his eyes move over my entire face. "How would it work? In theory?"

My stomach slowly climbs back up from the floor. "From what I understand there are some forms, an interview." The biggest piece of information comes out a little squeaky: "You'd stay with me. I mean, on my couch is probably the . . . way we would do it. Not, *it* it—but. Sleeping." I clear my throat. "Arrangements."

Calvin considers this, smiling down at the table. "Do you have cats?"

I blink. "Cats?"

"I'm allergic."

"Oh." I frown. This is really where his brain goes first? Mine went straight to bare skin and sex sounds. "No cats."

"That's good." He pushes a few pieces of lettuce around on his plate, scoops up a tomato and drops it again. "A year?"

I nod. "Yeah, unless we don't want to go that long."

He sniffs, fidgeting with his knife and spoon, straightening them over and over on the table beside his plate. "And when would we do it?"

"Soon." The word rushes out a little louder than I'd have liked, but I push on. "We couldn't put it off too long because of the hiring paperwork. Definitely before Ramón starts."

He nods, chewing his bottom lip. "Right. Sooner would be better."

My breath catches. Does this mean he's considering it?

"So we'd be married, and I'd get to be in the show?" he asks. "Just like that?"

"I think so. You'd have your dream, and Robert would have his new musician."

"I'd also have a beautiful wife. What would *you* have? Other than a famous Broadway musician husband, that is."

He thinks I'm beautiful? I hold his gaze from across the table, not blinking, barely breathing. "I'd get to help my uncle. I owe him so much."

I conveniently leave out the part where I would get to look at Calvin daily—*and that would not be a chore at all*—hear him play, be near him. Yes, I wanted him for months before ever speaking to him, but he's so clearly full of joy, and passion, and a playfulness I never could have predicted. I'm even more attracted to him now that we've spoken. He's witty. So talented . . . but not arrogant. *Way too sexy.*

Calvin looks down at his salad and I can tell he's mulling this crazy offer over. *Oh, my God, he thinks I'm a headcase.*

My stomach turns to concrete.

"Holland," he says slowly, more somber than his previous impish tone. "I appreciate what you're offering, I really do, but I worry that it's a burden that you really shouldn't have to bear. I wasn't trying to butter you up earlier—you really are beautiful. What if you meet someone in the next twelve months, and you want to date him?"

It's hard for me to imagine wanting anyone other than him right now. But maybe he's asking this from his own perspective. Maybe he doesn't want to be stuck in a situation where *he* can't date and sleep with other women.

"Yeah, I mean . . . if you want to date other women in that time . . . maybe you could be discreet?"

"Shite. No. No, Holland, that's not what I meant. This is beyond generous. I'm still in shock. That Robert Okai wants me in his show . . . that *I* impressed *him*. But you, wanting to make my dream possible?"

He lets out a long, controlled breath.

I'm not sure what else to say. I've laid it all out on the table and am holding my breath in these long, painful spans, just waiting to hear what he says.

Finally, he lifts his napkin and wipes his mouth again before setting the cloth neatly at the edge of his place mat. His face explodes in a grin. "I'm in, Holland. On one condition."

I feel the way my brows disappear into my hair. "A *condition*?"

"Let me take you out."

I nod, waiting for him to elaborate. When he doesn't, I look around the restaurant. "You mean like . . . a date?"

"Call me old-fashioned, but I like to date a girl before I marry her. Besides, to pull off this mad plan of yours, I reckon we need to look like we're in love?" When I nod, he continues. "Come out with me tomorrow night and let's see if we can stand to be near each other. You're not going to want me in your apartment if you can't handle me at a bar."

He has a point, but I laugh at his wording. "Handle you at a bar? Are you trying to scare me away?"

Calvin leans in. "Not in the slightest." His eyes move to my mouth, and his voice goes low and warm. "Besides, something this big warrants at least a twenty-four-hour think, yeah?"

Swallowing, I give him a trembling "Absolutely." We're

talking about a transactional marriage, but I feel like we've just enjoyed a tumbling round of foreplay.

Sitting up, he nods to where my phone is resting on the table, and I slide it over to him. He types in a message and a moment later, his phone vibrates with a text. "There"—he slides mine back across the table—"I'll send you the details and we'll see each other tomorrow night."

- - - -

I'm supposed to meet Calvin at Terminal 5 at eight o'clock. I'm a little better at handling the cast by now and get dressed on my own, deciding on a pair of loose ripped jeans for easier bathroom excursions, a black sweater, and my favorite boots.

It's a long walk, even by New Yorker standards, from the train to the venue on Eleventh Avenue. I have a cab drop me off as close as the crowds allow, and text Calvin that I'm here.

With an arm up in a wave, he steps off the curb in front of the building, his long legs wrapped in dark jeans, a gray jacket over a white T-shirt. His hair is shiny beneath the flickering neon sign, and when he's close enough to take my hand and lead me inside, I smell soap and fabric softener. I give myself precisely three seconds to imagine how it would feel to press my face to his neck and huff him.

"This okay?" he asks.

I pull my eyes up to his face and then look around, really taking in our surroundings for the first time. Calvin has managed to get us into a show that—according to the signs outside—is completely sold out.

"You're showing off, aren't you?"

His laugh is a bursting, delighted sound. "I'm *absolutely* showing off."

We check our coats and head to a sweeping balcony that looks out on the stage and the general admission area below. There's an identical level just above, with industrial steel railings, a bar, restrooms, and small clusters of couches scattered around.

"Are we here to watch?" I ask, looking out at the giant disco ball suspended from the center of the massive ceiling. "Or are you playing?"

"I'll be in for one set, yeah. It's a miniature festival. One of the bands I play with was invited." Calvin pays for our drinks and hands me my glass before leading us to a VIP section roped off next to the railing. "This time there will be no spandex or dangly earrings, I promise."

I laugh and peek out over the railing. The floor is starting to fill. Those lucky enough to get in are already crowding their way to the front near the stage.

"You guys weren't bad. Despite all the crotch-strangling Lycra. How many bands do you play with?"

"It changes," he says, "but four, at the moment. Funny enough, the crotch stranglers do pretty well for themselves. I was only brought in a few weeks ago when their original guitarist threw his back out doing a fancy high kick." He takes a sip of his drink and the limes jostle against the ice cubes. "The pay is good, so I didn't ask too many questions."

"Do you have a favorite?"

"I just want to play music." He looks down at me, and his

eyes are so wide and earnest. "It's all I've ever wanted." The way he says this plucks at a tender spot in my chest, the part that sees my laptop rusting away under a pile of takeout menus and junk mail. My degree sits useless in the proverbial box under my bed. Music is Calvin's passion and he's found a way to do it, no matter what. I've always been obsessed with words—so why can't I seem to write a single one?

"So what exactly do you do at the theater?" He gently bumps my shoulder with his. "Besides sell T-shirts and scout talent, that is."

I set my drink down, right next to where someone has written the words *P.L.U.R.*—*Purity, love, unity, respect* on the metal table between us.

"I'm basically peon number three. I take pictures backstage and work front of the house."

He tilts his glass to his lips, smiling over the rim. "Very cool."

I wonder how big a lie that is for him to tell. Calvin, with so much talent and passion that he stayed here illegally hoping to get a job, telling me—a twenty-five-year-old selling T-shirts—that my job is *very cool*. It almost makes me feel more ashamed.

"It isn't what I want to do forever," I say quietly. "It's just what I'm doing for now."

He opens his mouth to say something just as the house lights go out, and the stage lights come to life.

The first act is an EDM group. Three DJs stand onstage, each behind a laptop and various mixers, heads bowed and obscured by giant headphones. The floor erupts at the first beat and even though I'm not too familiar with this genre, I totally get it. There's a high that comes from live shows, a collective energy in a large group of people all gathered for one reason. The beat slices through the melodies and then drops; the crowd bounces and undulates like ripples in water.

I look over to see Calvin with his eyes closed, body moving to the beat, lost in the notes along with everyone else. I close my own eyes and let myself dance. The bass is so loud it feels like a monster heartbeat pounding through me. By the time the last song ends and the lights go up again, I'm flushed.

"They are so good," I say, finishing my drink. "I would never have pegged you as an EDM guy."

"The thing about this music is that if you just stand here and listen, you'll never appreciate it. You're supposed to be part of it—part of the party. I think that's why I like it so much." He does a quick check of his watch. "Listen, it's almost time for our set. Will you be okay here?"

"Absolutely."

"We're playing three songs, so if you want to come down during the last one I can meet you backstage."

I nod and smile up at him.

Am I really here? On a date with *Calvin*?

I'm momentarily light-headed. We're negotiating getting married.

He wraps a hand around my upper arm and gently squeezes. "You're sure you're okay?"

"Yeah." I pull a few strands of hair out of my face, and notice when he glances at my lips. "This is just sort of surreal."

"I know." He pauses, seeming to be on the verge of saying

something more about this, but in the end just tells me, "I'll give them your name and see you in a few?"

"Good luck."

At this, he gives me a grin and leans in, pressing a kiss to my cheek that nearly annihilates me, before heading down the stairs.

– – – –

Calvin's band is on about twenty minutes later, and when he looks up while tuning his guitar to offer me a little wave, my knees grow rubbery.

He was right about the distinct lack of animal print. There are four guys in total, all of them in varying degrees of distressed skinny jeans and vintage band T-shirts, all of them hot. Calvin is playing a guitar I've never seen him use before—it looks acoustic but plugs into an enormous amp near his feet.

Within the first notes of the opening number, I can already tell these guys are good. The singer is a gritty baritone, but impressive on the higher notes, too. The songs are short and range from indie rock to a bit heavier, and each one showcases Calvin's incredible fluidity on his guitar.

Unlike in the station, Calvin is playing to the audience here. He grins wickedly, lifts his chin in greeting to the screaming women up front, and steps into the spotlight during his solos. It's such a starkly different version of him— and still so obscenely sexy—that I can barely drag my eyes away.

And I'm not the only one. A girl with platinum hair and a

nose ring stands next to me at the railing, her gaze locked in on the stage. "Is that the new lead guitar?"

The girl next to her is equally impressed. "Jesus Christ. Is he going to be at the after-party? Because if he is, so am I."

At this, I essentially sprint down the stairs and toward the backstage entrance.

"Um, Holland Bakker?" I tell the security guard. "I'm supposed to meet Calvin McLoughlin."

He looks down at me—seriously, I think he's seven feet tall—and then at his list. With a bored sigh he steps to the side, allowing me to pass.

Calvin is just coming offstage and spots me immediately. Having known Robert all my life, and worked at the theater for the last few years, I'm familiar with the adrenaline rush that comes with performing. It's a high as good as any drug, and is the only explanation I can find for the way Calvin's eyes light up when he sees me, the way he makes his way straight to where I stand and picks me up in a squeezing, sweaty hug.

"Could you see all right? How did it sound?" he asks, amped.

"It was amazing." Being this close to him makes me legitimately dizzy. I now know how hard his chest his, how strong his hands are.

He sets me down again. "Yeah?"

I don't even need to exaggerate my breathlessness. "*You* were amazing."

"McLoughlin."

Calvin turns to find the lead singer standing right behind him. "Devon, hey."

"Thanks for filling in on such short notice. We would have been screwed without you."

"No problem." Calvin tucks an arm around my waist and pulls me closer. When my sweater rides up, I feel the rough press of his hand on my skin, making me grow as hyperaware of each of his fingertips as if he's just brushed them across my nipples. "I appreciated being asked."

Devon wipes his face on a towel and lays it over his shoulder. "Do you think you'd want to make this a permanent thing?"

Calvin takes a moment to consider before looking down at me. He blinks, and a beat of silence passes between us where I think he's asking, *Well? Are we doing this?* His fingers rub my waist gently, as if to remind me there's no pressure.

I swallow, giving him a smile that says: *Fuck yes we are.*

Calvin turns back to Devon. "Dev, this is my fiancée, Holland. Holls, this is Devon."

Holls.

Fiancée.

And I die.

Devon's eyes disappear into his artfully styled mop of sweaty hair before he reaches out, and I return the handshake awkwardly with my cast.

"Fiancée?" he asks. "Well done, man."

Calvin laughs. "Thanks, mate."

"So what do you think?" Devon asks.

Another glance in my direction before Calvin grins. "Thanks for the opportunity, Dev. I really appreciate it, but I'm going to be pretty busy for the next several months."

nine

The coldest day of January also happens to be my wedding day.

What a strange, strange sentence.

It's one thing to say, *Oh hey, I should totally marry this guy so I can save the day*. It's quite another to make it happen. Despite what I told Calvin—a few forms, an interview—Google happily informed me that this process is arduous. There are a *million* forms. There are a *million* requirements. And although there are visas specifically for this situation—where someone in the arts wants to hire a foreigner and an American citizen can't fill the role—Calvin having lived here illegally makes that option unlikely. Which is why just yesterday we were here, getting our marriage license.

Marriage license. Holy hell, this is happening.

"I know I'm always encouraging you to get a life," Lulu says, sliding her hand into mine, "but this is like me suggesting you eat something and you go and scarf down three dozen donuts."

My heart is in my throat as we climb the stairs in front of City Hall, and I grip Lulu as if she's keeping me above water. I am so grateful that she's here: she got a great deal on simple gold bands from her shady uncle and came over early this morning to do my hair.

"You did say it would make a great story for my biography one day."

Her dark hair—blown out and curled for the occasion—falls in a polished wave over one shoulder. "I said *my* biography," she says.

Tipping her head back, she takes a final draw on her cigarette before snuffing it out. Her exhale plumes into a dense cloud in front of her, and I let go of her hand and subtly step away. Lulu quit smoking twice this year—going from Marlboros to vaping, to nothing, and back to Marlboros again. According to her, it's not so much that she's addicted as that auditions make her nervous, the wait after the audition makes her nervous, working in a restaurant in Manhattan and dealing with people's shit makes her nervous.

"Just giving you a final chance to back out." She fishes in her small bag for a box of orange Tic Tacs. "We don't have to go in there."

Her suggestion would be the easy choice, and certainly the smart one, but I can't back out now. For as nervous and as terrified as I am, there's another side that's secretly, shamelessly giddy.

Self-consciously, I smooth the front of the pleated chiffon

skirt I'm wearing as we pass through the glass doors. I'm still not sure it was the right choice. Trying too hard? Not trying hard enough? What does one wear to a fake wedding, anyway?

"You look good, kid." Lulu pauses to spare me a glance. "What underwear are you wearing?"

"*Lulu.*" Seriously, how is it possible she is both the good and the bad angel on my shoulders?

"It's an important question. Wedding night, Appalland."

I've already explained to her a thousand times that it's not going to be that kind of marriage (I mentally pour one out at the sorrow of this truth). We step just inside and I point in the direction of the Marriage Bureau, leading us down the corridor.

"I admire you for this decision, so don't take what I'm going to say the wrong way." Her shoes click on the tile floors. "But I can't believe you didn't at least tell *Jeff.* I plan on lying like a politician if either of your uncles ever asks me whether I was here."

"I'll tell them both everything as soon as it's done. It'll be like a little surprise party. 'Hey, look! You get your star and oh, by the way, we're married.'"

She loops a sympathetic arm around my shoulder and gives me a little squeeze. "I do not envy you that conversation."

A hint of movement catches my eye, and I see my groom at the end of the hall. His light brown hair is neatly combed and he's wearing a blue suit with a purple gingham shirt and blue bow tie. With my blue skirt and pink silk top, we match.

"*Jesus,*" Lulu stage-whispers.

My pulse takes off like a rocket.

His stride is long and purposeful, and in just a few steps, he's standing in front of me. My eyes move from Calvin's freshly shaved jaw to the tan column of his throat. I imagine him with his guitar in the park in the summer, the dappled shade in his hair and blades of grass clinging to his shoes and the bottoms of his pants.

"You look nice," I say, in dramatic understatement.

"You look . . ." His green eyes take a casual stroll down the length of my body. I feel the attention as surely as if it were hands moving on my skin. "Stunning."

A throat clears at his side.

"Hello." A man with acres of black hair and pale blue eyes steps in front of him, taking my hand. "I'm Mark. The better man."

"Is that right?" I say with a laugh.

"Witness," Calvin clarifies, and sidesteps him. "This is Mark Verma. A friend."

I smile up at him. "It's nice to meet you, friend."

He aims a set of dark, raised brows in Calvin's direction. "I like her."

I can feel Lulu hovering just behind me and pull her forward. "This is my best friend, Lulu."

"It's nice to officially meet you," she says to Calvin, stepping forward to take his hand.

They talk among themselves for a moment, and it's only now, with Calvin standing just a few feet away, that I notice what he's carrying.

He follows my attention down to the circle of pale purple blooms in his hands. "It's an Irish tradition for brides to wear flowers in their hair—in my family, at least. I know we're not . . . that this isn't traditional in that sense. But Mam would be heartbroken if I didn't at least ask."

My brows go skyward. He's going to tell his parents about this? My folks live in the same country and I've already concluded it will be easier to lie my face off than live with their inevitable disapproval and concern. His parents live on the other side of the world. A gesture like this feels like we're doing Till Death Do Us Part, when really, it's only Till the Fat Lady Sings. Why on earth would he tell them? My immediate reaction—and surely the most mature, here—is to want to press pause and talk about how we each see this going. In hindsight, we hardly talked about it at all, and telling our families makes this something much bulkier that we have to manage.

But he looks so earnest and uncharacteristically unsure, I decide to put him out of his misery quickly.

"Of course I'll wear it. Thank you."

It's made of loosely braided lavender, and I take it from him, settling it carefully on top of my hair.

Lulu reaches out to adjust the silky purple spikes, tilting her head to inspect her handiwork. "There. Perfect." She snaps a few photos. "Let's get you two married."

I'm overly aware of the way my palm fits against Calvin's as he takes my hand and leads us through the crowd toward the clerks.

Sidestepping a woman in a jewel-toned sari, I smile at a passing man wearing a yarmulke. There are couples of every composition and age. Some wear traditional dresses and suits, others are in jeans and T-shirts.

"Busier than I expected," I say softly.

Calvin exhales a little laugh. "Yeah. You'd be surprised how many wedding dresses I see at the station."

The room is long and narrow, with a row of sleek green couches on one side and marble counters and swiveling stools on the other. The ceilings are white-paneled with gold filigree detail. A marquee suspended from two chains shows the number now being served and at what station, and a ticket machine sits on the counter below. There's even a small gift shop that sells last-minute items like flowers and emergency bow ties.

Calvin pulls a number from the machine and shows me: C922. A flash goes off and we both startle.

"That's going to be good," Lulu says, looking down at the screen of her tiny camera. She catches my bewildered expression. "What? The candids are always the best ones. A wedding is something you want to remember." She looks at me pointedly. "Any couple would want photos to commemorate that."

"Right." This needs to be official. I've put so little thought into the logistics of this. Man, when I try to be spontaneous, I steal a lighter and throw it blindly into a pool of gasoline. "Good thinking."

Calvin and I sit on one of the narrow couches, waiting and trying to ignore the click of the camera every three seconds. We make polite small talk:

"Did you have a good morning?"

"Yeah, didn't sleep, though."

"Me either."

"It's so cold outside."

"I know. I nearly forgot my coat."

Awkward laugh. "That would have been . . . bad."

And on, and on, for a half hour, about what we ate last night and how we weren't sure what to wear today. The only time either of us seems to relax and fall into easy conversation is when Calvin mentions he almost brought his guitar with him.

"It seemed oddly fitting," he admits, "but then I worried it would be a hassle, or seem odd."

"I wish you had."

I really do. His music magically loosens that knotted ribbon inside me; I already miss hearing him play in the subway.

While we trip our way through the Holy Shit We Are About to Be Married awkward dance, Lulu and Mark chat unobtrusively to the side, having no apparent problem making entertaining conversation. Mark—like most people—seems completely charmed by Lulu, but every time Lulu snorts and loses it over one of his jokes, the more anxious I feel.

From this moment forward, no matter what happens after, I am combining my life with Calvin's.

Finally, our number is called. We step up to the counter and I watch Calvin fill out the last bit of paperwork. Alongside our witnesses, we sign our names—mine is a lot less legible than everyone else's, thanks to the cast—and after another small wait, it's time. The New York City Marriage Bureau is very efficient.

We're led into a small room with peach walls and pastel watercolors. Our officiant is a smiling woman with dark hair and rosy cheeks who greets us with a friendly welcome. There's no music or fanfare, but she gently instructs us to stand opposite each other, while everyone else can stand or sit where they'd like. Calvin takes both my hands.

"Calvin and Holland," she begins, "today you celebrate one of life's greatest moments, and give recognition to the worth and beauty of love, as you join together in the vow of marriage."

I look up at his face; his eyes are crinkled in amusement that is oddly masked as joy. I bite my lip, grinning back despite myself.

"Calvin," she continues, "do you take Holland Lina Bakker to be your wife?"

His voice comes out hoarse at first, and he clears his throat. "I do."

I love the way his accent curls the words.

She turns to me, and he squeezes my hands in his. "Holland, do you take Calvin Aedan McLoughlin to be your husband?"

I nod. My breath is tight in my chest, and for the first time since the ceremony began, I feel a pang of loss that Jeff and Robert and the rest of my family aren't here. "I do."

We promise to love, honor, cherish, and protect each other—forsaking all others.

We promise to have and to hold, in sickness and in health, for richer or for poorer.

My stomach drops, and Calvin twists our fingers together— a tiny loophole on these promises.

With a shaking hand, I slide the simple band on his finger, and he returns the action on mine. At the bases of our fingers, the rings are so unblemished and innocent, gleaming proudly. I have the hysterical thought that I wouldn't have the heart to tell these shiny, happy rings that they're just props.

The ceremony is over with a flash of the camera as the officiant pronounces us husband and wife.

"Calvin, you may kiss your bride."

I do a double take toward the officiant before I can help it. It never occurred to me that he would. That *we* would.

Calvin laughs a little at my wide eyes. "I promise to make it nice."

It takes every bit of focus I have to remain upright. "I . . . believe you."

A tiny cocky grin curves his mouth. "If you can't be good, at least be good at it." His hand comes to rest at the back of my neck; his fingers thread into my hair. "So come here," he whispers, licking his lower lip. As he leans in, I have to tip my head back to see him. His eyes are closed, his breathing even, and there's a moment of hesitation where I know we're both thinking, *This is it. We're really doing this.*

I bring my hand to rest on his chest and it's that solidness that spurs me on, has me closing the last bit of distance between us. His lips are warm, smoother than I imagined, and tiny explosions travel along my body like a rush of caffeine filling my veins. It's a perfect kiss, not too wet, not too soft, and I count to two before he pulls away, his forehead resting against mine. And just as I'm wondering whether he'll ever kiss me again—unprompted—he whispers a sweet, nearly imperceptible *"Thank you."*

A flash goes off to the sound of cheering and applause. More couples wait their turn, so we're rushed out the door and down the hall to a small backdrop of the historic building. We pose for photos, of me and Calvin, Mark and Calvin, me and Lulu (she threatens dismemberment should I let Jeff or Robert find them), and all of us together.

"You did it," she says into my ear, hugging me tight. Holy shit, she's right. I got married. Me. I've never even *considered* marriage before and the word sounds so foreign I can barely wrap my brain around it. She hands me a small bag. "Your first wedding present!"

Inside and buried beneath what has to be an entire package of tissue paper is a red magnet with a white heart that reads:

Married in New York City.

ten

S o what now?

  Ahead of us, Lulu and Mark are trading small talk—about jobs, New York, weather.

 Calvin and I are in a weird bubble right behind them. The wind is sharp and cold, and we're bundled up, heading down the last block to Gallaghers Steakhouse, unspeaking. He's a nice person, I'm a nice person. As our two dates have demonstrated, we get along just fine . . . but I'm sure we're both reeling with the awareness that we're *married*.

 Married. Calvin is my husband. I am his wife.

 I glance down to the ring on his left hand and, in response, the metal on my finger seems to grow bitingly cold.

 "You all right?" he asks.

 Startling at the sound of his voice, I shift my attention to his face. His nose is pink, and adorable. Ugh. I've married him, and he has no idea I've been writing Holland/Hot Busker fic in my head for months. How is this a good idea?

I go for breezy: "Yeah, of course—it's my wedding day."

When he turns his face forward again, I can barely see it peeking out from the hood of his black down jacket. But I do catch the smile. "You're quiet. I haven't known you that long, but what I do know isn't quiet."

Well. He spotted that quickly.

"You're right, I'm not." I smile faintly back. My face is numb, it's so cold outside. "I'm just thinking about all of this."

"Regrets?"

"No, more of the 'What now?' kind of thinking. I need to tell Robert."

"Maybe we could talk out here, away from prying ears."

I look over at him again. We're less than half a block away from Gallaghers now, and he's got a point. Once we get in there, everyone will be able to hear us, and will for sure see the awkward navigation through the *What now?* if we leave it until the end of the meal.

I stop, bending as if adjusting the strap on my shoe. Calvin calls out to Lulu and Mark. "Yeah, keep going," he says. "We'll catch you inside."

And then he crouches, meeting my eyes. "This is big, what you've done."

"Yeah." I'm caught in the intensity of his expression.

"I can see why you'd be left a little speechless."

"Yeah."

"Maybe I could go with you when you talk to your uncles?"

"Okay."

Use your words, Holland. Tell him it isn't so much that you're feeling regret as you're feeling sheer panic at the prospect of sharing an apartment with a stranger who also happens to be the hottest man you've ever touched. What if you fart in your sleep?

"I want you to know," he continues, "despite my misdemeanor candy theft, I'm not a creep. I would never hurt you. But if you would feel more comfortable staying separate places—"

"We can't." Although it's true, there is a vague tremor of nausea in my thoughts now. I'm ninety-nine percent sure Calvin isn't a rapist or rampant drug abuser. But now taking him into my apartment seems somewhat impulsive—and not just because I might fart in my sleep.

"I want you to know how much I appreciate this," he says, "and I won't take anything for granted."

I'm unaccustomed to being thanked so profusely, and stammer out a few sounds before nodding.

"Is the plan that I come home with you tonight?"

Heat spreads up my neck and over my cheeks. "I think so."

"You have a couch?"

I nod.

"Your bedroom door locks?"

I pull back, looking at him. "Do I need it to lock?"

He shakes his head quickly. "Of course not. I want you to feel safe."

"You must think I'm a maniac."

His grin charges something to life inside me. "Well, aren't you? I think that's why I like you, Holland Bakker McLoughlin. That and your freckles."

We straighten in slow unison, and the whole time he grins

down at me from several inches above. I finally manage to respond to this: "You think I'm taking your name?"

"I'm sure of it."

My jaw drops through a grin. "I married a caveman?"

"Just a personal preference. Want to make a wager on this?"

"As in," I say slowly, "I lose and take your name. You lose and I keep mine? What's really in it for me?"

"If I lose, I'll take yours."

What is even happening right now?

He slides his hand around my fingers. "So . . . uncles tomorrow?"

I blink up from our joined hands. "I'll make sure they're home."

"Good. Now let's get inside and make that wager. I'm freezing my bollocks off."

I nearly trip on the sidewalk.

- - - -

As Calvin holds the door for me, I hurry inside where Lulu and Mark wait and a blast of warm air hits that's so amazing, we groan in unison.

Lulu walks over, cupping my elbow. "You okay?"

"Yeah, just had to fix the strap on my shoe."

"Okay, good." She seems placated and motions to where a group of busboys are clearing a table. "About five minutes, they said."

"Cool, thanks for doing that. And thanks for coming with me today. I don't know what I'd have done without you."

Her smile goes soft and she wraps her arms around me. "Are you kidding? The craziest thing I've ever seen you do is try to change the date on your expired Saks coupon so you could still get half off. I wouldn't have missed this."

I laugh and press a kiss to the side of her cheek. "You can be kind of great sometimes. Not often, but . . ."

"Very funny. Now pardon me, but I'm gonna go live it up and harmlessly flirt with your husband's friend."

Calvin watches Lulu leave and returns to my side, taking my hand. The touch is so unfamiliar and awesome, it makes my stomach vault around in my belly.

"Hungry?" he asks.

"The wager?" I remind him.

"I'm getting there—it's related to my question." He lifts his chin to the meat locker. "They have good steaks here."

And just like that, I'm interested in whatever he's suggesting. "They do. What're you thinking?"

"They have a porterhouse for two, three, or four."

I haven't eaten in nearly twenty-four hours, and the idea of a big juicy steak has me salivating. "Yeah?"

"So, I say we split the one for three, and whoever eats more wins."

"I'm going to guess their porterhouse for three could feed us both for a week."

"I'm betting you're right." His adorable grin should be accompanied by the sound of a silvery *ding*. "And your dinner is on me."

For not the first time, it occurs to me to ask him how he makes ends meet, but I can't—not here, and maybe not when we're alone, either. "You don't have to do that."

"I think I can handle treating my wife to dinner on our wedding night."

Our wedding night. My heart thuds heavily. "That's a lot of meat. No pun intended."

He grins enthusiastically. "I'd sure like to see how you handle it."

"You're betting Holland can't finish a steak?" Lulu chimes in from behind me. "Oh, you sweet summer child."

- - - -

As we get up, I groan, clutching my stomach. "Is this what pregnancy feels like? Not interested."

"I could carry you," Calvin offers sweetly, helping me with my coat.

Lulu pushes between us, giddy from wine as she throws her arms around our shoulders. "You're supposed to carry the bride across the threshold to be romantic, not because she's broken from eating her weight in beef."

I stifle a belch. "The way to impress a man is to show him how much meat you can handle, don't you know this, Lu?"

Calvin laughs. "It was a close battle."

"Not that close," Mark says, beside him.

We went so far as to have the waiter split the cooked steak into two equal portions, much to the amused fascination of our tablemates. I ate roughly three-quarters of mine. Calvin was two ounces short.

"*Calvin Bakker* has a pretty solid ring to it," I say.

He laugh-groans. "What did I get myself into?"

"A marriage to a farm girl," I say. "It's best you learn on day one that I take my eating very seriously."

"But you're only a tiny thing," he says, looking from my face to my body and back again.

It's as though his gaze drags fire over me.

"Not *that* little." At five seven I'm on the taller end of average, and while I've never been overweight, I've never been thin, either. Davis used to say I came from sturdy stock, not the most flattering description, but not the worst. In short, I have a body made for sport, but hand-eye coordination made for books.

We push out of the restaurant and convene in a small huddle on the sidewalk. It's too cold for a prolonged goodbye. Mark asks if we want to go out for a bit longer, but when Calvin hesitates, I jump on board, saying—honestly—that I'm sort of wiped, even if it's only ten.

But that means they hug us goodbye, give another congratulations, and then turn, hailing cabs and going their separate ways.

It was easy for Calvin and I to play at comfort during dinner—we had a distraction: the bet. And nearly as soon as we sat down, Lulu ordered wine, Calvin ordered appetizers, and conversation exploded easily, as it always does when Lulu is around. I used to refer to her as social lubricant, but Robert made me promise to never use that phrase again.

Now it's just us—me and Calvin. There's nowhere to hide and no one to hide behind.

I feel the warm slide of his gloved hand around mine.

"Is this okay?" he asks. "I'm not trying anything, I just feel fond."

"It's fine." It's more than fine. It's making it hard to breathe, and—shit—this is a terrible idea. Every bit of that disarming honesty and affection he shows me is going to make it that much harder when the run of the production ends and we can part ways.

"Which way are we?" he asks.

"Oh." Of course. We're just standing here in the freezing cold while I internally melt down, and he has no idea where I live. "I'm on Forty-Seventh. This way."

We walk quickly, strides matched. I forgot how weird it is to walk while holding someone's hand. Weirder still when it's cold, and we're rushing, but he holds on tight so I do, too.

"How did you meet Mark?"

"We played in a band together while I was at school." His shoulder brushes mine as we turn on Eighth. "He just did it for sport, though I was quite intense about it. After he graduated, he went on and got an MBA." After a pause, he adds, "I've been living at his flat in Chelsea."

Well, that answers one question.

"Paying rent," he quickly adds. "He was sad to lose the extra money, but as he put it, will not miss the sight of my white arse." He laughs. "He suggested I invest in pajamas."

My eyes widen and he quickly clarifies. "Which I have, of course."

"No . . . I mean"—I press my palm to my forehead. My face feels a thousand degrees. "I want you to be comfortable. Maybe just warn me if you're going to . . . be—I'll knock before I come out in the morning."

He grins and squeezes my hand. "Anyway, I can put that money into yours now. It's only fair."

My stomach clenches. This is all *really* weird. I know sterile details about Calvin from the marriage license, like his birth date, full name, place of birth. But I don't know anything relevant, like how he makes money other than street performances and cover bands, who his friends are, what time he goes to bed, what he eats for breakfast, or—until just now—where he's been living.

And of course, he doesn't know these things about me, either, but from what I understand he'll *need* to. Immigration will want us to know things some couples don't know even after years together. Is this how we do it? With this sort of frank, transactional honesty?

I dive right in, blurting: "Robert and Jeff pay about two-thirds of my rent."

"Really?" He lets out a low whistle.

"Yeah. Surprisingly, I don't make much selling T-shirts and taking pictures of people backstage. Not enough to live in Manhattan, anyway."

"I don't imagine."

Nausea rises. Is this a good thing to admit, or bad? Have I just revealed to him that Jeff and Robert are totally loaded?

"I try not to take advantage," I say, oddly humiliated. After all, Calvin just admitted to relying on a friend, too, and I know he makes money, at least in part, from playing gigs. "I was going to live in New Jersey and commute, but they found me this place when a friend of theirs moved out"—died, actually—"and . . . yeah."

"Do you like living alone?"

I laugh. "Yeah, but . . ."

It seems to register what he's just said and he laughs, too. "I promise to stay out of your way."

"No, no. I like it," I clarify, "but I'm not someone who *needs* to be alone, if that makes sense."

Calvin looks over at me, smiling. "It makes sense." He hesitates. "I make decent money for what I do. Probably make fifty bucks every time I busk. Make a couple hundred for the bar shows. But it's not a real job."

I look over at him. He's got his face tilted up to the sky, like he's inviting the shock of the cold.

"What do you mean, 'real job'?"

He laughs. "Aw, come on, Holland. You know what I mean. I like that, actually, that you know exactly what I mean." Looking straight into my soul, he says, "I make money, but it feels like cheating, like I have this ability I've worked so hard for, and I'm not doing shite with it."

"Well, now you are."

A smile spreads over his face and I wish I could describe it. It's the expressive equivalent of an eraser, wiping away any doubt I had about this.

"Yeah," he says. "Now I am."

- - - -

Because there was no way I could sleep before the wedding, I cleaned the hell out of my apartment last night. I'm not a slob, but I'm not meticulous, either, and cleaning kept me occupied for a solid two hours until there wasn't even a bit of dirty grout left to scrub with an old toothbrush. So I started writing out a list of pivotal moments in my life.

To date, my longest relationship was with a guy named Bradley. He was from Oregon, and I met him during undergrad at Yale. We dated for two and a half years, which I now know to be the point when you've heard most of the stories and some of them you've heard a few times. But with Bradley—who was a completely nice guy but sort of boring (also his penis turned dramatically to the right, and as much as I tried to pretend it wasn't a big deal, it always felt in my hand like a bone that needed to be reset)—I learned those things gradually, over time. Our getting-to-know-you had happened in sleepy doses during pillow talk, or at a bar, as we got progressively drunker and more physical. We broke up under completely pedestrian circumstances: I just wasn't feeling it anymore. After a week of quasi-dramatic begging, he gave up and within a month was dating the woman he would eventually marry. Two and a half years, and the entire thing—from start to finish—was completely unremarkable.

I'm thinking about all of this—the strange way we'll spew out our histories almost as if we're downloading data—as I walk inside with Calvin, so when I see the list on the counter, I want to burst out laughing.

"Wow." Calvin steps in, eyes wide as he looks around. My place is tiny, but it *is* pretty great. I have a giant bay window in the living room, taking up the majority of the wall. The view isn't postcard-worthy or anything, but it looks out over rooftops, and into other apartments. I have a sleeper sofa, a coffee table, a television. Beneath the coffee table is a rug with swirling oranges and blues that Robert and Jeff got me as a housewarming gift (despite my protestations that the apartment itself *was* the housewarming gift). There are two bookcases loaded with books that bracket the television, and then nothing. That's all I have in here. It's clean, and simple, and cozy.

"This is so nice," he says, moving closer to read the spines of my books. "Mark's place is amazing, but he's got twin two-years-olds who visit, and it's super cluttered."

I mentally file this bit of information away in my Immigration Interview Bank, and he runs his fingers along the edge of a book by Michael Chabon.

"This . . . I like it sort of simple, like this." He wanders to the tiny kitchen, peeks in at the minuscule bathroom, and then stops, turning to me. "It's really nice, Holland. Well done."

He's being so adorably awkward, I can't help but say, "You can look at the bedroom."

Beneath his olive skin, blood rushes to the surface. "That's your space. That's all right."

"Calvin, it's just a room. There aren't, like, naked posters of me in there or anything."

I can't tell if the sound he makes is a cough or a laugh, but he nods, joking, "Well, that's a shame," as he moves past me into my bedroom.

It's my favorite space. I have a wrought-iron-framed double bed with a white coverlet, a dresser, an antique standing mirror, a couple of lamps on the nightstands, a few photos of my family, and that's it.

It's bright and sparse.

"I think I expected it to be girlier."

"Yeah." I laugh. "I'm not super girly."

He picks up a pair of pink scissors from on top of a pink photo album. Sets them down next to a pair of rose gold sunglasses. He glances dubiously to my doorless closet; it's clear that pink plays a leading role inside there, too.

"Well," I amend, "except for a few things, I guess."

He motions to my arm. "Purple cast." And then, quieter, "And you were wearing pink the night you were shoved."

My fingers tingle in this weird way when he says that, like blood has evacuated my extremities and rushed to fill my chest. He meets my gaze head-on, like he wants to cover this now, first, before we do anything else; our conversation at the bar was such a scratch of the surface, and now I know that he didn't intervene because he wasn't here legally.

"Tell me what happened that night," I say. "I don't remember much."

"Well, yeah. You were rather unconscious." With a little beckoning tilt of his head, he turns, leaving my bedroom and heading out to the sofa. He pats the seat beside him.

For a few seconds filled with blinking embarrassment, I realize this means he saw me in complete disarray.

My saggy tights.

My skirt at my waist.

And, later, my shirt unbuttoned to my navel.

"Oh God."

He laughs. "Sit."

"I was such a mess." I drop down beside him.

"You landed on the subway tracks and knocked your head." He looks at me quizzically. "Of course you were a mess."

"No," I say, groaning into my hands. "I mean you probably saw my saggy crotch and my boobs."

A strangled laugh comes from beside me. "I wasn't really thinking about crotches and boobs at the moment. I jumped up, telling the bum to wait, but he ran. I tried to reach you but couldn't. I worried if I tried to fetch you, we'd both be stuck down there. I called the paramedics, called the MTA. The ambulance arrived, and that was that." When I look back at him, I find him studying me. "It happened so fast. I wasn't sure what he was doing at first, but then he came for you. I don't have a legal ID or residence. I was paranoid. That's really it."

"Okay."

He nods to my cast again. "How much longer do you need to wear that?"

Tracing a finger along a line in the hardened bandage, I say, "I get it off in three weeks."

"Does it hurt?"

"Not anymore."

He nods, and the silence swallows us.

We look around. At the dark television, the window, the bookcases, the kitchen. Anywhere but at each other.

My husband.

Husband.

The more I repeat the word in my head, the more it sounds fake, like it's not a real thing.

Calvin clears his throat. "Do you have anything to drink?"

Booze. Right. This is the perfect situation for some booze. I jump up, and he laughs, awkwardly. "I should have thought to get champagne or something."

"You bought the dinner," I remind him. "Obviously the champagne was on my list and I dropped the ball."

Pulling a bottle of vodka from the freezer, I set it on the counter and then realize I have nothing to mix it with. And I finished the last beer the other night.

"I have vodka."

He smiles valiantly. "Straight-up vodka it is."

"It's Stoli."

"Straight-up mediocre vodka it is," he amends with a cheeky wink.

His phone buzzes, and it sets off a weird, giddy reaction in my chest. We both have full lives beyond this apartment, which remain complete mysteries to each other. One difference between us is that Calvin likely doesn't care about my life outside of this. Yet I care *intensely* about his. Having him here feels like finding the key to unlock a mysterious chest that's been sitting in the corner of my bedroom for a year.

Buzz. Buzz.

Looking up, I meet his eyes. They're wide, almost as if he's not sure whether to answer.

"You can get it," I assure him. "It's okay."

His face darkens with a flush. "I . . . don't think I should."

"It's your phone! Of course it's okay to answer it."

"It's not . . ."

Buzz. Buzz.

Unless, maybe, it's some Mafia drug lord and if he answers

his ruse is up and I'll kick him out. Or—gasp—maybe it's a girlfriend calling?

Why had this not occurred to me?

Buzz. Buzz.

"Oh my God. Do you have a girlfriend?"

He looks horrified. "What? Of course not."

Buzz. Buzz.

Holy shit, how long until his voicemail puts us out of our misery?

". . . Boyfriend?"

"I don't—" he starts, smiling through a wince. "It's *not*."

"'Not'?"

"My phone isn't ringing."

I stare at him, bewildered.

His blush deepens. "It's not a *phone*."

When he says this, I know he's right. It doesn't have the right rhythm to be a phone.

I lift the vodka to my lips and chug straight from the bottle. The buzzing has the exact rhythm of my vibrator . . . the one I tucked beneath that cushion on the couch days ago.

I'm going to need to be pretty drunk to deal with this.

eleven

roll over onto my side, right into a solid, warm body. It's black all around us, and the darkness only amplifies his quiet moan. Against me, Calvin is completely bare; we both went to bed clothed, but somehow I ended up back out in the living room—naked—and the unbelievable heat of him seems endless in the tiny sofa bed.

The springs creak when he rolls to face me, nibbling a path from my shoulder to my jaw. "Well this is unexpected," he says.

I want to ask him how long I've been out here, but he wipes away all organized thought, leaving only a trail of fire behind as his hand slides up from my hip, over my breast to my neck.

"You didn't want to fuck in the bed?" he asks, speaking into a kiss against my jaw. "I would have come to you."

He shifts away just enough to let me explore with my palms: the solid expanse of his chest, the hair on his navel, and lower, to where he's hard for me, shifting into my palm when I curl a fist around him.

Like this he moves for a few tight breaths, sucking at my neck, cupping my breasts in his rough hands. But every inch of my skin feels tight and aching—I need him over me, *inside*.

"I want . . ."

His mouth hovers over my nipple, teeth bared. "Want?"

I try to blame my impatience on the fact that it's the middle of the night, and I've somehow wandered into Calvin's bed, and *he's totally fine with it*—I don't want to lose a single second of this by either of us overthinking it. So I urge him over me, staring up at him in the dark.

"Did you get enough dinner?" he asks, kissing from my breast slowly up to my neck.

I don't know why he's joking about the steak right now, but it doesn't even matter because I can feel him press against me, and then he shifts his hips and he's sliding inside with a moan that vibrates against my throat.

The stretch of him inside me is so new, so unexpected, that I cry out and he turns his head, covering my open mouth with his. He says something I can't make out, but it's probably less about the words themselves than it is about my inability to process beyond the feel of him sliding in, and back out of me.

It seems unreal that he's here, *moving*, pulling my legs around his waist. He's not quiet—he lets out a gust of pleasure with every thrust, and I don't think I've ever been this wild: pushing up into him, digging my nails in his back, begging him for faster, for harder.

Then he's behind me—*how*, it was so fast—and I feel the sharp sting of his hand, the satisfied grunt he makes when I cry out. And then I'm over him, his hands on my breasts, fingers drawing maddening circles around the peaks.

"Are you close?" His voice is tight with restraint.

"Yes."

"Fuck. *Good.*" His hands come to my hips, and he starts working himself up into me, hurried and deeper. "It feels so *good.*"

And it does. My skin feels staticky, my spine is tight with the spiral of pleasure.

"Jump on me," he groans.

". . . Jump?"

"Rabbit," he growls. "Like in a field. *Carrots.*"

With a gasp, I startle awake into the darkness of my bedroom. The sheets are a tangle at my feet. My door is still closed, and I am completely alone with my hand down my pants.

Bolting upright, I lean forward, listening for any sound of activity outside the door. There's a quiet rustle, a squeak of the sofa bed springs. According to my clock, it's 1:48 a.m. Is Calvin awake? *Oh my God*, did I wake him up by moaning? Was I loudly . . . masturbating?

I want to throw myself off the fire escape outside my window. This is only the first night having Calvin outside my room, and already I'm having sex dreams about him.

I am so fucking doomed.

- - - -

Nobody thinks they're a morning person—I'm no exception. I'm not mean or one of those people who requires a sonic boom to get me out of bed, I just tend to stumble around, blurry, for a few minutes before the hamster wheel upstairs starts rolling smoothly.

Wednesday morning, I wake, push myself up, scrub my face, and stand. Like I do every morning, I walk to the kitchen to get the coffee started. No doubt my straight hair has been teased into a campfire. My pajamas are twisted around my torso. I have dragon breath.

A deep, gravelly voice mumbles, "Hey."

I jump back, pressing my palm to my chest. "*Ohshitthat's-right—*"

Apparently I'd completely forgotten that I have a husband. A husband with a penchant for showing skin.

And as soon as I see him, I remember my dream—the *You didn't want to fuck in the bed?*—the endless length of him sliding inside, the sting of his hand across my ass—and a blistering flush spreads across the entire surface of my body.

Calvin is folding up the sofa bed, his hair standing up as if he's been electrocuted by my couch. His pajama bottoms hang low on his hips . . . very low. I get an eyeful of navel hair before my eyes dart away.

I'm impressed with how accurately my dream hands predicted how he'd look naked.

I affix my attention to the tip of his nose. "Morning."

He reaches up, wipes his nose self-consciously. "Mornin', Holland."

"You sleep okay?"

He nods. "Like a rock."

I struggle not to look when he reaches down, absently scratching his stomach.

"You going in to work today?" he asks.

"Ah." I'm overheated. "No. We'll need to talk to Robert at some point, but I took the rest of the week off to, um . . ."

I have to turn away to reach for the coffee filters. His body is insane. His body hair is the best balance of there-but-not-furry.

Calvin is half naked in my apartment and I am completely losing my shit right now. I need to get some distance and some caffeine.

I gesture vaguely to him across the room. "To study."

"To study *me*?" he asks playfully. I'm not looking at him, but I hear the grin in his voice.

"Yeah. Your life, and things."

"'Things'?" he repeats, and laughs. My brain fills with the memory of his happy trail and our dream sex.

"Are you headed to the station later?" I blurt, desperate to change the subject.

If he notices how I've just demonstrated my knowledge of his schedule, he doesn't show it. "No, think I'll stop doing that."

My heart is a wilting flower in my chest. I mean, of course, it makes sense that he'd stop performing at the station now that he's about to have a full-time job, but it also means the end to this little tiny joy I have.

I pour another out for Busker Jack.

I hear an odd dissonant scratch behind me, and turn. Calvin has pulled his guitar out of its case and now sits shirtless

on

    my

        couch.

He plucks at the strings and grins boyishly at me. "You put the pot on, I'll provide the soundtrack?"

My controlled exhale comes out of me in tiny, sharp splinters. "Sure. Yeah."

One of the few things Calvin has put in the kitchen so far is a box of tea labeled BARRY'S, so I assume that's what he wants, putting the teapot on the stove and dropping a teabag in a mug. Round, warm music begins to fill the apartment, sending a wave of goose bumps down my arm. I intently study the thin stream of coffee filling the pot to keep from turning and gawking while he plays his guitar half-naked.

"Holland," he says, slowing the meandering tune, "can I ask you something?"

"Sure." I risk a look over my shoulder at him. Big mistake. "I figure that's what we're doing today."

"This question is different."

I smile in encouragement. "Go for it."

"Are all female sex toys bright pink?"

Gah.

Gahhhhhhhh.

"Or is it just you? Like the scissors and your coat and—"

"I . . . Are you fucking with me?"

He holds up one hand, with a guitar pick wedged between two fingers. "I swear I'm not trying to embarrass you."

"Embarrass me?" I look back to the coffee and grab a mug to pour it into. "Man, I'm totally used to having guys come over and find my vibrators in the couch. That's why I keep them there."

"Really?"

I turn and look at him flatly.

"Right," he says through another delighted laugh as he returns to his strumming. "The colors of these things strike me as odd."

"How do you take it?"

His eyes go wide. "Pardon?"

I hold up his mug and bite back a laugh. "Your tea."

"Black." An adorable giggle bursts out of him. "Oh my God, this conversation. I'm so sorry. I'm not fully awake yet. I don't know what I'm saying."

Returning to the living room, I hand him the mug. "Have you been thinking about this since last night?"

Last night: when I pulled my enormous, pulsating pink vibrator out of the couch, sprinted to the bathroom to wash the couch lint off it, and then shoved it under the sink, in the very, very back. Last night, when I went to sleep and very nearly got myself off dreaming that he was having sex with me.

"No, just since I woke up." He thanks me, and takes a sip before leaning over his guitar to place the mug on the coffee table. "You'd think the colors would be more masculine if you're getting a fake cock—"

My brain goes all wavy when he throws that word into my living room like it's not a live bomb.

"—but—and my sampling isn't huge here—the majority seem to be pink."

With his easy chatter and judgment-free tone, my embarrassment slowly, slowly drains away.

"I think the flesh-colored ones have a weird sense of sadness to them." I sit down beside him. "Like a penis separated from its host."

"That is a very sad prospect, indeed."

"They also grow discolored?" I say, remembering. "I had a flesh-toned one I kept in my underwear drawer and it sort of took on the colors of the fabrics around it until it eventually looked tie-dyed."

He laughs, nodding as he works his fingers up and down the neck of his guitar.

I want to understand why I feel so easy around him. Calvin is the human equivalent of a joint. It must be the soothing sound of the guitar. "Maybe it's because women want pleasure for themselves," I say, "and not to feel like they're owing it to a dude, even when it's a toy."

He stops playing at this, turning to look at me. "That's astute."

I purse my lips at him, playfully. "You're pointing out how astute I am for understanding my own sexuality?"

The grin that comes over him is probably the best thing I've ever seen. It's wide, showing teeth, crinkling his eyes. "I knew I'd like you."

I knew I'd like you, too, Busker Jack.

I nod to his guitar as I stand up to start breakfast. "Then keep playing."

- - - -

By midmorning we're headed toward the theater. It's freezing out, but the cold keeps me from dragging my feet and putting this off any longer. No doubt Robert was tipped off that something was different when I didn't show up with coffee from Madman, but I doubt he's expecting *Hey, I got married yesterday!* as an explanation.

I remind myself that the hard part is over. Telling Robert will be easy because he'll be thrilled . . .

Right?

Jeff, on the other hand . . .

"So they'll both be here?"

It's the first thing Calvin has said since leaving the apartment, and the sound of his voice jerks me out of my anxiety spiral. Clearly we are both on the same page.

"Yeah." I texted Jeff this morning, asking for a good time to check in with both of them . . . he said he'd be at the theater with Robert all morning. "Robert's barely left since Seth quit. Jeff threatened to drag him out if he didn't at least let him bring fresh clothes and food that didn't come from a vending machine."

Calvin gives me a tiny wince. "Does it make me a terrible person if I'm relieved they're still stressed about replacing Seth?"

We reach the front of the Levin-Gladstone and I turn to face him. "If you are, then I am, too, because it just occurred to me last night they could have found a replacement in the time it took to do all this." I lift my hand and wiggle my ring finger. "That would be . . . inconvenient."

Calvin gently grips my elbow, stopping me from opening the door. "Thanks for letting me come along this morning. It feels like the right thing." He hesitates. "You don't reckon they'll murder me?"

"They wouldn't murder you. They'd murder me."

Just inside, Brian's eyes land on me like a heat-seeking missile.

"Brace yourself," I mutter under my breath.

Calvin follows my gaze to Brian barreling down upon us. "Who is that?"

"It's my boss, the stage manager. Imagine Mr. Plankton and Effie Trinket rolled into one. He hates me."

"What in the hell are you doing here?" Brian asks, pointing to the door. "You took four days off. *Go take them.*"

"I came to see Robert. Is he upstairs?"

"He's upstairs with the rest of your family. I swear to God, are we running a show here or hosting a reunion?" His eyes shift to where Calvin is standing just behind me. I register the exact moment he recognizes him and puts the pieces together, because he glances at my left hand and his face contorts in glee. "*Shut. Up.*"

"Brian—"

"You *actually* did it." He takes a step closer and I step back, colliding with Calvin's chest. "You let me sit there and get my ass handed to me in front of Michael *and* the Law brothers, and then you went out and did it anyway."

I nod, taking these lumps. After all, he isn't wrong. But the difference was, in the end, it was *my* decision, rather than some bartering chip Brian gets to claim as his.

"Well." He takes a dramatic step to the side, throwing his arm out as if to point the way to Robert's office. "By all means, head upstairs and inform your uncle that you did exactly what I suggested. I cannot *wait* to hear what he says."

I take Calvin's arm and lead him to the stairway, making a mental note to steal the lifts from inside Brian's fancy Gucci loafers.

"Seems like a good chap," Calvin says dryly, and despite everything, I burst out laughing.

Robert's office door is half-open; I stop just outside. "Wait out here, okay? Just for a few minutes."

Calvin hesitates before giving me a reluctant nod, and I lift my hand to knock.

Robert calls out almost immediately. "Come in."

"Hey." I walk in, taking a deep breath. Robert is seated at his desk eating a bagel, and Jeff is folding a pair of pants before tucking them into a leather duffel bag.

Robert looks up when he hears the door click closed behind me. "Hey, Buttercup. I thought you were off this week?"

I walk over and kiss Jeff's cheek before rounding the desk to kiss Robert. "I came to talk to you."

"Are you hungry?" Jeff asks. "There's fruit and coffee and a bag of those little quiches you like."

"Thanks, but . . . I already ate." The idea of keeping food

down at the moment is comical. I turn to face Robert. "How's the search going?"

Jeff looks at his husband with an expression that says he's been living with this particular mood for a few days. "Please don't get him started."

Robert rubs his eyes with the heels of his hands. "We've auditioned a dozen musicians."

"And?" Hope mixed with anxiety burns a hole through my gut.

He sinks back in his chair; he looks exhausted. "And . . . we'll probably audition a half dozen more."

"Would it help if I said you didn't need to?"

I become acutely aware of Jeff going still off to the side.

"We've already gone over this, Holland," Robert says, and then adds, "He can't."

"Who can't what?" Jeff asks very carefully, but I'm sure he already knows.

I ignore this for the moment, focused intently on Robert. "But, let's just say—hypothetically—that he could?"

He watches me warily. "Well, I would be thrilled. Hypothetically."

That's all I need to hear.

Standing, I turn to the door, stopping with my hand on the knob. "I want you to know that I did this because I love you, and when I saw the chance to be able to help, I took it. I know you're going to be angry with me but it's done."

Robert's voice is a low, menacing rumble. "Holland Lina Bakker. What did you do?"

Judging from the look on his face, he already knows.

I turn the knob and Calvin steps inside, hands tucked deep into the pockets of his jeans. "Mr. Okai." He looks at Jeff. "Mr. . . ."

"Also Okai," Jeff finishes, looking back and forth between Calvin and me in confusion. "Would someone like to fill me in?"

I hold up my left hand, displaying my wedding ring.

One breath.

Two.

Three.

And then the burst of Jeff's incredulous voice: "You got *married?*" It's so loud I know even if Brian isn't standing just outside, more than likely he's still heard it.

I hold up my hands. "Only temporarily."

"You married a man you met in the *subway?* Does your mother know?"

"Absolutely not." I step closer, putting my hand on his arm. "I talked to Davis and he's assured me he won't say anything. I'm hoping you'll do the same."

Jeff whips to Robert. "Did you put her up to this?"

"Of course not!" I insist. "He was the first person to shoot down the idea when Brian suggested it."

"You did something *Brian* suggested?" Jeff is usually the calm one in our family, so I'm not really sure how to feel about the way that vein in his forehead is bulging. I do, however, take small pleasure in knowing that Brian probably heard this, too. Jeff looks at each of us. "Have you all *completely* lost your minds?"

"Honey." Robert stands, rounding his desk to take his husband's elbow. "Let's all take a moment to breathe."

Jeff wheels on him. "You're not seriously going to let her go through with this."

Robert throws his hands up. "What do you want me to say?"

"That she needs to undo this immediately?"

I point to my chest. "Hi. Grown woman, standing right here."

I feel Calvin shift behind me. "I am really sorry that we didn't involve you in the decision—"

"But it wasn't up to him," I interrupt, glancing over my shoulder before looking back at my uncles. "I made it clear Calvin can handle his family, I can handle mine."

Robert looks up at me, eyes searching. "You're *legally* married?"

I nod.

"I can't believe I'm hearing this." Jeff closes his eyes and takes a calming breath before reaching for his coat and folding it over his arm. "I'm going home to take a bottle of blood pressure medicine and try not to call your mother—*my sister*—who will want to kill me when she finds out." Turning to Robert, he adds, "We'll discuss this when you get home. Which—considering you have a new guitarist—will be *early* today."

Robert nods obediently and walks Jeff into the hallway. While he tells him goodbye—speaking too softly for us to hear—Calvin and I share a grimace.

That could have gone better.

With Jeff gone, Robert closes the door and moves to his desk, motioning for us to take the seats opposite him. Hands folded neatly on the chaos of portfolios and résumés in front of him, he looks crankily at each of us in turn. "Okay. You did this, so we may as well deal with it."

- - - -

I . . . think we pulled it off?

I mean, Robert is furious with me—with both of us—but I'm not homeless or on a plane back to Des Moines, so I'm calling it a win. Best of all? Calvin has officially been offered the part for *Possessed* and even if Robert won't admit outright that he's ecstatic, he's droopy with obvious relief. After we'd gone over the details, he called in the rest of the team. He was practically vibrating with creative energy. *I* did that.

Mission accomplished.

But we aren't done yet. Despite his anger at all of us, Jeff still forwarded the email he got from Sam Dougherty, his childhood friend who now works at USCIS—US Citizenship and Immigration Services. That's heartening, at least. But my mood wilts when I count the number of attachments; it feels like there are a thousand forms for us to fill out.

Calvin and I spend the rest of the morning gathering birth certificates and medical records and copying them in triplicate. By that afternoon, the coffee table is stacked with tidy piles of official documents. We haven't even started the process of filling anything out yet, and my brain is goo.

Calvin finds me blinking into the open kitchen cabinet, staring at the mugs there. I was listening to an audiobook as I put dishes away and *boom*—surreal slaps me across the face:

I see Calvin's Juilliard mug on the shelf next to the one Davis gave me for Christmas last year that reads WORLD'S MOST OKAYEST SISTER.

"Everything all right?" he asks, eyeing me.

"Just having a momentary freak-out. I'm great now."

Calvin laughs. "I hear that." He picks up an apple, absently polishing it with the hem of his T-shirt. I keep my eyes at chin level. Mostly. "Do you think everything with your uncles will be okay? Jeff seemed pissed off."

I close the cabinet door and turn toward the fridge. We stopped for some groceries on the walk home, and I grab two beers now. I don't care what time it is, it's five o'clock somewhere.

"Jeff might take a little longer to calm down, but the great thing about family is they have to forgive me." I hand Calvin a beer. "I think we both need this."

We crack them open and head back to the task in the living room. Calvin takes a seat at my side on the couch, stretching his legs out on the table in front of him.

He's not wearing any shoes, and has these screaming purple argyle socks that I immediately adore. Purple socks, happy trail, electrocution hair. I have this dream man in my apartment, and he is distracting as hell.

I can't wait to see how tonight's sex dream plays out.

I reach for my laptop and wake it up with a swipe of my finger across the trackpad. It's been ages since I've looked at this thing, let alone turned it on. The expensive novel-writing software sits in the toolbar with a little book icon reminding me how much I suck.

Ignoring it as usual, I open my email instead. "Jeff's note said there are forms for each of us. Did you get a link?"

Calvin takes a sip of his beer and sits back to click through to his account. "Form I-485. Check."

"I'm I-130," I say. "He has a note that we can file these two concurrently, and fill out the rest of the package for him to send off once we get the initial approval. There's also another list of things we need to make copies of, and a to-do list."

Calvin looks over at me and I try to ignore the way the lamp behind him makes the tips of his eyelashes glow. I like seeing him on my couch. I like knowing what color his socks are, and what his sleepy face looks like before he's had his tea.

He scratches his chin. "A to-do list?"

"You'll need a medical exam. And until you're officially on the books, I need to provide pay stubs to show I can support us both." I let out a hearty guffaw. "Which means Brian will need to give me a raise. If you think he was great today you should hang around for that conversation. It's going to be a doozy." I tap my pencil to my lips, reading. "And we'll need documents that prove our marriage is bona fide. His suggestions are a shared lease—easy enough—joint club memberships . . ." I look over at him. "Do you go to the gym?"

An amused curve shapes his lips and he folds his arms across his chest in that way all guys do when they want to emphasize the guns. "I do. I can add you to my membership, unless you have one of your own and want to add me?"

"Just go ahead and add me to yours," I say quickly, as if I

don't routinely have a king-size Snickers for lunch and view treadmills as a mindless way to run and never actually get anywhere. "He suggests we have emails and texts between us, so I guess we should do that?"

"Texts like 'Can you pick up a gallon of milk?'—or like . . . *personal*?"

I absolutely can't look at him right now. I fix my gaze on the far wall. "We want to be convincing . . . so a mix of both?"

He pulls out his ChapStick, drawing my attention back to his mouth. He's only about two feet away from me. I've never had the chance to look at his hands close up before. His nails are trimmed—thank God—his fingers long, but not delicate. He's wearing my ring.

"To be clear," he says slowly, recapping the lip balm, "so they don't arrive and scare the hell out of you, we're talking about *I can't wait to get your kit off* kind of personal?"

My heart stands up, waves the white flag.

"Uhhh . . . yeah, I think so." I immediately return to the safety of my bullet-point list while he picks up his phone, typing something. "What else . . . ? Letters or cards congratulating us on our marriage, bills in both our names like utilities, credit cards, that sort of thing."

My phone buzzes with a text from Calvin. Are you coming home before work?

I type in casually, I'll be home in about 30.

He replies, Good. I want to taste you again before you leave.

I choke, sliding my phone back down on the coffee table. "That's—good job. I . . . approve."

Honestly . . . how often has he done this?

He laughs, his face a little pink. "I feel sort of bad making you go to all this trouble."

I wave off his concern. "It won't be bad. Some sexting, a couple more copies, a couple yes-or-no questionnaires. Honestly, how hard can it be?"

- - - -

Shoot me in the face.

Have you ever tried to do your own tax returns? Immigration paperwork is a lot like that, but with less math and far more opportunities for perjury.

My form was easy enough to fill out—names, addresses, and former employers. But Calvin's are so in-depth that even when we split them it takes over an hour to get through the first two.

I look up at him from the other side of the coffee table. I'm on my second beer of the afternoon and my pencil is lost somewhere in my hair. "Can you list past and present memberships or affiliations with every organization, fund, foundation, party, club, society, or group you've been a part of since the age of sixteen, along with the location, nature, and dates of said affiliation?"

He stares blankly, exhausted. "I don't even know the name of the band I was in last year, let alone from when I was sixteen."

I check the form before glancing up at him again. "You better remember, because it wants that, too."

Calvin leans back and runs a hand through his hair, laughing. An apple core sits on a plate in front of him, along with a handful of orange peels, the empty wrappers of two granola bars, and a bit of crust from one peanut butter and jelly sandwich. Calvin revelation: he eats a lot.

I move on to the next section. "Tell me about your parents."

"They're called Padraig and Marina. They're . . ." He trails off, shrugging. "They're nice."

"Padraig?" I say, doing my best to repeat his pronunciation.

He turns to face me, tucking a purple-socked foot underneath him. His hair is standing straight up, almost as if it is as delighted as he is by my mistake. "*Pat-rick*," he repeats in an obnoxious American accent, emphasizing each letter this time.

I feel my face heat. "Oh. *Patrick*. I am an idiot."

"You Americans speak at the back of your mouth and crowd all your consonants together. Where you might say 'How are you?'" he says, now using an almost perfect American accent, "an Irishman would simply say, 'Hawarya?'"

My voice comes out shaky and soft: "I like that."

Close your mouth, Holland.

He continues as if he hasn't noticed my swoon. "The accent is stronger some times than others—like when I've had a few pints and I have to remind myself to slow down. If we were in Galway, you wouldn't understand a thing I said."

"I'm sure we sound fairly boring in comparison."

He gives a slight shake of his head. "I like the way you sound, though."

Oh.

I clear my throat and look down to the forms.

We spend the next fifteen minutes going through his

phone, looking at photos of his family while I write down the full names and birth dates of all his siblings. He's twenty-seven, the oldest of four: Brigid is twenty-five and closest to Calvin, Finnian is twenty-three, and Molly is nineteen.

"So is the birth order rule true?" I ask him. "Are you the dependable oldest child? The conscientious, overachieving, structured . . ."

He laughs and tips his beer to his lips to take a swallow. "I'm here on an expired visa and had to marry a stranger to get the job of my dreams. 'Conscientious' might not fit me to a T." Pausing, he scratches his jaw. "But yeah, I was a know-it-all with them, and a bit of a bossy little shite, especially when our parents weren't around. But they retaliated sometimes. Once, a girl I fancied was outside with a friend in the street, and Brigid and Finn stripped me bare and pushed me out the front door."

"Oh my God."

"Eh, I'm sure I deserved it." He tilts his chin to me. "What about you, baby of six? Are you the classic youngest child?"

"I'm sure Davis would say I am. I mean, Robert created a job for me and my uncle pays most of my rent, so . . ." I trail off and motion to the room around us, as if to say *see?* "I'd say that's a yes."

"I don't know," he says, elbows on his knees while he looks at me. "This feels pretty selfless. Giving up half your space and putting yourself at risk."

"I think you're giving me too much credit." I busy myself straightening a pile of papers. Guilt is like a little stopwatch *tick-tick-tick*ing away in the back of my head. In my heart,

I know I did this for Robert. But having Calvin here so close . . . and feeling like I've finally done something useful for the production . . . I can't deny that I also did it at least a little for me.

"Thomas," Calvin mutters, tapping his list of my siblings' names with the tip of his pencil. "Bram, Matthew, Olivia, Davis, Holland."

"That's right," I say, and stand to get us each another beer. "Thomas is an ophthalmologist in Des Moines. Bram is a high school math teacher in Fargo. Matthew is in tech support at the University of Iowa . . ."

He cuts in: "Davis lives in Wisconsin, and Olivia is . . . ?" He shuffles through his notes, but I know he won't find anything.

"Who knows," I tell him, returning with the bottles. "Last week she wanted to go to massage school. Before that, she decided she was going to turn Mom and Dad's land into an organic farm."

"Every family needs one of those." He points his thumb to his chest.

"Some of these yes-or-no questions are really easy." I motion for him to hand me his laptop, and he does, almost gladly.

"Cheers." He leans back again, wiggling his purple socks.

"Never been arrested . . ." I click the box marked NO and move on to the next one. "While in the United States, do you plan to engage in espionage?"

He gives me an evil smirk.

I grin, and then look back to the form. "Plan to engage in any activity a purpose of which is opposition to, or the control or overthrow of, the Government of the United States, by force, violence, or other unlawful means?"

He pretends to think, and I move on. "Have you ever been a member of the Communist Party?" He shakes his head and I click the correct box. "Do you intend to practice polygamy in the United States?"

"Let's see how this one goes first."

Butterflies twist into a tornado inside me. "Within the past ten years, have you been a prostitute or procured anyone for prostitution, or do you intend to engage in such activities in the future?"

"I'm trying to cut back."

He can't see over my shoulder, and I know this could be a golden opportunity to get a little Calvin info. "Have you ever conspired to engage in, or do you intend to engage in any form of terrorist activity?"

"No."

"Counterfeiting?"

"No."

"When was your last relationship?"

He stops with his beer halfway to his mouth. "It wants to know that?"

I hold my hands up in mock innocence. "I didn't make up the questions."

"Erm, a while ago."

I pause with my fingers hovering over the keys. "It wants a date."

"About ten months ago, I suppose. Though it wasn't very serious."

"Have you ever joined or do you plan to ever join the mile-high club?"

Calvin opens his mouth to answer, but seems to figure out what I'm doing. "You little shite!"

I laugh, ducking the pillow he lobs in my direction.

twelve

M ore often than not, it's me pounding at the door of Robert and Jeff's apartment with arms full of groceries. But Friday night—three days after the wedding— Uncle Jeff shows up loaded down with takeout.

Although he's silently forwarded communications between us and Sam Dougherty, we haven't spoken since the morning he left Robert's office, fuming. Jeff and I have never gone this long in an anger-induced silence, and I'm so grateful to see him that I throw myself into his arms. More accurately, since he's holding bags from Pure Thai Cookhouse, I hurl myself at him, pinning his free arm at his side with my non-casted one.

"I'm sorry," I say, taking a step back and swiping at my eyes. Calvin is there to rescue us and slips in, taking the food from him with a smile. Jeff nods in thanks before pulling me into a genuine hug.

"You're an idiot," he says into my hair. "But I suppose you're my idiot, and I'm pretty grateful for that."

I press my face into his dress shirt, smearing tears and mascara onto the blue-and-white-checkered cotton. "So you're okay with all this?"

"I'm definitely not *okay*." He pulls back enough to swipe at my cheeks with his thumbs. "But I understand it a little better. There's nothing I wouldn't do for him, either. Anyway," he says, stepping back. "I come with an army." He gives me a silent look of pleading.

Robert is, of course, at the theater, but it's true that Jeff isn't alone. Behind him, Lulu holds up two bottles of tequila, and behind *her* is Gene, Lulu's . . . bed-friend, holding a bag of limes and sporting the world's most enormous mustache.

I take the bag of limes from him. "Are you guessing my weight tonight?"

Jeff laughs in a loud bark before heading into the kitchen, but Gene does a bewildered double take. "What?"

"Do I get to shoot a water gun to knock down the ducks?"

I see the moment he gets it because his giant mustache twitches under his suppressed grin. "I'll take my limes home if you're going to be sassy, miss."

"You look like an old-timey auction barker," I say. "Or Yosemite Sam. I have this sudden urge to buy a few head of cattle." Behind me, Calvin snickers.

"You *wish* you could grow a 'stache like this."

I burst out laughing. "I'm sorry, I can't even hear what you're saying through that thing."

"I told him it's awful." Lulu tugs at it and Gene leans away.

He smoothes it down proudly. "I'm so lazy, and this is much more low maintenance than shaving."

I don't need to look that closely to see he's clearly waxed and styled it with a comb. It's really not an afterthought mustache; it's the kind that a person chooses from a book on various mustache styles—the perfect accessory for his *very* carefully crafted *I don't care enough to even glance in the mirror* look (which Lulu tells me takes him a long time in front of the mirror).

Gene steps inside and Lulu stops in the open doorway. I don't think I have to ask how she ended up coming along with Jeff tonight. "He called and yelled at you, didn't he?"

She leans in, pressing a kiss to my cheek. "He sure did. But I appeased him by sending him all the photos. He said I did a great job with your hair."

I laugh as she makes her way into the kitchen, and I close the door in time to see Jeff step up to Calvin.

"I don't believe we were properly introduced." My uncle extends his hand. "And I want to apologize for being rude. Holland is my youngest niece, and more like a daughter to me, so I'm very protective of her."

"No, no." Calvin balks at this, returning the handshake. "I completely understand."

"And, congratulations." Jeff smiles with a twinkle in his eye. "You've passed a three-step criminal background check." He looks over at me. "Holland, I emailed you a copy."

Calvin's eyes go wide. "Honestly?"

With a laugh, Jeff walks into the kitchen to unpack all the food.

"Oh!" I pull Gene forward. "I'm so sorry, Calvin. This is Gene, he's Lulu's, um . . . friend?"

"*Boy*friend," Gene corrects.

"Fucktoy," Lulu says with a smile, smooshing his face in her hand before walking away to help Jeff or—more likely—pour some alcohol.

Calvin and I exchange a look, and something giddy is born inside me at the way it feels like we have an unspoken language of snark.

Calvin extends his hand. "I'm the husband."

"Not the fucktoy?" Gene says, throwing a bucket of ice-cold awkward over the conversation.

"Erm, no," Calvin says, giving me a comical *Eep* face.

"Not yet!" Lulu calls from the kitchen.

"Lulu," I call back, "you and Gene will be banned from this apartment if you continue to make tonight weird."

"It's already weird enough," Jeff says.

Leaning in close enough that only I can hear, Calvin says, "I did find a sex toy in the couch."

I smack his arm.

Lulu returns with four tequila gimlets and Gene asks us how our first week of marriage is going. Despite the mustache and obsession with looking like he doesn't care about appearances, Gene is twenty-nine and, admittedly, pretty hot. But standing next to the God that is Calvin in his dark jeans and faded T-shirt, the boy doesn't compare. For a couple of seconds, I catch Lulu looking at Calvin the way my old retriever used to eye my dinner plate, and I move a little closer to him.

I cup my hand around my mouth, calling out, "Jeff, there's wine above the fridge!"

"Already got it," he answers. "I'm just putting out the food."

"A warning," I stage-whisper to Calvin. "The drunker Jeff gets, the more honest he'll be about how horrifying he finds this whole thing."

Calvin glances across the room toward Jeff. "He'll be *more* honest?"

"I can hear you, Holland," Jeff says, choosing that exact moment to join us in the living room. "I just worry that this won't end well. Not to mention I hate lying to my sister."

"I guess we could tell Mom and Dad," I say, and motion for everyone to head to grab some dinner. I'm totally lying, and have my fingers crossed in my pockets hoping that I'm calling Jeff's bluff. "Mom's pretty chill—she's not going to disown me . . . It just . . . it didn't feel official yet, maybe because we haven't had the immigration interview. Why worry them?"

"I told my parents," Calvin says casually.

I squint up at him. This surprises me, given how fast everything happened. "When?"

He sips his drink, lifting it in thanks to Lulu. "Before the wedding."

"They were fine with it?" I ask.

He nods. "They were thrilled."

"You told them *why* we got married?"

"No," he says, setting his drink down so he can fill his plate. "I told them I met a girl. It's true enough, innit?"

It *is* true enough . . . but not a surprise to them how fast it happened? I study him for a second longer, at his easy calm, his constant smile. Maybe it's that he's a son instead of a daughter, or the oldest instead of the baby, or maybe he seems confident enough about every move that his family stopped questioning his decisions a long time ago.

The conversation shifts as we grab food and head back to the living room. I don't have a dining table, let alone enough chairs, so we all find spots on the floor around the coffee table.

Everyone tucks in, and I get up to grab some supplies for the evening. The plan was for Jeff to be able to share information about me with Calvin, but since Lulu came along, I quickly devised a game based *entirely* on keeping Lulu from dominating the conversation: Lulu, Jeff, and Gene will each have a bag of poker chips. They have to bid to share a story in the category Calvin requests, and are free to outbid the others if they think their story is better. I haven't known Gene that long, so I'm only giving him a bag of chips to be nice, but Lulu and Jeff have some pretty great—and some pretty terrible—stories about me, and they're going to need to share the stage, so to speak.

After I explain the rules, we all look at Calvin.

He swallows a bite of dinner, wipes his mouth with his napkin, and then pulls a small notebook from his back pocket. "Can't we start with some basics everyone can answer?" He pulls the cap off his pen with his teeth.

"I guess so." I point to Lulu. "But you are limited to a minute per answer."

She flops dramatically back onto the throw pillow behind her.

"So, first," Calvin says, "I want to know what you admire most about Holland."

"Besides her rack?" Lulu calls from the floor.

Jeff groans; Calvin grins, and then, without any subtlety whatsoever, checks out my chest. "All right, yeah. But besides that."

My pulse riots in my throat.

"Her backbone." Lulu pushes up onto an elbow to look at me. "She does what she says she'll do, and doesn't do things she doesn't want to do."

"Cheers. Good answer." Calvin jots it down before turning to Gene, who shrugs.

"I mean, she's a really good cook?"

Calvin laughs. "Are you asking me, or telling me?"

Jeff clears his throat and then coughs into his fist, looking at me. "That's going to be hard. I admire so many things."

"Aww, Jeffie." I lean over and kiss him on the cheek.

"I think I admire that she, more than anyone I know, tries to be circumspect about her successes and failures, and who she is. She tries to see herself clearly—both kindly and critically—and I think she's generally pretty spot-on."

It's one of the best, most unexpected compliments of my life, and I'm left momentarily speechless.

"She's also pretty funny," Jeff adds, and Lulu is already protesting.

"You only get *one*," she says, but Calvin is quick to interject.

"Yeah, but she's class," he says with a cheeky smile in my direction. "So I'll let that infraction slide."

Calvin asks a couple more general ones—what's their favorite thing to do with me, what sort of music do I listen to, what sort of movies do I hate, what do I always order at restaurants—before ending with "What bothers you about Holland?"

"Hey!" I protest.

He takes my hand, squeezing. "Come on. I think this is really interesting."

Damn him. It's impossible to deny him when *think* comes out as *tink*.

"She won't take risks," Lulu answers immediately.

"Hello?" I point to Calvin. "Risk, *right here*."

She snorts. "I dunno. That's a pretty fine-looking risk."

Calvin leans a little closer to me.

Gene thinks for a minute before giving yet another shrug. "She, um, I don't know, won't ever call me Lulu's boyfriend?"

"To be fair," I argue, "*Lulu* doesn't call you her boyfriend."

Gene laughs. "True. Why won't you call me your boyfriend, Lu?"

"Because we're not sixteen? Would you be happier if I called you my manfriend?"

"Yeah, actually."

While they're bantering, I look at Jeff, unsure whether I want to hear his answer. He's already doing that thing where he licks his lips in preparation for saying something difficult.

"What I said before was true," he says quietly, as if he's speaking only to me, "about how Holland tries to see herself clearly and seems to end up in a pretty good place. But I also think she sees herself as a supporting character, even in her own life story."

Just as I was thrown by his compliment, I am equally—and

conversely—thrown by his criticism. It lands with a resonating *bong*. Has Jeff just hit on the truth behind my biggest road-block? For nearly a year I've been trying to come up with an idea for my first novel, and nothing is there. Is it because books aren't about side characters, and those are the only voices in my head?

The room has gone quiet.

I lift my drink, finishing it and holding it out to Lulu to refill. "I feel like an insect under a microscope now." With Lulu and Gene here, this is way more uncomfortable than I'd antic-ipated. "Let's get the fun part going."

The bidding begins. Calvin starts out easy—what's Hol-land's favorite movie?

Even Gene knows this one—we saw it down at the Beek-man together a few weeks ago. At Lulu's pointed stare from across the room, he tosses in a chip. "Is it *Blues Brothers*?"

"Correct," I say.

"A time Holland cried," Calvin prompts.

Jeff throws in a chip, but Lulu throws in two, and he gives her this one. Instead of saying something heartfelt, she tells the story of the time I got wasted and slipped while cross-ing Madison and Fifty-Ninth, and started sobbing because I couldn't find the sunglasses that were on my head.

"Thanks for that, Lulu. And for what it's worth, they were pink and limited edition. It was more about frugality than feel-ings."

She salutes me.

Calvin takes another bite of dinner and swallows before asking, "Something Holland is sentimental about?"

Without throwing in any chips, Jeff and Lulu call out, "Gladys" in unison, and Jeff explains: "She has a stuffed dog named Gladys that she's had since she was three. It was a birthday present from Robert, who, you will learn, is Holland's favorite person alive."

"It's true," I agree. "I'm not really sentimental otherwise."

"Your most embarrassing story?" Calvin asks.

Lulu throws in a chip and starts speaking before Jeff has a chance to bid: "Oh, I got this one. She had sex with a guy one night and there was a ton of air in her—"

I smack my hand down on the coffee table. "*OH MY GOD, LULU.*"

Everyone goes deathly silent, and it might be because we've killed them all with the horror of this visual. Lulu looks around as if she's only now registering the audience.

"I can live a thousand years," Jeff says, "and never hear the rest of this story."

"Why do I ever confide in you?" I ask her, genuinely annoyed.

She sounds surprisingly contrite. "Because my stories are always worse?"

"I was thinking less about 'Holland with a boyfriend' type of scundered," Calvin says, "and more inebriated hijinks."

I look over at the sound of his voice—sort of tight and thin—and catch his peeved expression. I'm starting to sense that Calvin doesn't care for Lulu's brand of crazy.

And I'm not sure I like it tonight, either; she's dialed up to eleven.

"Well," I say, putting my hand on his arm, "there was the

time my *grandmother* didn't recognize me because I'd gained the freshman fifteen." Jeff coughs, and I amend, "Freshman twenty-five."

Calvin looks at me gratefully—"That's brutal"—and bends to write it down in his notebook.

We drink more, tell more stories—about what sports I played (volleyball, briefly), what books I love (many), where I've gone on vacation (fewer places than I'd like)—and Calvin shares a few of his own: He used to fish on a lake with his father every Friday morning for Friday dinner; his youngest sister, Molly, has cerebral palsy; he saw *Possessed* seven times because he was lucky in the lottery twice, and has a truly generous former professor who took him five other times; he doesn't understand the appeal of sitcoms— particularly *Friends*; his favorite movie is *The Godfather Part II*—and I love that this makes him sort of average in at least one way; he doesn't eat lamb and thinks it's an abomination to mix anything with whiskey. He also used to help his mom out a lot when he was younger and is apparently quite the knitter.

"You *knit*?"

He nods slowly, relaxed by the food and the alcohol and the company. "Could knit you a scarf and a cap to go with it."

It could feel like we are taking in information in giant gulps—like one might drink from a fire hose—but the way the stories unwind with tangents and jokes and side stories also makes me realize we truly are getting to know each other, in the intense way that happens when people are cooped up together, like at summer camp.

Jeff stands, beckoning Lulu and Gene to leave when he does, and I appreciate my uncle's ability to be frank without being rude: "Let them get some sleep. Imagine how exhausting this is."

He gives Calvin a wary smile before hugging me tightly.

Lulu grabs the remaining full tequila bottle, and Gene sends air kisses on their way out.

When the door closes behind them, Calvin exhales heavily. "Wow. I feel full." He taps his temple, indicating his meaning. But if the way he looked gratefully at Jeff is any indication, I think he also feels full of social interaction.

"I bet."

Together, we pick up the plates and clean the kitchen. He washes the dishes; I pack up the food and clean the counters.

This feels so easy. Hanging out with my people with Calvin there, cleaning up afterward. Is it because we know how fake it all is, and there are no pretenses? Or is it something more, some matching chemistry?

See, Holland, this is where you'll get in trouble.

He grabs a beer and moves to the couch, dropping onto the cushion, and I flop down on the opposite end.

"Did you have a good time?" he asks.

I rub my forehead, counting out the four gimlets I drank over three hours. "Yeah. It was fun. I'm tipsy, though."

His laugh is light, like he finds this charming. "Your nose is all pink."

And then, unexpectedly, he shifts so that he's lying down and he carefully lowers his head into my lap. "This okay?"

"Sure." Tentatively, I lift my hand, brushing his hair off his forehead.

He hums at the contact, and his eyes fall closed. "What a crazy week."

"Yeah."

This moment is so surreal I actually bite my bottom lip to make sure I'm not imagining it. I wonder if it will feel more or less like real life when he goes to rehearsals and I'm back at work, and we come home together every night.

One year. A voice inside warns me to cocoon my heart and expectations in bubble wrap.

"I had enough drink to be comfortably sleepy," he says. "Maybe loose-lipped."

"That's a good thing. Let me go get my list of deeply personal questions."

He laughs, looking up at me. "I learned a lot about you tonight. You can tell a lot about a person by what their loved ones say."

I groan, remembering. "Lulu was a beast. Clearly that does not reflect well on my character."

"I was going to ask about that." He lets his eyes fall closed again as I comb my fingers through the front of his hair. "She seemed okay at the wedding but was acting the maggot tonight. Is she always so crude?"

"Yeah, Lulu's emotions can be all over the place, but tonight it felt almost aggressive, like she was trying to out-drama me."

"What we've done *is* pretty dramatic. From the outside it seems to me that Lulu is used to being the wild one."

"It's true." I look down at his face, enjoying being able to study it without him noticing. His nose is straight and narrow, lips full but not feminine. I love the shape of his eyes. I don't know how to describe them other than roman, mildly hooded. His lashes are thick but not distractingly long. His stubble grows in darker than his hair, which is light brown, but in the sun it's cut with red. And, at the back, I know there is a surprising streak of silver there, like crystal forking through dark stone.

He reaches for his phone, typing something quickly before saying, "We should probably talk about the things that new lovers always discuss first."

"You mean such as *past* lovers? Do you need to get your notebook?"

Calvin waves this off with a smile. "Jeff made passing reference to a lad named Bradley earlier." He crosses one ankle over the other. "So I assume he was long term."

I blink, trying to figure out when—and why—Jeff and Calvin would have been discussing my relationship résumé tonight. But my phone buzzes on the table. I reach over him and read the text that has just arrived . . . from Calvin.

> Are you ready for me?

I stare at the screen, bewildered, before I realize what he's doing. Adding to our normal-couple sexting. Playing the game. I reply with a warm blush.

> If by ready for you, you mean naked, then yes.

"You were telling me about Bradley," he prompts when I put my phone on the couch next to me.

"Right." I clear my throat, looking down at him. He's suspiciously pink, too. "We were together just under three years."

"Did you ever think you'd marry him?"

It's such an obvious question, so there's no excuse for the way it catches me off guard. "No, not really. He was nice, but . . . we were boring in similar ways."

He narrows his eyes at me when I say this, and I wonder what he's thinking. "So what about others?"

Others. So much mediocrity there.

"You first," I deflect. "How many women have you been with?"

He sucks in a quiet breath when he glances at my text, quickly typing something else, and then sets his phone on his stomach, facing away so I can't see.

"Like, relationships?" he asks. "Two." Calvin scratches his leg. He's taken off his socks, and has nice feet; they aren't calloused or knobby. Just smooth and tanned, nails trimmed.

My phone buzzes.

> I want to feel the heat of you next to me when I go to bed tonight.

These words detonate in my blood. My crazy brain finds this . . . *applicable* to our situation.

> I want that, too. When will you be home?

"Only two?" I ask, trying to maintain the thread of our actual conversation.

"Well, two real girlfriends. Aileen and Rori."

"Those are very Irish names."

This makes him grin and then let out a big belly laugh. "They were very Irish girls."

"No one here in the States?"

"Rori moved here with me when I started school, but went home after a few months. Since her . . . there were a couple I mostly just got off with, but not many." Calvin winces as he lifts his head and tilts his bottle to his lips, adding, "One girl from school, Amanda." He squints as he thinks. "Six months, maybe? But she was a bit diabolical. And bossy."

"I would think a bossy woman is a good thing in bed."

"You'd be right. That aspect wasn't the problem." He takes another sip, not meeting my eyes. "What about you?"

"Me?"

He looks up at me, eyes narrowed. "Men."

"Oh. After Bradley . . . hundreds."

He sits up a little. "Really?" His voice is full of dramatic, drunken interest, but it dies when he sees I'm joking and he lies back down. "I mean, it wouldn't be unheard of. Sexual freedom and all."

"Not hundreds. Some."

"You know," he says sleepily, "secrets are currency."

"Are they?"

Briefly, he glances at his phone, typing something out with rapid fingers. My heart seems to erupt in my chest. Calvin nods when he looks back up at me. "Mam says that secrets unlock something between friends."

I look down at him in playful exasperation. "You're bringing sweet mother-in-law Marina into this talk of my sex life?"

"She's grand."

I glance at my phone and the words that appear there.

> I'll be home as soon as I can.
> You're all I can think about.

My breath is trapped in my throat, a thick, cottony presence.

"Besides," he says quietly, "you're too beautiful to be inexperienced in love." Before I can let the full flush of this roll through me, he adds, "I only know of Bradley, and then whoever Lulu was talking about tonight."

I groan at the memory of Lulu's mortifying outburst. "Okay, so: I lost the V-card to a guy named Eric on my sixteenth birthday. Jake was my boyfriend my last year in high school . . . we were only together for about eight months. Bradley was most of college. Since then . . . a few more, but—as you say—they were relationships mostly in bed, including the one Lulu was talking about." I look down to see his reaction, but it's clear he's waiting. He seems to want a number. "I've had sex with six people."

"Six isn't so bad."

"For who?"

He looks up at me and gives a self-conscious wince. "Me, I suppose."

I look away. I'm honestly not sure what to think of all this.

We've been acquaintances for a time that can be counted in days, not years, and it's still so insane to me that he's here in my apartment—*in my lap*. Beyond that, there seems to be a genuine commitment he's made to this marriage, and a genuine interest in me as a person. Given my desire to protect myself, I don't know how to feel about this.

Touched, maybe. Similarly possessive. Also wary.

We've never established that we'll be faithful in any way.

"I spent so much of the last four years trying to get a job," he says quietly. "Relationships absolutely took a backseat. I think I auditioned for everything. But classical guitar is tricky. People want guitar to be rock."

"You play rock, too."

He eyes me. "Yeah, but not as a passion."

"No," I say, "of course not. But you could do rock if you wanted."

"The problem isn't only that I didn't want to do that, it's that there are a million people playing rock guitar."

"Well, now there's only one person playing classical guitar down at the Levin-Gladstone."

He does a cute little fist punch in the air.

"But speaking of," I say, nudging his head off my lap, "tomorrow you head down and start rehearsals." I point to the clock that tells us it's far past midnight. "You should sleep."

He looks up at me. "Tonight was hatchet."

I laugh. "Is that a good thing?"

"Aye, means I had fun."

"Me too."

His smile straightens. "I don't like to think of you playing a side part in your story."

I bite my lip, struggling to not look away. I'm not entirely sure what to say to this.

"You've suddenly become a very large part of mine," he says quietly. "And I yours. No? Why not make it epic?"

Calvin sits up, leaning forward to press a chaste kiss to my cheek that I feel long after he's walked into the bathroom.

I head to my room to put on my pajamas and then sit on my bed, staring at my phone. His last text has gone unanswered. I reply impulsively.

> I feel the same way.

What am I doing? I'm less afraid of getting in trouble for this fake marriage than I am of falling in love with someone who could be playing me completely.

I have no idea how long I sit there, but when I step out to use the bathroom, I see Calvin on the sofa bed, tucked under blankets, eyes closed.

My phone lights up again.

> And I despise every night I
> go to sleep without you.

thirteen

I remember the first time I saw *Working Girl*. It was at Robert and Jeff's—of course—and they had the VHS tape of the film. There are so many classic lines ("I am not steak! You can't just order me!") but my favorite scene is the end—spoiler alert—when Melanie Griffith and Harrison Ford are in the kitchen together, making coffee and packing lunches for her first day on the job. They're all private smiles and shoulder bumps and it's obscene how cute it is.

I'm going to be honest with you and say that our morning before Calvin's first rehearsal is not like this. For one, we both oversleep. Our panicked sprinting around each other in the tiny apartment—to brush teeth, to make coffee, *Go ahead, you shower first; Oh shit, Holland, can I use your razor?*—is interrupted only when my cell phone rings. It's Robert: Calvin's phone is on silent and my uncle's been calling, asking him to come in an hour early to rehearse before Ramón shows up.

Calvin emerges from the steamy bathroom with a towel around his waist. I have the absurd thought that he reminds me of the plastic torso from an anatomy course I took: each of his muscles seems perfectly defined beneath his skin.

He shuffles past me. "I forgot my clothes out here."

What was I supposed to tell him again . . . ? Oh, right.

"Robert called," I say, and part of me wants to warn him to hold that towel tighter because he might drop it when I pass along the request. "He wants you to come in earlier."

Calvin blanches. "When earlier?"

I peek at the clock over his shoulder. "Now earlier?"

He explodes into action, grabbing his clothes from the couch, jogging back to the bathroom. I catch a flash of bare ass and find religion. I throw on whatever clothes are on top of my clean laundry pile—no one cares what I'm wearing today, or any day, for that matter—and pour coffee for each of us into travel mugs, waiting by the door.

And then we're off.

It's so cold outside that I'm legitimately worried about his wet hair freezing. Apparently he is, too, because he tucks it into a knit cap and bends into the cracking wind, cradling his guitar case to his chest. We pass the Fiftieth Street station without comment—he doesn't even look at it this time, but I do—and my heart is pulled into a bittersweet knot.

"What else did Robert say?" he asks, wincing in the wind.

"Ramón is coming in at ten. He wanted to go through a few things with you first."

Calvin stops abruptly on the sidewalk, stunned. "Oh my God. It's Ramón's first rehearsal, too."

Once he's said it aloud, he seems to come to the same realization I did when Robert mentioned it—there's no point in Ramón rehearsing with Lisa if Calvin is coming in. Today, they'll begin working together in earnest.

Calvin turns, continuing on his frantic march to the theater, and I jog to keep up with his long strides.

"You're going to be amazing," I assure him.

He nods into the warmth of his scarf. "Keep telling me that."

"You're going to be amazing."

This earns a tiny grin.

"I'll get you drunk later, regardless."

Calvin laughs. "Keep telling me that, too."

- - - -

I can tell Calvin is intimidated by the crowd that's gathered near the stage to hear his first rehearsal. He seemed so much more laid-back at the audition—but of course he did. He'd had nothing to lose, then.

With a little shoulder-squeeze of solidarity, I let him go at the top of the center aisle and watch him make his way toward Robert. I'm relieved to see that Ramón isn't here yet.

In the distance, my husband and uncle shake hands, and then Calvin is pulled into a hug. Bless Robert's intuition for nerves, and bless Calvin for collapsing into him so readily.

Brian comes up beside me, lifting his chin toward the stage. "Well. That certainly looks chummy."

I roll my eyes but otherwise stay silent. He's wearing a

dark blue shirt covered in suns and tigers and snakes and I don't care that it's probably Gucci, it's ridiculous. I'm not sure if the idea of him paying eight hundred dollars for a cheesy polo makes me happy in a really catty way, or sad about the state of my own finances.

Either way, Brian is a dick.

"How lucky for him that there was an eligible young lady with spinster tendencies and a poor outlook on the future."

"Did you need something?" I ask, curling my hands into fists so I don't reach out and slap him.

He raises a single brow in warning at my tone. "We'll make sure everyone knows you're married. Robert mentioned we can't have rumors that it's fake."

I don't even know what to say to this, so I just mumble, "Thanks." I can already feel the way Brian wants to insert himself into this craziness, wants to collect truth and gossip like coins in a treasure chest.

He turns and looks at me. "I have to tell you, even at that meeting . . . I never thought you'd actually *do* it."

We so rarely stand this close and look at each other so evenly, but there's a perceptible shift in the dynamic this morning, and once I understand it, everything snaps into focus: He can't deny I did something of value. He needs to bring me down a peg again by pointing out how insane I am to marry a stranger.

"You seemed pretty sure it was an *out-of-the-box* idea," I remind him.

"I was fucking *joking*," he says. "I mean, who does something like that?"

He snorts out a laugh and disappears back out to the lobby. His superior attitude always makes me want to scream, *You know it's pronounced supposedly, right? Not supposably? You know there's no 'r' in Washington? You realize you have your read receipts on your text messages so we always know how long you draw out your power trip before responding?*

And yet, I don't. I carefully pull my camera out of the bag at my hip and head down the aisle to capture some pictures of Calvin and Ramón: day one.

- - - -

For a while, Robert and Calvin talk quietly, heads bowed. It reminds me of watching Dad coach out on the football field, with my oldest brother, Thomas, the high school star quarterback: their heads together, plotting out plays, feeling the pressure of hundreds of eyes on their every move. In some ways, this seems not altogether different, except the scale of celebrity here is colossal.

The thought of Dad and Thomas makes my chest hurt a little with homesickness. I've stood still for so long, and suddenly my life is this moving train; having a secret this enormous makes them feel even farther away.

In front of me, Calvin steps away, pulling his guitar out and tuning it with mannerisms that seem oddly familiar already. I get a phantom whiff of coffee and tea—he's been tuning in the morning, wearing barely anything while I pour our respective mugs—and I know what he's going to do next before it happens: he rolls his neck, squeezes his hands into fists, and then flexes his fingers. My heart is drumming in my throat, and when Calvin looks up to Robert for guidance, the drumming melts into fire.

Robert lifts his hands, counting down, and then music seems to spill out of Calvin's instrument and along the aisle, a river overflowing, flooding us all. No one moves, no one speaks, and the richness of the music gives me that odd sense of déjà vu, of something far away that's suddenly so close again, and I'm smothered by it in this way that makes me turn my face to the ceiling, trying to inhale it, swallow more.

He doesn't need the sheet music; he rolls through the pieces. Every time Robert stops him to correct something it leaves me feeling like a sneeze has been cut short, or a breath punched out of me. At one point, when Robert stops Calvin again and again during a single four-measure stretch, the gathered mass groans, unconsciously, together.

Robert turns and playfully tells them to be quiet. "Let me run this show."

Someone calls out, "He's giving me chills."

"The chills will be better when he gets the syncopation right." Robert turns back around and counts down for Calvin to start again.

It's so much like a dance—conductor and musician. Robert moves like water where he stands, and music pours out of Calvin. It's an hour into the rehearsal before I remember I'm supposed to be doing something. I lift my camera up clumsily, balancing it on my cast to look through the viewfinder. Through the tiny square, I watch a six-foot-seven, Broadway-baby-turned-Oscar-winner, grinning, clapping Ramón Martín step onstage.

fourteen

Calvin is really drunk.

Not just goofy, jokey, and smiley, but blurry—with a heavy arm draped across my shoulders as I help him up the three flights of stairs to the apartment.

"*Ramón. Martín.*" He's slurred this, with dreamy emphasis, at least seventy-five times tonight. To be fair, Ramón was *with* us until an hour ago, when we poured him into a cab. The two of them were drunken, hugging mutual fanboys.

"I can't believe this is my life." He leans his full weight into me and I groan. "Holls. This day was madness. Like a dream."

I struggle with my keys, propping him against the wall to get the lock open before my next-door neighbor, Mrs. Mossman, comes out and demands we shut the hell up. As tipsy as I am from my own share of martinis, I am even more intoxicated by what I witnessed today. Calvin alone was stunning. Calvin and Ramón together were prodigious. Ramón is already an impressive baritone, and with the unfurled richness of Calvin's guitar, his voice opened up and rolled across the theater: bottomless and infinite. They brought the house down—and this was a house full of people who have seen and heard these songs hundreds of times. Even Luis Genova came by to watch the last half hour or so, and was nearly weeping with relief that the beloved show wouldn't die in a whimper when he left.

"And I owe it all to you." Calvin presses his thumb below my lip. "My sweet Holland and her magical ear." It seems to require a good deal of effort for him to focus, but when he does, he murmurs, "Your freckles really are lovely."

Just as my heated blood seems to press up against my skin, I manage to get the door open and he trips inside, sprawling past me and onto the couch.

I stare down at him already half-asleep. Even in his rumpled clothes and his untied sneakers, I can't help thinking, *Look at you. Just look at you here in my apartment, being.*

"'S Lulu here?" he asks.

"She went home with Gene."

He laughs, rolling to giggle into a pillow. "Gene."

I'm unreasonably pleased that Calvin is as tickled by Gene's old-man name as I am.

I'm less pleased, however, with Lulu's behavior tonight. Once again, she was on obnoxious overload, teasing me in biting, passive-aggressive ways, buying shots for Calvin and Ramón, sitting on their laps, flirting shamelessly.

Lulu's always been my wild friend, but never this sharp before. Seeing her through Calvin's eyes is embarrassing; I want her to relax and back off, just the tiniest bit.

"She's so jealous of you," Calvin says, tugging his shirt up and over his head. He tosses it past the couch; a puddle of blue lands somewhere near the bay window.

I shuffle to the kitchen, getting us each a glass of water so I can pretend I don't need to respond to this—his comment about Lulu or his apparent preference for bare skin. Calvin hiccups from the couch and then groans; thank God he doesn't need to be at the theater until Tuesday afternoon.

"Why's she like that?" he mumbles, and I press the glass of water into his hand.

I wonder if he's thinking of the same moment I am, from early in the evening: Lulu climbing on Calvin, straddling his lap, pretending to dance on him, and the barely masked revulsion that spread over his face before he urged her to stand back up. I hate that Lulu flirted so brazenly with him, but even more, I hate that she made such a mockery of our marriage tonight.

"I don't know, really."

He opens one eye, squints at me. "I don't think that's true."

"Maybe it's what you said, she likes being the crazy one." I mean . . . tonight definitely counted as crazy. I return to the living room and hand him the water. "Did you have fun?"

His full lips push out in a thoughtful pout. "I liked being with Ramón. I like being with *you*."

The alcohol dims my natural reflexes and instead of sprinting away, my heart gives a single heavy punch to my ribs. "I like being with you, too."

He scrunches up his nose. "But I don't like *her*."

This makes me laugh. In less than a week, I've discovered

that Calvin is incredibly chill about nearly everything, but when he doesn't like someone, he has zero poker face. "I can tell."

"I've had friends like that," he says, "the ones you outgrow but keep anyway."

When he says this, a wind blows through me. I can't tell if it feels happy or sad to realize he's right. Lulu and I met nearly three years ago at Columbia, and have clung to each other in these months post-graduation when we're told we're supposed to have some idea how to adult. She's my only girlfriend here, and I've wanted it to be great even if it didn't always feel like we fit so well anymore.

"I think you're pretty drunk to be making such sweeping statements."

He giggles. "I'm your *husband*, don't I get a say?"

He stops laughing, and for the duration of an inhale looks completely sober—in this exact moment we're both struck by the absurdity, the incomprehensibility of our situation. And then he closes his eyes and the hysteria bubbles out of him, round and unstoppable. I have to take the water glass from his hand so he doesn't spill it or drop it on the carpet. Calvin gets control of himself again while I watch in amusement, and then without warning he reaches up, tugging me down over him, tucking me so that I'm trapped sweetly between his body and the back of the couch. An ache spreads up my thighs, and settles heavily between my legs.

His breath is humid on my neck. "I think you might be the best girl there ever was."

The heat of his bare chest against me sends a paradoxical

shiver from my throat to my toes. I open my mouth to respond, trying to find words through the haze of the *reality* of him—the virtuoso musician, this silly boy rolling around on my couch, his shirtless form pressed so easily to mine—but when my simple "Thank you" makes its way to the surface, he's already asleep.

"I think you're the best boy there ever was, too."

fifteen

"For the love of God, who do I have to blow to get a fucking electrician over here?"

It's nearing the end of rehearsal and there's barely a hiccup when Brian screeches this into the backstage abyss. Coming from anyone else, this rhetorical would be met with an array of saucily raised hands, but none of us can even get it up to joke about getting sexual where Brian is concerned.

I click a surreptitious photo of his rage face and then show it to Calvin, who's standing beside me, waiting for Robert to finish up auditioning a new percussionist.

"Wow," Calvin whispers. "That one's sour as vinegar."

"Don't even get me—"

"Holland." Brian materializes like a dementor in front of me, and I lower my camera as inconspicuously as I can. "You think this is the time for photos? You have seventeen boxes of merch up front to unpack, and two hours until tonight's show."

Mortified, I glance quickly to Calvin.

"Don't look at *him*," Brian growls, and snaps crisply in front of my face. "He's not going to touch a box with those hands. Get up front, and get unpacking."

I feel so belittled; I can't even meet Calvin's eyes right now. With a tight "Sounds good," I turn and head toward the front of the house.

I hate Brian.

I hate Brian.

This is why no one corrects you when you say expresso, or ex cetera, I think, all the way down the aisle. *This is why even Robert didn't tell you when you had toilet paper on your shoe.*

Is it time for me to start looking for another job? The thought makes me laugh, because that time came and went about two years ago. If I haven't started my novel by summer—a lofty goal, considering I don't even have an *idea*—maybe I can find something as an intern at a magazine? I think of the connections I have and wonder if it's time to send out more feeler résumés.

Turns out Brian was exaggerating *slightly* about the loads of boxes to unpack: there are four, and they're tiny. I'm guessing they're full of key chains and embroidered knit caps. Even with only one arm it will take me, at most, ten minutes to put this stuff away.

A low whistle comes from the other side of the counter and I look up to see Calvin surveying the span of merch beneath the glass case. "I forgot how much of this stuff there was."

I look up, humiliated all over again for him to see me

standing out here unpacking overpriced crap with my compa-rably untalented hands. "Hey."

He picks up a key chain and spins it on an index finger. "Do you ever think of taking some of this stuff and selling it on eBay?"

I look around wildly, making sure no one heard him. To even joke about something like that is a huge no-no. "God, no."

"I was kidding. I mean, I'd only encourage that sort of thing if you set it up under Brian's name." He leans his folded arms on the glass case, bending so he's level with me. He never rushes to speak, this one. Green eyes search mine before he quietly asks, "You okay?"

I busy myself with unpacking the box. "Sure, why?"

"You seem a little tense."

Ripping at a stubborn piece of packing tape, I growl, "Why would I be tense?"

Calvin reaches out, bracing a hand on each side of the cardboard to steady it. "Because your boss is a twat?"

Embarrassment and gratitude flush through me and I look up at him. "He's pretty abhorrent."

"D'you like your job, though?" he asks, and looks away, back down at the contents of the display case.

The reprieve from eye contact allows me to answer hon-estly: "I like hearing the music. I like taking the photographs, but out here . . . I feel like I'm wasting my brain."

"You know, that night, what Jeff said . . ."

Jeff's words come running back to me, and they ache: *She sees herself as a supporting character, even in her own life story.*

Calvin continues, "I mean, in all the time we've talked

about who we are, we've never talked about what you studied, what *you* want to do with your life."

This makes me pause in surprise. "Yes, we have."

But when he looks back at me, eyes narrowed, I realize he's right.

"I have an MFA in creative writing." I bite my lip and pull a strand of hair away from my face while he gazes at me intently. "I want to be a novelist."

"Wow," he says, looking slightly taken aback. "I always assumed you wanted to do something with music."

"Why?"

He looks at me like I'm dense.

"I promise," I tell him, "I'm not a musician."

"Well, a novelist is amazing all the same. And an MFA. That's really impressive, Holland."

I rarely admit this ambition anymore because it seems to always garner this exact reaction: an odd combination of surprised and impressed. And I can't tell whether people respond this way because they like the idea that I want to do something difficult and creative, or because nobody looks at me and immediately thinks *She's got stories buried inside her.*

When I graduated, I had dreams of writing something fun, commercial, entertaining. Now I'm a twenty-five-year-old glorified concession worker who hasn't finished a short story or poem or, hell, a *sentence* in months. If I had a quarter for each time someone told me *The only way to write the novel is to just sit down and do it,* I'd be able to afford a penthouse overlooking Central Park. Sometimes well-intended advice is so supremely unhelpful.

"It's only impressive if you do something with it," I say.

"So *do* something."

"Easier said than done." I let out a little growl. "I want to write, but it's like my brain is empty when I try to think of a story. Lately I feel like I'm not qualified to do anything, not like you, or Robert."

Instead of responding to the unmasked vulnerability here, he—thankfully—laughs. "Don't ask me to write an essay, or solve any maths. I'd embarrass you." He sobers. "We're all good at different things, *mo stóirín*. I think you undervalue your own gifts." He looks back down at the case but reaches across the glass, twisting his pinkie with mine. "You're doing all this stuff for me, and Robert—not for yourself. There's enormous generosity in that. And it seems to me that you know music better than a lot of people around here"—he tilts his head back, indicating the theater—"so obviously your brain is creatively driven. Trust your muse."

He's just poked at the tender spot in my emotions.

"But what if I don't have one? There's a part of me that worries I don't love to write enough to do it all day, my entire life." I've never said those words to anyone, and the clawing honesty of them leaves me feeling untethered and bare. "I think part of what's keeping me from starting is the fear that I *won't* actually love it, and then I'll be left with a degree I won't use, and no other prospects."

The problem is I know he can't relate to this. He picked up a guitar when he was four, and has played out of sheer love for it ever since. I love to read, but whenever I pick up a novel that blows me away, I think, *There's no way I have something like*

that inside me. Is Jeff right? Am I unable to create anything because I see myself in a supporting role? Doomed to always be
the friend, the daughter, the linchpin in everyone *else's* story?

As if he realizes he can't say anything to this, Calvin points
to a glossy collector's-edition program that shows Luis and Seth
standing onstage, grinning at each other after the performance
that earned them their first, thunderous round of applause.

"Did you take this photo?"

I did, actually, but I'm surprised this is his question.
It's like it hasn't occurred to him yet that *he's* going to be
the new sweetheart of Broadway. That there's going to be a
photo of him and Ramón jubilantly grinning at each other
on these commemorative programs, selling for twenty-five
dollars a pop.

"Yeah, I did."

He smiles down at me, proud. "It's a great shot. You've got
all these gifts you don't even realize."

– – – –

Rehearsal done, and with the crowd thickening outside, Calvin
holds open the door, and we take a right down Forty-Seventh.
Robert is handing the reins over to the assistant musical director tonight because he's been working ridiculous hours getting
Calvin and Ramón ready for their start while still running
every performance.

I suspect Jeff jumped in and put his foot down, insisting
his husband take the next few nights off to breathe.

It's freezing out. I wrap my scarf a little tighter around my neck, pushing my hands into a pair of gloves. Calvin—who seems to still be running on adrenaline from rehearsal—doesn't seem to notice the chill at all.

"How was the rest of your afternoon?" he asks, glancing over at me as we wait to cross the street.

A puff of condensation escapes with my laugh. "I plotted Brian's murder—"

"An excellent idea for a *book*," he cuts in.

"Unpacked some merchandise—"

"And may I say the display looks *exquisite*."

I watch him out of the corner of my eye. "You're being awfully complimentary."

His gloved hand comes up to his chest. "I'm simply impressed with how much you do around the theater, that's all. It's like you're born to be here."

I tuck my arm through his, huddling against the wind. "One of Robert's favorite stories to tell is about the day I was born." I glance up at him and see how riveted his attention is on my face even as we walk. "According to Robert, and Jeff, and Mom, and anyone else who was there that day, Dad brought my five siblings into the room to meet me, and it was like a pile of puppies all over Mom, who looked so exhausted she could barely speak. Robert took me from her arms and told her she could rest. Apparently he said, 'How about you let me take care of this one?'"

Calvin laughs.

I grin up at him. "I'm being serious."

"I'm laughing because I can absolutely believe this."

"Whenever I wanted to do anything big," I say, "like summer camp, volleyball, a weekend trip with a friend and her family—I'd ask my parents, but they'd usually tell me to check with my uncles, too. I spent every day after school at their house in Des Moines. I was there most weekends. I went to work with Robert at night, and did my homework in my favorite seat—row H, seat twenty-three—while he conducted the symphony rehearsal."

"Did it bother your parents?" he asks. "Mam was so protective; I think this would have killed her."

He's not the first person to ask me that. My entire life, friends wondered whether there was some rift between me and my parents, and there never was. I just gravitated to my uncles, and they were family, so it never bothered my mom. "When I came around, Mom had so much less time to baby me. Thomas was thirteen when I was born. By the time I was only three, Dad was coaching Thomas in varsity football and they went to state, so that became the biggest part of our family life. Thomas got a full scholarship to the University of Iowa and Dad was there all the time. Olivia was seven years older, and always a handful for Mom. Davis was Mom's little cuddler and—"

"You got lost in the shuffle?"

I shake my head. "Maybe a little. I don't know. I guess it's easier to see it as an arrangement that worked out for everyone. Mom seemed happy to see me thriving with them."

"It must have been amazing, growing up in the symphony hall."

I nod. "I could probably name any classical piece within a few opening notes, but I wonder sometimes if it's devastating to Robert that I'm not more musical."

"That *is* musical, Holland."

"No, I meant talented."

I can feel him looking at me a bit longer before tucking my arm more tightly in his.

A car horn wails as it passes, and we move with the crowd like a school of fish down the sidewalk and to the restaurant where we're meeting Robert, Jeff, and Lulu. I'm mildly anxious to be together with my uncles and Calvin in the same place, only because the four of us haven't all been together since we dropped the news of our nuptials. I also hope Lulu has worked through whatever's been bothering her. I love Lulu, but I'm not sure how much more of her drama I can take.

Calvin motions for me to lead the way and we descend the small set of stairs that lead to Sushi of Gari. Restaurants in New York come in every imaginable size, molded to fit the space available. Here, the hum of voices is a monotonous buzz as we're led through a Tetris game of tables and past a narrow sushi bar to a booth of sorts where Lulu, Robert, and Jeff wait, sipping their sake.

Robert and Jeff both stand, each pressing a kiss to my cheek before we slip into the empty bench waiting for us.

"Sorry we're late," I say.

Robert waves us off. "We just got here."

Lulu raises her sake cup. "I didn't. I've been here for twenty minutes."

Answering my mental question, Jeff adds, "Lulu has been entertaining us," and gives me a little wink.

"You don't say." I slip out of my coat and toss a warning glance to her across the table.

She grins smugly back at me and holds out her phone. "Behold, I am technology."

Warily, I take it from her. "Oh my God." I stare down at the screen. It's a photograph of a couple on the beach, their toes in the sand and a fire crackling behind them. But it's no ordinary couple. It's *us*, Calvin and me.

Lulu smacks a hand on the table. "I knew that Photoshop class would be useful for more than just digitally enlarging my boobs."

In my peripheral vision, I see Robert and Jeff exchange a look. At best, they tolerate Lulu. But I'm actually relieved she's here; she's providing some social buffer from the elephant in the room—Me, Calvin, the Uncles: all of us here together as *family*.

"Christ," Calvin says, looking over my shoulder. His cheek is nearly pressed to mine and I can still feel the chill of the air outside on his skin. "This is pretty good."

"Your honeymoon," Lulu says. "To Florida, obviously, since you can't fly out of the country without getting busted."

Jeff gently shushes her and I swipe to the next image—a photo of Calvin and me together at an outdoor concert. He's standing behind me, arms wrapped around my waist, with his jaw pressed to my temple. In another we're on a bench in the park looking at each other, not the camera. "*You* did this? You can barely figure out how to record *The Daily Show*."

She ignores the insult. "I was inspired by this guy who inserts himself into Kendall Kardashian's Instagram pictures." Robert and Jeff appear to listen to her, but I can see from their glassy stares that with the combined utterance of *Instagram* and *Kardashian*, she's immediately lost them. "I used a bunch of pictures from your wedding day, and then a few of you I had on my phone. And that one you took and sent me of him at the bar."

I flash my eyes to her in warning, but Calvin doesn't seem to have heard, he's still studying the doctored photo.

"I'll tell you what," Lulu continues, pointing at the phone, "I'll never believe anything I see on the cover of a magazine again, but I'm excited as hell for my Christmas card photo with Prince Harry and Ed Sheeran."

We swipe one more time to the right and then freeze in unison at the pair of naked boobs on the screen before swiping back to the photo of us on the bench.

"Don't go too far," she says after quickly swallowing a sip of her rice wine. "There are pictures of my boobs on there, and then Gene sent some back."

Calvin grabs the phone—presumably before we get an inadvertent eyeful of dick—and returns it to Lulu. "Can you send them to Holland? The Photoshopped ones, not the boobs." He looks down to me. "We look like a real couple."

"A *hot* couple," Lulu adds, and my pulse does a tap dance across the room. Lulu is immediately forgiven. I know the photos have been helped by filters and a little computer magic, but I look like I actually belong next to him.

Across the table, Robert pours more sake into his cup— already. He's not usually a big drinker and I catch Jeff's eye. We both do a curious little eyebrow flicker.

"They're certainly convincing," Robert says distractedly, taking his glasses off and rubbing the bridge of his nose.

"Is it weird to see them?" I ask.

He looks up at me, eyes tight. "There's a lot about this that is weird to me." He pauses and then reaches for my hand. "I know I didn't want you to do this, but I can't pretend that having Ramón and Calvin together, playing the pieces I wrote . . . it's a bit of a dream."

Calvin makes a tiny sound of agreement in the back of his throat.

Letting go of my hand, Robert says more quietly, "But, God, I hope this works."

"Listen," Jeff says, and lifts Robert's hand to kiss it. "I might not be completely on board with how all this came together, but even I'm confident it will be fine."

I look between them, worried. Jeff isn't the PDA type. He's unflappable—yes. Calm and steady—yes. But he's never very outwardly affectionate in front of people. So seeing him reassure Robert like this gets my antennae up. "Is something wrong?"

The two share a quiet look before Robert squeezes Jeff's hand and replaces his glasses. "I worry it's going to be tight. Calvin should start officially next week, but who knows if we can swing it."

"We filed everything a day and a half after the wedding," I say, glancing at Calvin, who nods.

"I know you did, Buttercup, it isn't you. Work permits can take months, and we're asking for it to move through in two weeks, total. It's unlikely, and I'm not sure once Luis is gone that I can pair Ramón with Lisa until Calvin is officially hired. Ramón won't go for it."

One look at Calvin's face—affronted, possessive—and I know Robert is right.

Jeff turns to Calvin and me. "I talked to Sam down at immigration and he assured me they've got what they need for now. He can't guarantee approval, but he can give things a little nudge and make sure those forms go through in time."

My shoulders drop with relief. "Oh. That's good, at least."

"I know I've said it," Calvin says to Robert, "but thank you for everything you've done. I don't know how I'll ever repay you."

"None of that," Robert says, shaking off the tension. "I'm just having some pre-show jitters. Always happens. Circumstances are just a little different this time."

The waitress stops at the edge of the table and asks if we're ready to order appetizers. With little discussion Jeff and Robert order their usual, and during Lulu's turn, Calvin moves closer, pointing to my menu. "If I get the eggplant, do you want to split? Or even get a few appetizers and share?"

It's such a coupley thing to do, it catches me off guard.

"Holls?" Beneath his patient smile, there's an amused glint in his eye.

"Sure," I say. "What else did you want?"

He opens his mouth to answer, right as his phone vibrates in his pocket. He's so close, I actually feel it move through the cushioned bench. "Sorry," he says, pulling away and looking down to the screen.

I catch the name Natalie.

Calvin stares down at the screen in confusion for another ring, and then his smile slips as he seems to realize something. "Ah, bollocks."

My throat goes tight. "Is everything okay?"

"Yes. I . . ." He stops, seeming to have changed his mind, and turns to address the table. "Would you all excuse me for a minute? I need to take this." Back to me again. "Just order us whatever."

Calvin stands and I twist in my seat. "You're sure you're fine?"

"Of course." With a squeeze of my shoulder, he steps away and heads out of the restaurant. Through the glass doors I watch him climb the stairs—phone already pressed to his ear—before he's out of sight.

- - - -

I drop my keys on the counter and watch Calvin wordlessly duck in to use the bathroom before bed. I had this strange sense of a Plexiglas barrier between us the entire walk home and am trying to figure out what's bothering him. Other than the obvious, of course: the looming pressure of his first performance, the stress over our paperwork getting filed in time. Maybe that's all it is and he just needs some time to process it all. Keeping our sanity intact while we wait for the work authorization to come through is like watching someone hammer a nail through my hand one tiny blow at a time. It's excruciating, and I have no control. Imagine how it feels for *him*.

But Calvin finds so much joy in music, and he's so optimistic about all this, it seems hard to believe that he's quiet because he's worried about that. And what was the urgent phone call tonight? Is there another opportunity he's keeping on the back burner? Am I the only one who's planning to be faithful?

The prospect makes me want to vomit.

Calvin emerges, and does a double take when he sees me standing exactly where he left me, just inside the door.

"You feel all right?" he asks.

I attempt a smile. "Yeah. Dinner was fun."

Nodding, he moves to the couch, sitting down, untucking his dress shirt, and putting his head in his hands.

It's so weird to live with someone I don't know that well. He didn't drink very much, so I know he's not suffering any ill effects from alcohol. We just ate a half hour ago, so I doubt he's suffering from something he ate . . .

"Are *you* all right?" I ask.

He nods, and then looks up at me, eyes red and unfocused from exhaustion. "I know it's only been a little over a week, but seeing Robert nervous tonight made *me* nervous. What if we did all this for nothing? I feel like the waiting to start is killing me. I just want to perform. I just want to get *in* there."

I nod in understanding, but I get a weird twist of guilt, like I should be speeding this up somehow. And doing *all this for nothing* doesn't land entirely without impact, either. I realize we aren't actually together, but it's been nice to be with him, even platonically. It doesn't feel like *nothing*.

The name Natalie floats into my memory, paired with the way he dashed off . . . it leaves me feeling uneasy for a different reason entirely. "I hope that the phone call wasn't anything bad."

It seems to take him a few seconds to remember, and then he looks up, sheepish. "Oh." He grimaces. "I was supposed to be on a date, and completely forgot."

This leaves me momentarily speechless.

"Hold on," he corrects, holding up a hand, "that came out wrong. It was a date I made a few days before we had that first lunch. I forgot to cancel it. I'm sorry."

Well, this is awkward. I sit down next to him on the couch, picking at a tiny hangnail.

"I guess, if you wanted—but, yeah, I don't know—we probably shouldn't—" I trip over my words and can feel him turn to look at me. "Date. Shouldn't. I mean, just for appearances."

"Bloody hell, Holland," he finally says, incredulous. "I'm not apologizing because I'm feeling regret that I wasn't with her tonight. I'm apologizing because another woman called me when I was out to dinner with you and your lot."

"Oh."

He bursts out laughing. "Do you think I'm an absolute gobshite?"

"No?" I say, and can't help smiling back at him because I have no idea what a gobshite is. The unease slowly dissolves. "But it's true that our situation is a little unprecedented."

"It is, but I'm not going to be unfaithful . . . even if we're pretending."

Although he's used the word *unfaithful*, it's the *pretending* that sends a tiny hot poker through my side. I'm not pretending—or, I am; I'm pretending that I don't have feelings for him.

"How did you meet her?"

"Through a friend," he says easily. "There wasn't some long story building up to this. I've seen her once. That reminds me," he begins, and waits for me to look up at him.

Finally, the burn eases, and I can. "What's that?"

"We never discussed what to say when someone asks us how we met."

I nod, looking back at the coffee table. I remember the intimacy of our texts the other night, how it felt to curl up against him on the couch, the heat of his skin, the firm press of him next to me, and have to remind myself that *we're pretending*. "I guess we should keep it as simple as we can. We met at the subway station. It doesn't have to be more complicated than that."

sixteen

Every day, Calvin has three hours of rehearsal with Ramón before Luis and Lisa take over for the evening performance. And after each rehearsal, Calvin locates me backstage, and he's smiling like he's been plugged into a generator. The music makes him glow in a way I find hard to believe; sometimes it seems there is a candle burning just beneath his skin.

Robert rehearses with them sometimes, but once or twice a week, he hands over the reins to the assistant musical director, Elan. Because Robert composed the music, he feels the notes physically, and directs the musicians with instinctive, fluid movements. But I notice that Elan focuses on technical precision more than artistry, and the days he is there, the music loses some instinct, some deeper emotion that hasn't been fully transferred from Robert to Ramón and Calvin.

I've seen it happen before, how Robert's passion is slowly

fed into his musicians; how he trains them to feel it, not just see the notes. The key, the rhythm, the dynamics become an action themselves: a deeply drawn breath, a sob, a triumphant fist in the air. They are no longer individual notes, but constellations of them pulled together to make something nearly otherworldly.

Today was not an otherworldly day.

"What didn't work out there?" Calvin has barely exited the stage when the question is out, and he stares at me with intense expectation. He shifts his guitar in his hands, nodding to the stage behind me. "Something felt off, and I'm not sure where."

Normally I'd balk at the idea of advising him at all on how to more masterfully play his guitar, but I'm wrapped up in his glow and feeling emotional from the impending start of his theater run. "Lean into the deceptive cadence in 'Lost to Me,' to draw out the tension just a bit more. You and Ramón are both letting it resolve too soon."

He stares at me for a full ten seconds without speaking, and my stomach sinks. I've never criticized him before, not once.

I think I've just done something catastrophic.

- - - -

The quiet continues over dinner. He eats quickly at the coffee table before reaching for his guitar and, bending over it, forming a private cocoon. Retreating to my bedroom, I hear him playing the section again and again until I fall asleep to the sound of it, and dream of chasing him through the woods.

But the next day, onstage during rehearsal, he meets my gaze just as he's playing this section, and the emphasis of the notes, the astonishing beauty of them, makes tears spring immediately to my eyes.

I was right, and this is how he tells me.

Trust your muse.

Later that night, for the first time in months, I'm able to write. It's only a paragraph, and it isn't the fictional world I'm desperate to find—it's about the way it felt to hear Calvin and Ramón play, the sensation of having my chest so full of emotion that I nearly felt weightless—but I typed. I put words on a page.

Every evening, from the wings, Calvin, Ramón, and I watch Luis and Lisa perform together. I can almost hear Calvin mentally reciting the lines and cues, and—at the opening note of each show—counting down the remaining nights before he and Ramón debut.

- - - -

Months ago, Michael Asteroff released the news that Ramón would replace Luis in mid-February. But the showrunners have made no statements yet about the changes in musical direction—namely Calvin on guitar. While it's common knowledge that the lead violinist left, the press seems to assume that Lisa will continue on in his place. I know Robert is waiting until the work permit comes through before announcing anything, but given the crew's reaction to Calvin and the way he's treated like a new celebrity backstage—not to mention the way Lisa is being mildly bashed on social media in the more hard-core Broadway circles—I don't think it would hurt the production to get some buzz rolling about Calvin soon.

Three weeks after he started rehearsals, and just under a week away from his first performance, there is an official-looking letter waiting for us when we get home. We tear into it like starving dogs.

Our application has been accepted and, according to Jeff, that's good enough to move forward with the paperwork Michael needs to submit to get my *husband* officially hired.

Within hours, Michael's assistant has called to schedule joint photo shoots and interviews for Calvin and Ramón, to launch during their opening week. Although the primary media focus will be on Ramón, Calvin still gets a haircut, a fancy shave, a manicure—though he politely declines a chest wax.

We've opened a joint checking account, which required that we share the very basics of our finances, and they are equally bleak. Other than the three hundred dollars in our shared account, I have some money in savings that I never touch. Calvin is in much the same boat . . . minus the savings. For various interviews and appearances, he'll have to buy a suit, some dress shirts, new shoes. Our balance dwindles, but it's so much less stressful with someone else at my side . . . and any stress we do feel dissolves as soon as we step into the theater and frenetic energy explodes around him.

Our last few days before the debut performance should be

accompanied by a soundtrack. Ideally *Chariots of Fire*. More realistically, *Jaws*.

There is a looming baseline thunder, and I swear it's not just in my head. Social media is on fire speculating about the person replacing Seth—that it's a guitarist is sparking a lot of controversy. Fans mob outside, hoping to hear any bit of music to quench their curiosity. We practically live at the Levin-Gladstone. Michael, who rarely comes by the theater, paces the aisles, listening in on every note of rehearsal. The Law brothers—who, before, were never around and trusted Robert to run the production just fine with their money—are occasionally spotted in the balconies. Brian is a maniac backstage, barking out orders, laying into the crew if they're caught hanging around when they should be moving things. Robert is tense and bellowing at the smallest mistakes. Ramón is a perfectionist and demands to do something again, and again, and again until he's nearly hoarse and Calvin's fingers are practically bleeding. But Calvin still finds me backstage after every grueling rehearsal, with a giant grin. It's as if he's been waiting years for this, and he is Pressure Teflon, or maybe the thrill outweighs the terror.

I see the cast and crew eyeing him, eyeing *us*. We look like any other married couple. Calvin touches me freely and kisses me—*on the forehead*. We come together and leave together, even though I'm not needed here a fraction of the time I'm around. And while I'm not completely unfortunate-looking, I know everyone is half wondering how I ended up with someone like him. I'm that girl with the freckles, the one with snagged tights who spills her coffee awkwardly on her boobs, the one who knocks into everyone with my camera. Calvin, by contrast, drifts gracefully in and out of spaces, and we've already established how he can eat a salad without greasing up his chin.

It really is unfair.

– – – –

I find Calvin leaning against a wall backstage, talking to Ethan—a member of the ensemble who I'm sure would love to pull my husband even farther into the shadows for a far more *private* interaction. The fact that Calvin is straight seems to cause acute physical pain to many of our male co-workers.

He immediately spots me, expression relaxing as he steps around Ethan to come to my side.

Ethan gives me an annoyingly fake smile. "Hey, Holland."

I mimic the expression. "Hey, Ethan."

I nearly jump out of my shoes when Calvin pulls my back to his front and presses his mouth to my jaw. "I'm going to take my beautiful wife to dinner."

I can't even look at him over my shoulder because he's so close: we'd nearly be kissing.

"Take me to dinner?" I step forward, putting a little distance between me and he who is my husband, he who smells like the woods and fresh air, he who sleeps practically naked only a room away from me every night.

"A proper date."

Imaginary Holland stands up and waves the *That Means*

Sex! flag, but I tell her to have a seat until we obtain clarification. "'Proper'?" I say faux-demurely.

He seems to get the meaning the same time I do, and with a little cough pulls his lip balm out of his pocket, smoothing it over those lips I really, *really* like. "Proper." He snaps the cap back on with a grin. "Food. Drinks. Fun."

Did he lean into the word *fun?* Did he growl it a little? I look to Ethan, wishing there was a way I could ask him to corroborate this, but in our surprising moment of flirtation, I don't think either Calvin or I noticed that Ethan has already disappeared.

"I'm always down for food and drinks and fun."

"It's why I like you." Calvin threads his arm through mine, and I catch a longing, droopy look from another one of the stagehands. Tugging, he leads me toward the side exit. "You need to put on a proper dress, with proper heels, and put your hair up."

My brain is still trying to compute all this, to decide whether I love or hate that he's telling me what to wear, but then his hand slides around to cup the back of my neck, and his lips land on my cheek, lingering there, warm and soft. When he speaks, he speaks against my skin. "Your neck is my kryptonite," he says, and I feel his smile curve against me. "I suppose I should text you more about that."

- - - -

I emerge from the bedroom in the only *proper* dress I think I own: it's black, hits just above my knee, and has a fitted bodice with a flowy, pleated chiffon skirt.

And clearly Calvin likes it, too, because when I step out, his mouth hangs slightly open like he was about to launch into a thought and has completely lost the thread of it. I admit to being stunned stupid, too. He's wearing his new suit with a lavender shirt he's left unbuttoned at the collar, letting the sharp edges of his collarbone flirt with my eyeballs.

After a few seconds of scanning every inch of me, he simply says, "Right."

"This works?"

His eyes land on my neck; I have my hair in a high, messy bun. "Christ, yes."

We walk a few blocks to Taboon, and even though there is a line of at least ten parties waiting outside, Calvin shakes hands with a man at the door, who points us to a table in the back. I follow, noticing how heads turn slightly when the Irishman casually slips out of his tailored navy blazer and folds it over his arm.

When he pulls out my chair for me, I ask, "You knew that guy?"

"Juilliard." Calvin makes a faintly sour face. "Brilliant cellist. He's not had the best luck since."

I feel the impulse claw its way up my throat; the desire to help every stray. But no matter how amazing Robert is, or how elaborate his orchestra is for the modesty of the Levin-Gladstone, he can't hire every out-of-work musician we meet.

Still, even if I suppress it, Calvin reads the reaction in my eyes and it softens the tight line of his mouth. "He'll land on his feet. Maybe we can help, down the road."

We.

Down the road.

I swallow thickly, working to give a neutral shrug. In unison, we look down, scanning the menu, and butterflies land in my stomach, tensing.

A proper date.

We've had so many nights on the couch eating takeout. So many happy hours spent with Robert and Jeff or even Lulu before we head home together. What about tonight makes this . . . different?

Calvin looks up at me. "Want to share the cauliflower starter and the branzino?"

Holy crap, I love having a decisive eater as a husband. "Done."

He slides his menu onto the table and reaches over, taking my hand. "Have I said thank you?"

This makes me laugh. "Once or twice."

"Well, I'll say it again, just in case." His eyes take on a glassy, sincere glow. "*Thank* you."

"You're welcome. Of course."

After a little squeeze, he lets go of my hand and sits back to smile up at the waiter who's materialized at the table. This married game we are playing sure does seem easy, and Calvin sure does seem sincerely dedicated, but I get these tiny pulsing flashes of awareness that remind me I don't *really* know him all that well. I've memorized his face—the olive skin, the greenish eyes, the perfectly imperfect teeth—but his brain feels like a mystery still.

We order our shared dinner, and he turns to pull something out of the inner pocket of his blazer, producing a small pink box. "For you."

I am the worst about accepting compliments and gifts, so as expected, Appalland makes an appearance and I stammer out a few things that vaguely translate into *Oh my God, you're so ridiculous, how dare you.*

Inside the box is a delicate gold claddagh ring, and a storm erupts inside me.

"I realize it seems stereotypical to wear these," Calvin says through my stunned silence, "but we do. Please don't think I'm being trite. This doesn't just represent love—with the heart— but I suppose we think of the hands as friendship, and the crown as loyalty." He makes a self-deprecating little grimace as he slides it on my right ring finger, exposed from the cast, with the point of the heart toward the wrist. "Like this, it means you're in a relationship." With a smile aimed at my hand, he fusses with it a little, twisting it straight on my finger. "Normally, because we're married, you'd wear it like that on your other hand, but you've got the wedding ring there."

I'm so afraid of saying something inappropriate or flippant that I don't say anything, I just touch it with the fingers of my left hand and smile up at him.

"Do you like it?" he asks quietly.

This is where I could so easily reveal that I'm completely infatuated with him, and that his giving me a ring has essentially Made My Life Complete, but I just nod, whispering, "It's so pretty, Calvin."

He leans back, but the vulnerability doesn't entirely leave his expression. "Do you enjoy watching me in rehearsal?"

An indelicate snort escapes. "Is that a serious question?"

He gives that self-deprecating grimace again. "Well, yeah. Your opinion is the one I value most. Your advice is . . . everything."

This leaves me momentarily stunned. "I *love* watching you rehearse. You're spectacular—you have to know that."

The waiter brings our wine, and we each take a sip to approve the bottle, thanking him. Once he's gone, Calvin looks at me over the rim of his glass.

"I think Ramón and I sound great together, yeah." He bites his lip thoughtfully. "But—I mean—the entire time I've been here, I've wanted this—*exactly* this. Did I ever tell you, once *Possessed* debuted, I would play the music alone and imagine being in the production?"

Something squeezes my heart in its fist. "Really?"

He nods, quickly swallowing another sip. "After I graduated, I thought something like this would come. I thought that break was only a few months off. Or I would run into someone at a party, and give them my information and hope it would change everything. A year turned into two, and two turned into four, and I wanted to be on Broadway so much I just stayed. I really screwed myself, I know I did."

"I can completely see how that would happen, though." *It's like me with the book,* I think. *I expect the idea to sprout tomorrow, next week, in a month. And here I am, two years out of graduate school with nothing written.*

"So, I suppose what I mean is that this is so obviously worth it to me. Whether we are only friends or . . . you know.

I want this marriage to be worth it to *you*," he says gently, "and I'm not quite sure how to make that happen."

Whether we are only friends or . . . you know.

Whether we are only friends or . . . you know?

My brain is on a loop, barricaded from working past what he's just said in order to help assuage the guilt I can tell he's feeling. The reply *We could start having regular sex* is so close to the surface. So close.

I take a few deep gulps of wine and wipe my hand indelicately across my mouth. "Please don't worry about that."

"I could help you think about your book?"

I get that sinking feeling in my stomach that I always get when I imagine opening my laptop and working.

We could have sex tonight.

I take another deep drink of wine.

"I'll try to think of something," he says quietly.

seventeen

Calvin and Ramón's first performance is on a Friday.

When I find him tying his tie in front of my bedroom mirror, he looks calm and rested—but I know it's a sham, because I heard him pacing most of last night.

"You ready?"

He nods with his bottom lip trapped savagely between his teeth. Smoothing the tie down his chest, he says, "What do you think? Do *you* think I'm ready?"

He's said my favorite word of his—*tink*—twice in one sentence, as if I need to be further charmed.

"I *tink* you're going to be amazing."

He meets my eyes in the mirror. "You *tink* you can give me shit for my accent?"

"I *tink* you sort of like it."

He turns, and for ten seconds, we stand there like this, staring at each other. We're maybe a foot apart; I can see his hands shaking. He's been waiting his entire life for this moment.

"Tell me something I need to remember tonight."

He seems to need something to focus on, some advice to loop through so that he doesn't spiral downward in nerves for the next two hours. I reach out, fidgeting with his tie. "Don't rush through the bridge in 'Only Once in My Life.' Make sure to breathe in the opening solo of 'I Didn't Expect You,' because you hold your breath sometimes, and I think the notes come out looser when you remember to breathe." I think for a few seconds in his absorbed silence. "Trust your hands during 'Lost to Me.' Don't be afraid to close your eyes and feel the notes. When you do that, it comes out like water easily moving over a stone."

I slide my hands from his tie, over his chest. I can feel his heart pounding.

Calvin lets out a long, slow breath. "You should see the way you glow when you're talking about music. You just—"

I laugh, interrupting him. "We're talking about you right now."

He tilts his head, bending his arms so that he can capture my hands in his. "Are we?"

I blaze over this. "You're ready, Calvin. No question."

He glances at my mouth, and a fire seems to start low in my belly. It feels like the kind of scene where I step forward, he steps forward, a kiss happens, something sweet and slow, born of feelings that have been building for months.

But oops, that's just me. We've been fake married for just over three weeks, which means we only have eleven months left of the charade. We've managed to find an easy balance. No use complicating things.

- - - -

Even three hours before the performance, the theater is mobbed outside, and we slip in the side entrance. I looked earlier on StubHub, and tickets to see Ramón tonight were over six hundred dollars for the far-back balcony seats. Calvin is doing a good job looking relaxed, but even his calm facade has cracks in it: he keeps fidgeting with his tie.

Backstage is all motion and bustle. Calvin looks for his new buddy, but Ramón is in for makeup and able to offer only a final smile of support before Calvin is tugged away by a stagehand.

I give him a tight hug, a kiss on his smooth cheek, and then he's out of my sight. I won't see him until after the show. Instead, I'll be up front for most of the night, selling T-shirts. Sad trombone.

But I do get to sneak away and watch from the back. As I slip in, I wonder whether, in ten years, I'll hear a riff or an opening chord to one of the songs and be transported back immediately to this time in my life. It makes the shadow thought follow—what will I feel when I think of these times? Will I think, *Wow, those were the hardest days, trying to figure out who I was?* Or will I think, *Those days were so easy and free, with so little responsibility?*

I've had the thought almost without realizing it—the encroaching awareness that I feel settled but in truth can't see my future at all. I have a temporary job, a temporary marriage. Will anything ever be permanent? What the hell am I going to do with my life? I only get one shot at this, and right now, I'm finding my value only in being valuable to others. How do I find value for me?

Calvin told me to *do* something with my brain, but *how?* Threads of ideas appear on the edge and are gone as soon as my fingers settle on the keys. There's no connective tissue to string them together, no skeleton to hold them up. I want to live my life with the intensity I see on the stage up there, want to feel passionate about *something* in that same way. But what if it never happens for me?

My train of thought is derailed when the skyscraper set is shifted into place, the lights dim, and Ramón steps into a spotlight, center stage. He's already a giant in person, but on the stage he is towering. His dark hair is combed back from his face. His eyes are nearly black, but luminous all the way to the far reaches of the theater. I can tell his chest is rising and falling in excitement, and from nearly every body in my immediate vicinity I sense the vibration of static, the urgency of anticipation.

I suck in a deep breath; my heart is in my throat.

I can't see Calvin, but I hear the second he strums the opening chord of "Lost to Me"—one of the biggest hits from the soundtrack. Without having to see him, I know he's taken my advice and closed his eyes. The warm, honeyed melody rolls up the aisle like a wave of light.

It is sublime.

The crowd shifts in unison; a spontaneous smattering of

applause breaks out and then it grows: For a few moments, the audience is thunderous with surprise and approval. For Calvin, for Ramón, for the risk and beauty of the guitar and the salty richness of Ramón's baritone lifting the weight of the music up over his shoulders and launching it to the depths of the theater. My vision wavers, spotted with vibrating dots of light. I don't know what it is about Calvin's playing; listening to this feels so different from listening to Seth. And not just because of the instrument. Calvin's music gives an aching sense of time passing, the pain of finding love twice in a lifetime, of losing it in intervening years. It's exactly the way the story needs to unfold through music. It feels nostalgic . . . I'm already regretting the end.

- - - -

When the final curtain falls, there isn't just a standing ovation, there's a stomping one. I have the sense of light fixtures shaking, dust trickling from cracks in the walls. I have to rush back out to the lobby—we sell out of T-shirts tonight for the first time—but before I do I swear I catch Calvin's eye as he stands to take his bow.

Backstage there is champagne overflowing, and a hundred bodies trying to get to our stars. After the merch booth has closed, I join the melee, but am nudged to the middle of the mob, and then the back, where I stand on my toes to watch person after person embrace my husband. Jeff's words from our pseudo-poker game rise to the surface of my consciousness and bob there, refusing to be silenced. This is the very definition of being a supporting character. But I don't really mind that I'm this far away—I can still see the smile on his face as bright as a spotlight, and his joy seems to vibrate across the distance. Surely everyone knows what a big deal this must be to him, but I still look at him and remember the subway musician hunched over his guitar, sitting on a narrow stool, guitar case open at his feet. And now here he is, wearing a suit, standing beside Ramón Martín, and getting the praise and adoration of an entire cast and crew. I'm still on the sidelines, but *I* helped make that happen.

After each person approaches, Calvin looks up, searching. I think he's trying to find Robert; he gives his hunt a tiny flicker of attention before he looks back down to the person in front of him, thanking them, embracing them, listening to their praise. And then he looks up again.

Robert finds him, finally, and the two men embrace, clapping each other on the back. But again, when Robert pulls away, Calvin looks up and only then

only when Robert points

only when Calvin grins so wide

do I realize he's been searching for *me*.

Calvin's expression clears, and he pushes through, making his way over. The crowd parts to let him by, and I barely have time to appreciate his *Officer and a Gentleman* marching approach before his arms are around my waist and I'm lifted off the ground.

"We did it!"

I laugh, wrapping my arms around his shoulders. He is warm, his back is damp with sweat, and his hair tickles the side of my face. "*You* did it."

Calvin murmurs, "No, no," over and over, and then starts laughing. He smells like aftershave and sweat, and I can feel his smile against my neck.

"How was it?" he asks, voice muffled.

"Holy shit. It was . . ."

He pulls back to look at my face. "Yeah? Did you get to see me? I thought I saw you at the very end. I tried to find you."

I am so proud, I burst into tears.

This makes him laugh even harder. "All right, all right, *mo stóirín*. Let's go have some champagne."

eighteen

Rolling over, I straighten my legs and push my hair out of my face. A hammer inside my cranium bangs against my skull in protest.

Do not move, it says.

The sunlight beaming across the bed feels like it's coming from a star just outside my window. Calvin's groggy moan reaches me from the other side of the bed.

The other side of the bed?

I sit up, jerking the sheet across my bare chest, and my world tilts in a heaving, nauseating lurch.

Oh.

I'm naked.

I'm naked? I pull the sheet away from Calvin's facedown form . . . and . . . he is also naked.

The visual reminder is quickly chased by the more physical one: I am sore. *Oh my God* sore. *What the hell did we do* sore.

He presses his face into the pillow. *"Mmmmph.* I feel like I marinated in beer," he says, words muffled. And then he twists, looking over his shoulder, staring down at his body: "Where are my clothes?"

"I don't know."

He looks at me, and seems to surmise that I am equally naked under the sheet. "Where are *yours* . . . ?"

I keep my gaze carefully diverted from his muscular backside. "I don't know that, either."

"I think . . . I think I'm still wearing a condom." He rolls over and I get an eyeful of impressive morning wood before my gaze shoots skyward again, fixed on the ceiling.

He is, indeed, still wearing a condom.

With a whimper, he slowly peels it away and bends, dropping it in the trash bin near my bed. He rolls back, and the resulting silence pulls my attention over to his face.

He's grinning. "Hi."

I think my cheeks are going to melt under the heat of this blush. "Hi."

Saturday morning, late February, in my bed with Calvin McLoughlin. My *bed.* I have located myself in time and space but I still have no recollection of how we ended up here.

He scratches just below his eye. "Don't be surprised, okay? But I think . . ." He looks around at the mess of my bed. "I think we finally consummated the marriage last night."

"This theory is supported by the obnoxious hickey on your shoulder."

He turns his head to check for himself, and looks back

at me, impressed. "Do you remember . . . anything?" he asks, squinting at me through one eye.

Inhaling deeply, I think back.

Champagne at the theater.

He crossed the room, and everything inside me turned into tiny golden bubbles.

Dinner with about fifteen others.

Wine. Lots and lots of wine.

"Dancing?" I ask.

He hesitates. "Yeah."

More drinks and the deep pulsing of music.

Being tugged onto the dance floor. Calvin pulling me right up against him, his hands bracketing my hips, his thigh sliding between my legs. His mouth just below my ear, saying, *I can feel the heat of you. Is it the drink, or is it me?*

And then: watching him trip toward the bar and calling after him, *No more shots!*

The smile on his face when he returned, handing me a shot anyway. His gleeful *Just one more! This is called a Cowboy Cocksucker!*

More dancing. More of his hands on my hips, and my ass, and snaking up my waist, flirting with the sides of my breasts.

I remember sliding my hand up beneath his shirt, feeling the heat of his stomach on my palm. And I remember how our eyes met.

He said, *I want to take you to bed.*

A stumbling walk home at three in the morning.

I glance toward the doorway to my bedroom, finding my

discarded dress there. It's muddy, and that triggers another image. "I fell."

"Right." He reaches for my comforter, which has slipped onto the floor, and pulls it over his lower half, sparing me the effort it's taking to keep not looking. "Apparently I failed to save you."

I remember this. Oh God. I drunk-yelled at him for not having faster reflexes. He picked me up, threw me over his shoulder, and carried me back to the apartment. And then—oh.

Then it was a frenzy. I think we both remember it at the same time, but I can't look at him to confirm. I remember him walking in the door, the way he slid me down his body, his hands all over my ass, and then how we just stood there, weaving, staring at each other.

"I like you," he said.

"You keep saying that."

"Well, I do."

He bent in the only remaining tentative moment of the night, and pressed his mouth to mine.

It was like pushing my maniac button.

"I mauled you," I say.

He laughs, delighted. "I think you did."

"God, we were drunk."

A slideshow shuffles through my head: tearing off clothes, mouths everywhere, teeth knocking. Fingers, lips, and then him over me, pushing inside.

"Neither of us . . ." He trails off.

It takes me a second to figure out what he's saying, and then I blurt it out: "Finished."

"We gave it a good effort but after . . . a while . . . I think we just passed out." He laughs again. "What a testament to my masculinity."

My verbal filter is apparently gone: "Does that mean we *didn't* consummate?"

He giggles and pulls a pillow over his face. "The sex is the consummation, not the orgasm."

A hundred questions fly into my head, birds flapping in the confined space.

But, without the orgasm, did he like it?

Did he mean for us to . . . *yaknow?*

Does he feel weird about it?

Do *I?* I mean, obviously I've wanted to have sex with him since the beginning of time, but I didn't really want it to happen like *this*—drunk, messy, and where the emotional implication is so vague.

"You okay?" he asks, dropping the pillow. "I mean, mentally and . . ." He nods to my body beneath the covers.

"Yeah. You?"

This makes him laugh, like he doesn't even need to answer, and there's some consolation in that.

"Don't look," he says, grinning over at me. "I gotta pee, and I'm going to walk naked to your bathroom because I think you ripped my clothes off by the front door."

I squeeze my eyes shut. "It's your bathroom, too."

Once he's gone, I bend over, picking up my phone. I immediately want to text Lulu and tell her about this insanity, but I hesitate. Lulu used to feel like my bestie, the person I wanted to share every tiny detail with. But the past few weeks, she's been hard to read, and I don't like the sense I have that she would eventually use this story against me somehow.

I'm just starting to turn my screen back off when I catch the number of texts in my iMessage app.

There are 364.

"What the hell?"

I open it, reading the one up top from Jeff, delivered only three minutes ago.

> I'm assuming you're still asleep. Careful where you get your hangover breakfast today.

What?

There are seventy-three texts from Lulu, and the bottom ten are in all caps. I only need to read the most recent one to begin to understand what's going on.

> OPEN YOUR GODDAMN TWITTER.

I open the app. Oh my Jesus.

I scroll, and scroll, and scroll.

In the other room, the toilet flushes, the water runs, and the door opens. Calvin comes back into the bedroom, wearing only boxers.

"Let's head down to Morning Star," he says. "Get some greasy eggs. Some bangers. Some solid hangover food."

"I think we have eggs here."

"No, Holls," he says, flopping down at the end of the bed.

"*Food.*" I don't even care that the movement has tugged the sheet off my boobs and he's getting his own eyeful.

"I'm not sure we should go out and about today," I say, looking up. I'm trying to fight the hysterical bubble that's formed in my throat. "You're trending on Twitter."

nineteen

Honestly, despite the looming awkward of the drunken sex in our rearview mirror, it's all fun and games for two hours of social media surfing until we come across ads for penis enlargers in the #ItPossessedHim tag. With a surprised grunt, Calvin slams my laptop shut, and we turn to stare at each other in shock.

"I don't know where to start," he says. "Do we talk about the social media thing, the sex we sort of had last night, or whether or not I should invest in the penis enlarger?"

I can't maintain eye contact when he goes there because I think my brain starts bleeding, so I look over to the bookcases when I say, "I don't think . . ."

". . . that we should talk any more about the social media thing?"

I laugh. "That's the only safe topic."

In my peripheral vision, he nods. "So you're saying I need a penis enlarger."

"That's not what I'm saying." My face hurts from all the embarrassed wincing I've done since we woke up.

"I'm trying to make light of this. That's what I do."

"I'm getting that."

He nods slowly, licking his lips. "Good. Hungry?"

I'm starving. The problem is we're both hungover and terrified of exiting the apartment. It's not that he's recognizable yet; it's that, from my living room window, we can see three photographers lazily wandering back and forth in front of my building.

Calvin's Twitter account went from a paltry twenty-two followers yesterday to over sixty thousand this morning, and every time we look it's higher. He's tweeted three times in two years, and the third one—which he tweeted this morning and is a photo I took of him and Ramón after their first rehearsal together when they're shaking hands and laughing incredulously (because, really, the two of them together are magic)—has been retweeted over *seven thousand times*.

So, there's *that*. Also, apparently Lin-Manuel Miranda was there last night, as was Amy Schumer. I'm not sure I can rally my meager cerebral resources to comprehend this while at the same time calculating the true contrast of his talent to my *meh*.

I *think* I'm in some sort of shock. I can't interact like a reasonable adult even when Calvin is asking me direct questions. We had sex. We are married. He's a trending topic on Twitter. I honestly—truly—do not know how to proceed here.

On the one hand, I could just ask him: "Be honest: how much do you regret the sex last night?" The worst thing he could say is *a little,* which of course I would understand, and then we wouldn't even bother to pick up the pieces—we have a matter of months of required marriage left—and instead, we'd figure out how to move past them down the road.

On the other hand, it might be better for both of us if we just keep on joking and move past it without any serious conversation. His making light of it makes me think—

"*Hollllllllland.*"

I startle as Calvin leans into my field of vision. "Are you alive?"

Based on the playfully exasperated look on his face, I've missed something. "Sorry. What?"

He shakes his hair out of his eyes, and I get the full impact of both of them, smiling over at me. "I asked you whether you wanted eggs. And when you didn't answer, I decided you *would* want eggs, but then asked whether you wanted the bollocks American bacon in the fridge, or something greasier, like *delivery burgers.*"

"When did you say all this?"

"When you were mouthing your thoughts at the bookcases."

I frown. "I was mouthing my thoughts?"

He nods.

"What was I . . . mouthing?"

A grin flirts with the corner of his mouth. "I dunno. You tell me. I bet it was something about sex."

I don't even know what to say right now, so I just throw out: "Let's get burgers."

He seems to like this answer, snapping his fingers decisively and walking to the counter to get his phone.

I want to say something, not only to pull my brain out of the frantic recollection of every savory detail from last night, but because I'm not sure how to feel about how easily he seems to rebound from having emotionally murky drunk sex. "You have a performance tonight," I blurt. As if he could forget. It's a rare week without a matinee, but they had planned for Luis's departure, and the schedule is a little light as a result.

Looking around into the kitchen to the clock on the stove, he says, "Robert said I need to be there at five."

He's still wearing only boxers. I hear him on the phone, ordering our lunch—burgers and "chips, no—sorry—fries"— and I'm happily staring at him unobstructed—*Oh my God, we had sex*—when my own phone buzzes on the coffee table.

It's Jeff.

My heart slams against my sternum. Jeff doesn't often call; he's a texter. If he's calling . . . if something has gone wrong over at the immigration offices . . .

"Hello?"

"Hey, sweetie," Jeff says. He sounds happy. This is good.

"Hey, Jeffie, what's up?"

"Good news," he says, and then laughs. "I think."

Time slows. It's like I know what he's going to say, but I need him to say it anyway. "Yeah?"

"Your interview is scheduled."

I look up at Calvin, who's finished ordering and is headed back to the couch. The pleasure I take from him being in only underwear and the stress of what Jeff has just said are brewing a strange concoction in my belly.

"Our interview is scheduled," I whisper to him.

His eyebrows shoot up, and I swear his boxers slide another inch down his happy trail.

"But here's the bad news," Jeff says, and my stomach drops. "Sam had an opening, and he worked some magic for you to be penciled in."

"Okay," I say slowly, "when is it?"

Calvin watches my face to gauge my reaction.

Jeff clears his throat. "Monday at ten."

- - - -

We have two hours before we need to leave for the theater, and we'll have tomorrow to talk, but it's not enough. We expected we'd have at least a couple more *weeks* to prepare for the interview.

The internet is a godsend when it comes to sample questions, and Jeff assured me before he hung up that Sam Dougherty is really nice, and this meeting isn't something we should be worried about. But . . . how is that possible? We only have to lie convincingly to a nice person about our sham of a marriage? I don't want to be busted for this! I'm not a hardened woman; I would decay quickly in prison.

It's been so long since I crammed for an exam, and this one seems more important than anything in high school, college, or grad school. At least we had sex! There's one less thing to lie about. Too bad we barely remember it.

Swallowing an enormous bite of burger, Calvin looks as relaxed as ever. "You are Holland Lina Bakker, youngest of six." He wipes a napkin across his lips. "You're incredibly close to your uncle Jeff, who is your mother's youngest brother and married to my boss, Robert Okai. You were born the fifteenth of April," he says, "which is also Tax Day in the States."

"Extra credit," I say, and return his high five. "You are Calvin Aedan McLoughlin, born in Galway, Ireland—which is very interesting since according to most Americans, the only city in Ireland is Dublin—and are the oldest of four. Your mother is Marina, and she is a homemaker. Your father, Patrick, is in medical equipment manufacturing."

He grins, impressed. "Your favorite food is Greek."

I'm charmed he remembered this—especially considering I think I mumbled it as I was shoveling spanakopita in my face one evening. "Your favorite is . . . sushi?"

He laughs, shaking his head. "I hate sushi."

"Okay," I admit, "that was a guess. Chinese?"

"My favorite cuisine is German food."

I guffaw. "German isn't really a *cuisine*, is it?"

He crosses his eyes at me. "Let's pull up from the weeds, Mrs. McLoughlin."

"Mr. *Bakker*, you've played guitar since you were four." I chomp on a fry. "We met on a train—but this was six months ago, remember, not five weeks—and you asked me to dinner."

Calvin puts his feet up on the coffee table. "That first date was at Mercato, and we went home and had sex."

I choke on a bite of burger. "We did?'"

Calvin leans over, kissing my cheek. "Don't you remember? We couldn't keep our hands off each other."

"Oh, completely," I say, laughing so awkwardly the sound of it actually makes me want to punch myself in the mouth. "Okay, yeah, I mean of course we've had a *lot* of sex. Like, newlywed and so, *so* into sex . . . of course."

There's a beat of dead silence as Calvin tries to figure out what the hell is happening, and I can't help him because I have no idea what my mouth is doing, either. My brain has clearly checked out.

"*Right,*" he says slowly. "A lot of sex." His grin starts tiny and turns into a beacon of amusement. "Should I tell him you like it a little dirty?"

I swallow a bite of fry before I've even chewed it; my eyes water instantly. "What?"

"I mean, you do, don't you?" He licks his lips and stares at mine. "Certainly seemed that way."

I don't even know what's happening. I wipe my mouth, like there might be a line of drool there.

"I like seeing you speechless."

"I am . . . yes. Out of words."

His smile straightens and he licks his lips again, leaning forward a little.

With a jerk, I cough, and resolutely ball my burger wrapper up. "Moving on! You are now a part of the orchestra for *It Possessed Him,*" I say, "but formerly you were a *freelance performer* and played in various bands, including a cover band called Loose Springsteen—"

"Please don't tell them that. I don't want that a matter of government record."

I giggle. "And you apparently like to walk around the apartment mostly naked."

He looks slyly at me. "You keep the heat up pretty high."

I am no match for his verbal flirting. "Is it too warm in here?"

Calvin shrugs, and his greenish eyes are lit with tiny stars. "You're pretty red."

"You're embarrassing me."

"By being half-naked?"

"By bringing up the sex we had."

"The sex we *didn't* have," he corrects, becoming more amused by the minute. "That first date was pretend sex. Last night was real sex, without satisfaction for either of us. I'm wondering whether that has us both a little jittery. Maybe you'll find something to help you in the couch."

For a second, maybe more, I'm starting to think he's flirting. I'm starting to think that he's suggesting we go have some more real sex before we have to leave for work. He's certainly dialed up the charm this afternoon.

But as he holds on to the smile, it becomes a little forced and his eyes flicker away, to the clock, down to his phone. And *that* is not a smile I've seen on his face before. *Or have I?*

The bubble pops.

Calvin is good at this. It took him no time at all to say yes to my proposal. The kiss on the wedding day made my knees weak, but he's never tried to kiss me again. Well, not including last night's booze-induced mauling. But he's *really* good at the emotions, the intuition of feeling—it's part of what makes him such a good musician.

And I'm . . . not. I've never been a game player.

Our interview is Monday, and we need to crush it. There's a kernel inside me, holding steadfast, that knows he's playing a game, trying to get me to loosen up enough to be convincing. Yes, he's charming, and yes, of course, he's gorgeous. But he wants this job and this life more than anything. I think back to his words the other day. *"The entire time I've been here, I've wanted this—exactly this . . . After I graduated, I thought something like this would come . . . I wanted this show so much I just stayed."*

This is what is most important to him.

And that's when it hits me.

If playing me and flirting with me—and even sleeping with me—will get him that life, I don't doubt for one second that he would do it.

twenty

I peer down at my phone.

Brigid . . . Brigid?

Oh! Brigid, as in *Calvin's sister* Brigid.

"Calvin?"

I walk out of the bathroom and round the corner to find him standing in the kitchen. One can only assume he's wearing boxers, because from where I'm standing—and with his lower half currently obscured by the counter—he looks like he's eating cereal wearing nothing but his wedding ring.

Help.

When he sees me he lifts a forearm to wipe his mouth and my eyes zero in like tractor beams. With his arm out of the way I am confronted with an unobstructed view of pectorals, abdominals, obliques . . .

I see it each day—what is this extraordinary life?—but it knocks the wind out of me every time.

"I know you're not hungry so thought I'd grab something quick before we go." He points to the phone still clutched in my hand and drops his voice to a whisper: "Someone on the phone?"

I begrudgingly rip my gaze from his torso and meet his eyes. "Yes. Phone. Did you by chance give your sister my number?"

Calvin sets his bowl in the sink and steps around the counter. He *is* wearing boxers, but now I can see his legs, too. I'm not sure this is any better. Standing across from me in the doorway, he looks down, sheepish.

"She kept asking and since she doesn't know this is . . ."— he motions between us and I know what he's implying: *not real*—"I figured it best to give in. I hope you're not angry. She's not much of a texter so you'll probably barely hear from her."

"No, it's fine. And you're right, it would look weird if I didn't interact with them at all."

Calvin leans against the doorway across from where I stand, and is entirely too naked to be this close. I push away and turn to face him in the hallway. On the one hand, it's sort of lovely to have his sister's information. Our lives are becoming interwoven; we are marking up each other's history with permanent ink.

On the other hand, he hasn't been home in four years.

It's hard to know how much emotional currency he has really spent by connecting me with his sister.

"She won't get too personal," he assures me. "It's the Mc-Loughlin way."

I laugh at this. "Clearly it's the Bakker way, as well. And—upside—at least I won't have to lie that I'm in touch with them."

"True." His smile slips for a moment before it's replaced with one that doesn't crinkle his eyes the way I'm used to—it's the absence that makes it so notable. "Speaking of . . . I guess we should get ready to go?"

- - - -

Calvin stares ahead at the federal building, and together we look up up up. "I have the same feeling right now that I did as a kid hearing, 'Just wait till your father gets home.'"

I nod in agreement, congratulating myself on having the foresight to skip breakfast. It would just be coming back up right around now.

Calvin turns to me, and the faint color blooming across the tops of his cheekbones sets off a domino course of panic inside my chest. He looked completely calm at his audition, and only mildly anxious at our wedding. Seeing him nervous now only makes me more jittery.

"Before we go in," he says, "can we double-check that we have everything?"

Between us, we've checked and rechecked at least a dozen times, but I'm soothed that Calvin's need to be prepared is almost as obsessive as mine.

We step out of the main walkway and off to the side, next to a half-moon planter with a set of trees on each end. In the spring there would be shade overhead and lush branches heavy with blooms. Right now they're skeletal and stark against the looming gray sky.

Calvin closes in to block the wind, and I pull out the binder, careful not to let anything slip to the wet ground at our feet. "Copies of everything we've already sent," I say, turning past the first stack. "Photos, joint bills, copies of our applications." I nod into the cold. "It's all here."

He nods back and squints up at the building. "We ready?"

"No."

At least this makes him laugh. "What else can we sort out in the next . . ."—he pulls my arm up, sliding my coat higher to peek at my watch—"four minutes?"

Just this little gesture—that he knew I would be wearing a watch—gives me a measure of calm. "I guess we're good."

I still don't know that much about his family dynamic, I don't know much about his childhood, I still don't know that much about his time in the States. But I guess it's understandable . . . as far as they know, we met only six months ago.

He presses a single kiss to my brow—and my heart leaps into my throat—before he sucks in a breath and steps away, taking my hand. The flush in his cheeks has spread, and when he looks up again, I see that his neck is flushed now, too.

He gives my arm a gentle tug. "Let's get on with it, then."

- - - -

The gravity of what we're about to do really hits home once we're inside. There's an austerity in the air—an impression that this is not the place to expect to be charming and get away with anything. A set of metal detectors sits just inside the doorway and a stoic security guard watches while we sign in and pull out our identification.

We peel layers off in silence, placing coats and scarves and bags into gray plastic tubs that are shuttled away on a conveyor belt. Calvin motions for me to go first into the scanner. Once through, we silently find the elevator—my heart is a hammer now—we climb in—Calvin's hand grows sweaty in mine—and he reaches with his free hand to press the button for our floor.

I curse the hard-soled Mary Janes I'm wearing as they alternately squeak and then clunk across the glossy tiled floor. I try to adjust my footfalls and end up doing an awkward shuffle-dance down the hallway.

"Never a dull moment," Calvin quips at my side.

I growl through a laugh, trying to walk normally. "I'm not great with pressure."

"*No,*" he says in mock disbelief.

I shove him a little. "At least I don't have to pee. When I was a kid my mom knew where every bathroom in Des Moines was located. Even a hint of anxiety and I'd pee my pants."

He stifles a laugh. "I was a thumb sucker."

"Tons of kids do that."

"Not till they're four. God, Mam tried everything to get me to stop. Socks on the hands, bribery, even painting my thumb with this clear stuff that tasted awful." He scrunches his nose at the memory. "Then we visited my uncle and he told me to pluck on his old guitar when I felt the need to do it, and that was it. I never looked back."

We reach the office door and I tuck that piece of information away in my Calvin vault.

Understandably, this room has none of the optimistic charm found at the Marriage Bureau. The carpet is standard industrial gray and a handful of other couples sit in metal-and-fabric reception chairs. One couple seems to have brought a lawyer with them. Jeff told us not to. He said more often than not it tends to make the immigration officer suspicious, and that there was no need. I hope he was right.

At least twenty minutes go by. Calvin and I try to quiz each other in a way that looks more like flirting and less like cramming for a last-minute test—and get so caught up that we startle when our names are called. I'm assaulted by the mental image of cartoon characters with sweat spouting from their foreheads and the word *LIARS* flashing above. Calvin links his fingers with mine again when we stand, and we're greeted by a smiling man with more forehead than hair who introduces himself as Sam Dougherty.

Inside his office, Officer Dougherty sits down in a chair that creaks each time he shifts. "All right. Please repeat after me: 'I swear that the information I am about to provide is the truth, the whole truth, and nothing but the truth, so help me God.'"

We repeat it in quiet unison, and I wipe my sweaty hand on my thigh when we're done.

With his eyes on the file in front of him, Dougherty begins, "Calvin, may I please have your passport and driver's license, if applicable. And Holland, I need whatever proof of citizenship you've brought with you."

We huddle together, and despite knowing this file backward and forward, it takes a comical amount of time and repeated paper shuffling to find what he needs. I feel the tremor in my hands as I hand it over, and can see it in Calvin's, too.

"Thank you," Dougherty says, taking them. "And thank you for making copies. That's always appreciated."

Even though I sense that he's going out of his way to be nice, my heart is pounding in my throat. But when I glance over to Calvin, any trace of nerves seems to have left him. He sits comfortably in his chair, hands loosely folded in his lap, with one leg easily crossed over the other. I take a breath, wishing he could funnel some of that calm into me.

"When did you enter the country?"

Calvin answers honestly—eight years ago—and I note the tiny quirk in Dougherty's brow as he writes this down. I clench my own hands in my lap to keep from leaning forward and explaining, *See, he's a brilliant musician and kept thinking that the right opportunity would come along, and then it didn't, and before he knew it, he'd been here four years illegally and was terrified he'd lost any shot at playing music in the States.*

Calvin glances at me, lifting a brow as if he can tell that I'm on the verge of losing it. He winks, and my blood pressure backs off; the cold panic thaws along my skin.

I tune back in, following their conversation. *Where did you go to school? What did you study? When were you born? Where were you born? What do you do to make ends meet?*

Calvin nods, having prepared for this last question. Although street performance itself is protected under the First Amendment as artistic expression, we agreed with Jeff that busking didn't lend credibility to Calvin's plan to play the part of a classically trained musician. "I've been playing with a number of local bands," he says, "performing at various venues."

"Such as?" Dougherty asks without looking up.

"Hole in the Hall," Calvin says, and winks at me. "Bowery. Café Wha?, Arlene's Grocery. Tons of places."

Officer Dougherty turns to me and smiles. He seems completely satisfied with all of this so far. "Is this your first marriage?"

"Yes, sir."

"And do you have the marriage certificate with you?"

I fumble through the papers again and Calvin leans forward, gently pointing out the right document. "Right there, *mo croi.*"

I manage to mutter some breathy version of thanks, and hand it over.

"Were your parents at the ceremony, Holland?"

"My parents . . . no," I say. "They don't like to fly, and it was all sort of a whirlwind." I swallow down my nerves. "It was just us, and our best friends."

"No family there?"

A tiny stab to my heart. "No."

He writes something down on a sheet of paper, nodding. I suspect he already knew this.

"And what about your parents, Mr. McLoughlin?"

Calvin shifts in his seat. "No, sir."

Dougherty pauses, taking this in, before writing something down.

Defensiveness rises in me. "Calvin's youngest sister has cerebral palsy. Her medical expenses are enormous, and the family couldn't afford to come out. Our hope is to travel to see them this summer to celebrate."

Dougherty looks at me, and then turns sympathetic eyes to Calvin. "I'm sorry to hear that, Mr. McLoughlin. But I hear Ireland is beautiful in the summer."

Calvin reaches over, taking my hand and giving it a squeeze.

Dougherty goes through another round of questioning, where this time the goal is to verify that Calvin is of "good moral character," and he answers with flying colors. I'm just beginning to relax, to think, *Holy shit, what was I so worried about?*—when Officer Dougherty clears his throat, puts his notebook down, and looks us in the eye in turn.

"So, Calvin and Holland. Now we move on to the final part of the interview, and the part I'm sure you've heard the most about, where we hope to determine the authenticity of this marriage."

That sound? That was my heart falling like a brick from the sky and crumbling on impact.

"Believe it or not, some people *aren't* actually in love." He leans back in his chair—*squeak, squeeeeeak*. "They come in here trying to obtain a fraudulent green card." He says this like it's the most absurd thing he's ever heard. Calvin and I make a show of looking at each other, attempting to mirror his disbelief.

"And it's my job to figure that out, and identify red flags. I am required to remind you that you are under oath, and the penalty for perjury is up to five years in a federal prison, and/or a fine of up to $250,000."

I swallow, and then swallow again. A vision of me in an orange jumpsuit flashes in my thoughts and I have to resist the urge to laugh hysterically.

"I'm going to ask you some questions to assess whether or not you can satisfy your burden of proof as to whether your marriage is real. First of all, do you have documents to substantiate the marriage?"

"You have our certificate." I pull a stack of papers from my folder. "And here's the lease agreement." I slide it in front of him, followed by several more papers. "A copy of our utility bills and our joint account."

"So you have checks in both your names?"

"Yes, we have sex—CHECKS!" My face explodes in a fireball.

Beside me, Calvin lifts a hand to casually cover his smile.

"One would hope so." With a smile, Dougherty searches through a list of information. "Calvin, where did Holland study?"

"She went to Yale and then Columbia," he says. "She has a degree in English and her MFA in creative writing."

Dougherty looks up, surprised. "MFA. Wow."

"Yes, sir."

"And Holland, where did you and Calvin meet?"

"We met . . ." My brain is a slow-motion train wreck, coming around a curve too fast before completely careening off the rails. "At the subway." Our plan is to say we met on the subway, riding together. Our plan is to avoid mentioning that he was busking for money, and instead focus on his various musical gigs with local bands.

Our plan is to be *smooth*, for Christ's sake.

So I have no idea what's happening when the next words fly out of my mouth: "I used to watch him play."

I mentally scream as our carefully crafted, *simple* story somehow flies out of my brain.

"At one of the clubs?" Dougherty asks, brows raised.

Fix this, Holland. Say yes. "No." *Shiiiiiit.* "At the Fiftieth Street station."

"I would play there a couple times a week," Calvin covers easily. "It was more for fun than anything."

Dougherty nods and makes note of this.

"I could hear music when I'd pass, and one day I decided to see who it was." I swallow, wondering if that's the end of what has to be my complete mental breakdown. No such luck. "I couldn't take my eyes off him and so . . . I'd sometimes take the train when I didn't need to just to hear him play."

I'm afraid to look at Calvin, and instead keep my eyes straight ahead, to where the fluorescent bulbs are reflecting off Officer Dougherty's bald head.

"I have heard a lot of stories, but that is a new one," he says. "Very romantic. And how long before you talked to him?"

For Christ's sake, shut up, Holland.

"Six months."

Calvin slowly turns to me.

Ughhhhhhhhh.

"My goodness, that *is* a crush." Dougherty makes a few

notes in his file, and I swear I am sweating through my chair. "And Calvin, what did you first notice about Holland?"

"Her eyes," he says without hesitation, even though our story has dramatically changed. "The first time she talked to me we didn't say much, but I remember her eyes. They're hypnotizing."

He noticed my eyes? They're *hypnotizing*? Does he actually remember that I spoke to him that night before the zombie attack, or is he playing along? I don't even get time to savor this moment because the officer looks up at me as if to verify this. "And Holland, do you remember what you said?"

I feel the embarrassment all over again. "I think I blurted out something about his music."

Calvin nods. "She said, 'I love your music' and then sort of . . . shuffled away."

I look over at him and laugh. I feel jubilant: he remembers. "I'd been drinking in Brooklyn with Lulu," I tell him.

"I've figured that out in the time since, *mo stóirín*."

Officer Dougherty chuckles down at his papers. "A love story as old as time."

- - - -

We walk to the elevator in silence, and our steps reverberate down the hall.

I think we did it.

I think we did it.

I am mortified that I admitted to essentially stalking him, but it doesn't seem to have fazed him at all.

And who cares? Because we did it.

The elevator doors open and we step inside; thank God it's empty. I fall back against the back wall, stunned.

"Holy shit." He pushes a hand into his hair. "Holy shit. That was amazing."

I open my mouth. My body hasn't caught up with my brain yet; I still feel like I'm on high alert. "Oh my God."

"I almost lost it for a second when you blanked on how we met," he says, "but then you came up with that brilliant story about watching me for months."

Oh, shit. "I . . ."

"The idea of you coming to the station every day just to hear me play," he says, shaking his head. "It's insane. He ate it up like cake."

"Total cake," I mumble.

Would he like me less if he knew that it was the truth? That I watched him for six months? That I wanted him, in painful silence, for too many subway rides to remember?

He moves a step closer, crowding me against the elevator wall. "Do you know what happens now?"

With him so close, I want to tell him every embarrassing time I wondered what color his eyes were, what he'd sound like when he opened his mouth, what he looked like when he smiled. With him this close, my brain becomes a film reel of every second Calvin was naked in my bed. The smell of him and the sight of his face at this distance triggers the memory of how his skin felt sliding over mine, of him above me, moving.

"What?" I say, eyes glazed over.

His teeth press down on his bottom lip before his mouth curves into a beaming smile. "Now, we celebrate."

twenty-one

The plan is to go out for a celebratory lunch, but Calvin wants to stop at the apartment first. This morning I was too nervous to contemplate eating; now I'm too excited. We are both behaving like goofballs—racing from the subway station to the corner, play-wrestling outside the building, running up the stairs with enormous grins. I am aware, in this sharp sweep of clarity, how much *fun* I have with him.

In the time since we got married, I've discovered that I don't only appreciate his awesome face and hot body, but I genuinely adore being around him. We have fun because *he* is fun, and there's a little ache that chases that realization because I wonder where this can actually go.

Yes, he seems to enjoy being around me, but it's not like he has a *choice*—and Calvin seems like the kind of guy who can make the best out of any circumstance.

I fumble with my keys outside the door, and he leans into

me, breathless from the race upstairs, resting his chin near my temple.

"Are you starving?" he asks.

I shake my head, shoving the key into the lock. "I'm still too excited to be hungry."

The feel of him against me—his chest against my arm, his breath on my neck—would completely annihilate my appetite anyway.

"You were so good," he says, and kisses my hair. There's a little growl at the end of the word *good* that feels like fingers running up and down my spine, and I hear the echo of his words from two nights ago:

I can feel the heat of you. Is it the drink, or is it me?

I don't want to misread this situation because it could be devastating to think he's into me when he's really just being sweet and grateful, still high on adrenaline. But my pulse is rioting; the low ache in my belly is intensifying with every second. "You needed to grab something?"

He follows me in and closes the door behind us, saying, "I don't need to get anything."

Did I misunderstand him? "But I thought—" I move to put down my keys, but he reaches for my arm, turning me, gently guiding until I'm pressed with my back against the door.

"I didn't need to get anything from the apartment."

What?

Calvin bends, and his mouth hovers just below my ear. "I just wanted to come home before lunch."

Oh.

The ache explodes.

My body is pretty sure it understands his meaning clearly—my hands move up his chest and around his neck. But my brain—my brain is always the problem: "Why?"

He laughs, scraping my jaw with his teeth, and then kisses my cheek, my ear. "Do you realize you've been avoiding any casual physical contact since we woke up in bed together?"

"I have?" I pull back. It's surreal to be looking into his eyes when they're so close to mine.

This makes him laugh again. "I think I've made it pretty clear you can have me if you want me. I practically refuse to put on clothes when we're in the apartment."

"Oh. That's true."

He smiles, kissing my nose. "But if you aren't interested, I'll leave you alone and not ask again."

I hurl my words out like I'm bidding at an auction: "I'm interested."

"I've wanted this since the first time we had lunch."

What?

His smile moves up my neck, pressing parentheses into my skin. "I remember how nervous and sweet you were." More kisses. "I wondered whether you liked me that way. But you kept so calm with me in your house . . . and I'm out here on the couch thinking about you."

I don't even know what to say to this. I want to repeat the way he says *tinking about you*. He was out here feeling what I was feeling? My charade was too convincing; apparently I could have been getting Calvin Sex for the past month. I want to both celebrate and scream.

"And then we fell into your bed," he says, and his mouth

moves across my throat to the other ear. He sucks just below, pressing into me. Something hard digs into my hip, and I gasp.

It makes him hiss. "I like your sounds. I remember how many of them you made." His mouth moves closer to mine. "What do you remember?"

"Earlier," I say, and he kisses me once, "in the elevator, when you were close to me, I was thinking about . . ."

He pulls back, waiting. "Thinking about . . . ?"

"When we were in my bed."

"What were we doing?"

I push back the self-conscious doubt in my throat. "You were on top of me. We were already . . ."

Moving together, I don't say.

Calvin groans, sliding his hands under my shirt to grip my waist. "You were thinking about fucking me in the elevator?"

And just like that, I am hot everywhere. He's making this so easy. "I was remembering that feeling of skin on skin, where you can't get enough?"

His mouth comes over mine, and I remember this, too. It's not a new kiss, it's a kiss we've done before—teasing only at first and then sucking, and deeper, and hungry.

He slides his hands farther up my shirt, and around so he's unfastening my bra with a tiny pinch. My shirt and bra are pulled off together, and his mouth moves down, dragging words over my skin. I stare down at his shoulders, reaching for his shirt, wanting to see the way the muscles move as he grabs me and holds me, as he works his mouth down my belly to the clasp of my skirt.

My clothes are peeled off in front of the door again, but

this time I notice everything. I notice how his skin looks in the dim light coming in the living room window, and I notice how he smiles even when he's kissing me.

I notice the feel of his skin on my fingertips and how it's even smoother against my lips.

I notice he likes being licked on his chest, he likes being bitten near his hip, and his hands shake when he slides them into my hair as I move lower, taking him in my mouth.

But the things I learn about Calvin right now won't ever be shared in an interview; finally we have something that is just for us. I don't need to know that he's quiet while he watches, his breaths initially cut off and then gasping. I don't need to know that he begs sweetly when he's close, or that he warns me, trying to slow his body down before he comes—but I learn these things anyway. And I don't need to know for anyone but myself that he's a tease when he puts his mouth on me, or that he'll touch me with the same fingers he uses to strum his guitar and it's that knowledge that will send me over the edge on my living room floor.

We get a drink of water, we move to my bed, and his mouth is all over me again, along my thighs, over my stomach, sucking, sucking at my chest. I'm sure we'll talk later, but for now we're only sounds and breathing. It feels like all we've done is talk—in this instructional, memorizing way, knowing that everything we say needs to be filed away for a later date—but right now the only thing I want is to reconstruct that choppy memory of how it feels to have his weight on me and his skin all over mine.

The strange thing is that all of this feels so easy and famil-

iar, but when he's there—above me and then pushing inside—
that's where the familiarity ends. I know now that that night
we were nearly numb with intoxication, and I can say with
certainty that he didn't watch as he inched into me; he didn't
go this slowly. I can say with certainty that my eyes were probably closed and it was all wilder and rougher because we could
barely process a thing.

And I know for sure it didn't feel like this. I'm so sensitive
that he's only started to move and I'm clawing at him, pressing
into him to get closer, and closer, and we find a rhythm for so
long where everything feels so good we can't stop marveling
over it, and it blows over me, unexpected—

I'm coming and he's watching,

moving faster he's so focused—

his hips stutter against mine and he's there, following just
after me; his deep groan of relief vibrates against my throat. I
have one hand in his hair and the other on his neck; my legs
are wound around him, hooked together at his lower back: like
this, we go still.

It's raining outside, I didn't even realize. Heavy sheets of
water sluice over the eaves and down onto the sidewalk.

"Was it good?" he whispers, quietly reverent.

"Yeah." I swallow, catching my breath. "You?"

He pulls back a little and stares down at me. "Yeah." He
bends, kissing me. "I'm reeling."

Calvin's breath is warm on my neck, his back still slick
beneath my palms. The other night seems like drunken fum-
bling compared to what just happened between us, and I'm left
momentarily out of words.

He pushes up onto an elbow and reaches down between us with his other hand, anchoring the condom as he pulls out. When he shifts away to throw it in the bin, the entire front of my body goes cold, and I urge him back, pulling the covers over us.

"I don't think you'll ever be able to fake an orgasm with me." His voice is muffled by my shoulder.

This makes me laugh. "What? I mean—I wouldn't fake an orgasm—but what makes you say that?"

"You get this flush, up your neck and across your face. I thought I could go a bit more but then you started to come, and I was done for."

I curl into him. The feel of his arms around me is so insane. I want to look at him again and again, to make sure I'm not imagining this.

"What time is it?" I ask.

He stretches to see my alarm clock on the other nightstand. "Two."

We have twenty-seven blissful hours before we have to be anywhere. I nestle closer.

"Holland?"

"Yeah?"

"How did you know that my parents couldn't afford to come to the wedding?"

I pull back so I can see him. "I just made that up. I assume Molly's medical care is really expensive."

"It is." He leans in, kissing my nose. "It's been this enormous stress, her whole life."

This pushes a little ache into my chest.

"I've tried so hard to keep them from worrying about me," he says. I stare up at his face, watching his jaw tense as he swallows. "Didn't want them spending the money to come out to see me living in Mark's flat, paying fuck-all in rent. Little lies turned into big lies and—" He stops and looks down at me, searching back and forth between my eyes. "I'll tell it all to you someday but not now. It just felt good when you said that." He slides a hand up, over my breast and coming to rest on my sternum. "Feels like I don't always have to explain myself so much with you."

The thrill that blooms inside me when he says this feels like a kite pushing up into the sky, expanding beneath my ribs. "Well, for what it's worth, I can absolutely see how you stayed here for so long, and also why you wouldn't want them to worry about how you were doing, or who's taking care of you."

"Mam is really glad we're married," he says. "I haven't been so good about keeping her up to date, but I'm trying to do better. I told her how good it all is with you. But my father is a tougher sell. I imagine that's why Brigid texted you."

I wince, remembering. "I need to reply."

"You were a bit busy today."

"I haven't told my parents yet," I admit.

I can tell he's only mildly surprised by this. "Yeah?"

Up close, his green eyes seem so much more complicated—green, yellow, brown, bronze. It makes it hard to be flippant, or lie. "They barely trust me to run my own life, they'd automatically assume th—"

"That you're being used?"

In truth there are a dozen reasons; this is definitely one of them. "*I* don't think that," I quickly add.

"I was taking advantage at first, I suppose." Licking his lips, he seems to think on this for a few more seconds. "But I knew that I liked you, knew I'd be happy to score with you"— he laughs, kissing me—"I thought there *could* be more. I just put the marriage before the feelings."

"Arranged marriages do that all the time."

"They do." He looks down at me. "And you said a year, after all. It seemed to be what you wanted, but what an enormous thing to do for Robert, for me. I wondered whether there might be more you wanted, too."

I don't know how to interpret this; I hate my brain sometimes. Does this mean sex is the equivalent of him fulfilling his end of the bargain? Was he pretending to not believe me about my six-month crush, and decided this is the way to repay the favor? Or do I take him at his word, that he wanted this from the beginning?

My logical head wants to wait and see how I feel when I'm alone tomorrow, to not read too much into this. My heart and my heated blood want me to ask for more.

"My father thinks I should have stayed in Ireland," he says after a few ticking beats of silence, "gotten a proper job."

I glance up to him. "In manufacturing?"

He nods. "He reminds me I'm the oldest, that it's my responsibility to care for Molly when he and Mam are gone. I assume I'll go back, someday. Always have."

"Are you ever homesick?"

I miss Des Moines in these unexpected bursts. Like when the sirens wail past, over and over outside my window, and I just want quiet. Or on trash days, when all I can hear is the crashing and creaking and jostling of metal and refuse. Or when I leave my apartment and feel like everyone wants to stay in their bubble and not interact with another human on the planet.

"Yeah." Calvin rolls to his back, pulling me so I'm half on top of him. "It feels easier there in some ways, and harder in others. The world feels smaller there—which is good and bad. I suppose we choose our hardships. I thought it'd be easier to find work in New York, but I was wrong."

"I can see how the years just went by, though."

"Yeah." He inhales slowly, and my head moves with the expanding of his ribs. "It's so much less lonely now that I'm with you. Before, I felt rather untethered. Everything here feels so *aware*, if you know what I mean. Everyone pays so much attention to themselves."

"Well, it *is* the theater district."

He laughs like I'd hoped he would. "I mean more than all that. I mean how it feels like we're all always posing for a selfie, even when we're just talking."

"You're not like that."

He pulls back, looking down at me. "No?"

"No. You're this huge, larger-than-life presence and you don't even realize it." I run my hand over his chest. "You're a genius with that guitar, but you're also so . . ."

"Silly?"

"No, simple," I say, quickly adding, "and I don't mean that in a bad way. I want to think that, with you, what you see is what you get."

"I'd hope so."

"Everyone likes to think they're that way, but so few people *are*."

In my words, I can hear the small question, *Can I trust this moment right here?* I am suddenly so aware that we're naked. That we've just made love, and that I think he wants to again.

"You're just saying that because you like me." He smiles, rolling slightly to kiss me.

I think he means it to be a small touch, lips to lips, like punctuation at the end of the sentence, but I press for more, climbing over him. He's right, I *do* like him. In fact, I worry in this moment right here that I'm falling too hard and too fast.

"Well, yeah." I reach down, wrapping my fingers around the part of him that is hard again, so soon. "Haven't I heard you say you like *me?*"

He watches me lift my hips and lower them back down over him before his eyes roll closed. *"Mo stóirín*, I fear I'll like you too much."

"What does that nickname mean?" The question comes out tight, already out of breath.

His hands slide up my waist, cupping my breasts. "It's strange. I haven't ever used it before." My skin heats beneath his palms. "My granddad used to say it to my granny. It means 'my little darling.'"

twenty-two

The next few weeks are a blur of sex and takeout, of roaring applause and winter turning into spring, of quiet conversations in the rain on our way home. And every single time we walk in the front door, it feels like a warp back to surreal: Calvin isn't just staying in my apartment anymore, he *lives* there.

I've never had a sexual relationship like this: sex everywhere, every day, almost like we can't get enough. Instead of taking turns in the shower, we shower together. There's barely enough room for one, but as Calvin correctly points out, that's the best reason to do it. Some afternoons we have lunch with Robert and Jeff, but more often than not we're at home—preferring the quiet comfort of home pre-performance—reading, talking, watching a movie on the couch. Or tangled together in bed.

Calvin is a nearly insatiable lover, and his appetite for it calms the fever mirrored in me, makes me less self-conscious about the way it seems I want him again nearly as soon as we've finished. He kisses me constantly and brings me tiny gifts: bookmarks with quotes from books I adore, my favorite chocolate-covered oranges from the candy store around the corner, and tiny pink treasures—earrings, a woven bracelet from a street vendor, zany fuschia-rimmed sunglasses. He eats like a ravenous teenager and prefers to be completely naked when we're home—*Just for the craic of it*—insisting there's nothing like airing out after an intense day of rehearsal. *Ah, Holland*, he says, putting on a thick accent, *it feels amazen. T'ere's nothin' like going bollocks bare when yer sweatin' in yer trousers like da'.*

And then he tackles me on the couch and tickles me until I'm hysterically laughing . . . and naked, too.

I try to remind myself that this isn't real—and it certainly isn't forever—but every time he rolls over in the middle of the night and wakes me up with his hands and his weight over me, it *feels* more real. Every time he brings me a cup of coffee with his crazy bed head and pillow lines on his face, it feels more real. Every time he holds my jacket for me to slip into before we leave the apartment, and kisses my cheek, it feels more real.

Whether he's enthralling hundreds, or moving above me staring unfocused at my lips, or quietly plucking away at his guitar on the sofa at noon, I wonder how I lived such a solitary, mediocre life before him. Even then, watching him so briefly create magic as he played at the station was the highlight of my week. But now he's become this consuming force of nature in my world. *How could I possibly not fall in love with that?*

I reply to his sister, and despite Calvin's insistence that

she's not much of a texter, she writes me again. Back and forth like this every day—at first with little innocuous tidbits and then with photos and stories—we get to know each other. Each little bit of him in my life is another nail building the home our hearts can inhabit, and with a hunger that is nearly aching, I want to bring his mother and sister out here to visit. I know he misses them. I don't have a lot of extra, but together Brigid and I scrounge it together and buy two tickets to surprise him.

- - - -

One night, it's the climax of the second act and Ramón is singing near the lip of the stage as his character watches his daughters move farther into the forest. Calvin accompanies him in the orchestra pit just a few feet away. This is the moment everyone waits for, where the attention of an entire audience is held by a single set of spotlights focused on Ramón. I can barely breathe during this song, and make a point each night of finding my way to the door to listen, to watch, to wait for that single note that—

"Mama, is it going to be over soon? They're only singing for *hours*."

A ripple of laughter moves through the auditorium at the sound of this boisterous kid voice, but Ramón plays into the entire thing, nodding in sympathy as the sheepish mother waves and carries the little girl away. The audience erupts into applause.

Live theater is unpredictable, and most performers will say that's partly what they love about it. Whether it's an unruly child or a missed lighting cue or a wardrobe malfunction, the energy of the audience and these tiny uncertainties are exactly what makes it addicting.

For Calvin, performing seems to be an intoxicating aphrodisiac. He finds me that night after his final bow and can hardly contain himself, trapping me against the iron frame of the forest set. His eyes are bright with the mischievous joy I've grown addicted to. Dropping his arms to my waist, he lifts me just high enough for my feet to come off the ground.

By now, the theater is practically empty, but he walks us both deeper backstage, dropping sucking kisses up my neck.

"You were fantastic tonight," I tell him just before he puts his lips on mine.

He speaks into the kiss. "I dropped a few notes on 'I Didn't Expect You.'"

"Yeah, but only two," I say, pulling back a little, "and Ramón was really belting it out tonight, so I think only you and Robert noticed."

"And you," he whispers.

I nod toward the side exit. "Are you doing the stage door?"

Fans of the show wait outside behind the theater, hoping for a glimpse or a photo of one of the cast as they leave for the night. Ramón almost always stops by, and lately Calvin has had quite a fan club gathering there, too.

He places me back on my feet and the front of my body drags along the front of his. He's half-hard for me beneath his dress pants, and it's almost impossible not to wrap my legs around him and shimmy myself back up.

Just over his shoulder, I catch Brian as he looks away from

where we're tucked into the shadows. I see the tail end of his disgusted sneer, and the expression communicates so much that I feel, for a second, like I've been punched.

I can practically hear his voice: *You are such a fucking fool, Holland.*

I close my eyes, press my face into Calvin's neck.

This is real. It is.

"I'll go for a few minutes." He looks down when my phone buzzes in my back pocket.

"It's Lulu," I tell him, "asking 'where the fucking hell' we are."

"She's so demure," he says, deadpan. "I can't wait for her to come out of her shell and be more assertive."

This makes me laugh. "Go sign some autographs and I'll meet you out front in ten."

"I don't want to stay out too long." He brushes his lips over mine, lingering meaningfully. He shaved this morning but his chin is already rough, and I'm strung like one of his guitar strings—tight and vibrating—knowing how that stubble feels between my thighs.

- - - -

We're meeting Lulu only about a block from the theater, at Dutch Fred's for burgers and drinks, but when I slip out the side door to grab Calvin twenty minutes later, he's still surrounded by fans, and looks up at me with wild, helpless eyes.

I've never seen him look overwhelmed before.

"Sorry, everyone! Five more!" I yell, pretending I have the authority.

But sometimes pretending is all it takes. Calvin signs the last one, and apologizes to the twenty or more people holding their programs. We duck down the alley, escaping via a secret route I use all the time when I don't want to run into Brian on my way out at the end of the day.

"This way." I tug his sleeve, and he follows. There are a few puddles we avoid, and the smell down here isn't exactly fresh, but it will be a quick walk to the bar, and easy to avoid the crowds.

After only a few steps, though, we hear footsteps and I realize . . . people are following us.

I turn to look over my shoulder, and Calvin does the same; it's a mistake. Cell phone lights flicker blindingly as soon as he shows his face. At least a dozen iPhones are tracking our every move.

I hear him mumble a bewildered "What the fuck?"

"Where did Ramón go?" I ask.

"He left in a car a few minutes before me!"

There's nowhere for us to go but straight ahead or back into the mob. The alley narrows toward the end, where it makes a ninety-degree turn behind a Chinese restaurant, and from the right side of that building you can shimmy out onto Ninth. Are they going to follow us the entire way?

We start to jog.

"Calvin!" someone cries out, and a few teenage girls scream, and within an instant the moment crumbles into mayhem. The group begins to run after us, and I feel a few bodies pressing up on our heels.

He leads, and I follow, both of us sprinting as fast as we

can, shimmying along the grimy wall between the theater and the restaurant before pressing into the narrow space between Ying's Dumplings and a launderette. A girl reaches past me, catching Calvin's sleeve and jerking him out of my grasp so she can snap a selfie. I get a glimpse of it—she looks maniacal and he looks terrified; I have no doubt she'll still post it on every social media account she has.

"Easy," he says, trying to smile. "I always hit the side door. Every night. Please just come another time."

They press forward, their hands all over him, and he's trying to be polite but sweet Jesus I am suddenly *furious*.

I pull the closest hand off his jacket. "Don't grab him. Don't chase us. Come back another night and my husband will sign your program—if you're calmer."

The girl apologizes, staring wide-eyed at Calvin's face. It's like looking at someone in the height of Beatlemania. I know she isn't herself. She has that saucer-eyed, on-the-verge-of-tears air about her. But Calvin appears genuinely disturbed; and of course he is. There are at least fifteen girls standing not ten feet away from us, taking pictures of him every few seconds. A few are already crying.

I slide my hand into his and he looks down at me, anchoring.

"Ready?" I ask.

He nods.

"Don't follow us." I don't even recognize my voice. Never in my life have I been this firm.

We walk alone for half a block; at least it seems the mob has turned back the other way, or decided to be decent humans and not chase him anymore. Calvin isn't letting go of my hand, and I swear I can feel his heart pounding through his skin.

"That was insane," he says.

I stop, pulling him into a little alcove of a closed clothing store. He stares down at me, pulse hammering in his neck.

"You okay?" I ask.

He bends, hovering just in front of my lips before making contact. It isn't a morning kiss where we're sleepy and giggly, or a tipsy kiss where we're all teeth and filth. This feels like the way he would kiss me if he loved me: with both hands cupping my face, soft kisses all over my mouth with no need to go farther in. He pulls back, and in the light, his eyes seem to be the same exact color as his hair—a light brown, amber.

"You're unbelievable," he says.

"I was a bitch."

"No." He kisses me again. "I was literally terrified, and . . . you weren't."

- - - -

By the time we get to Dutch Fred's it is *packed*. Calvin and I cut a path through the crowd, ducking between diners in wicker chairs and people cluttered around the tiki-themed bar to a table in the back where Lulu is already seated.

"Fucking finally." She stands, giving each of us a hard, tight hug. When she drops back into her seat, the chair skids backward a little, but she doesn't seem to notice.

"Sorry. The crowd was huge tonight." I nod to Calvin as

he takes my jacket with still-shaking hands. "He was mobbed outside."

"*Ooooh,* fancy-pants." Lulu turns to the waitress, who has appeared to replace an empty wineglass with a full one, and mumbles her thanks. I'm tempted to tell her what happened, but it's obvious she doesn't care about anyone but herself tonight.

The waitress turns to us. "What can I get you guys?"

I nod to Lulu's drink as I settle into my chair. "I'll have what she's having, and . . ." I lift my brows to Calvin in question.

"I'll have the Left Hand Milk Stout, please." He unwinds a charcoal scarf from around his neck and gives her a shaky smile. "Cheers."

"*Cheers,*" Lulu repeats. "God. You are so adorable," she says, but she sounds faintly disgusted.

"How long have you been here?" I ask, covertly checking my watch. We're only about twenty minutes late, but it looks like Lulu is already a few rounds in.

She picks up her glass and brings it to her lips. "Awhile. I had an audition earlier and they interrupted me halfway into my first line to tell me they'd seen enough."

I slide my hand over hers. "Ugh, Lu, I'm sorry."

With a sneering eye roll, she pulls her hand away to cup it around her wineglass. "I figured since there's nothing else going on in my life, I might as well head over and get drunk."

I'm caught like a snag on her tone. Lulu is clearly in A Mood. Again. And after what just happened outside the theater with Calvin, I'm going to have to work to put on a convincingly sympathetic voice. "I'm sorry, sweetie, I don't remember you mentioning an audition. I would have helped you with—"

"Of course you don't."

I sit back in my seat like I've been shoved, looking to Calvin for confirmation. Am I misreading this? His small shrug tells me he's as baffled as I am.

I'm cut off from asking what the hell her problem is when the waitress returns with our drinks. Before she leaves, Lulu orders another glass of wine.

"And maybe some food," I suggest. "Have you eaten anything tonight?"

She regards me blankly over the top of her glass. "Is this your not-so-subtle way of suggesting I've had too much to drink?"

"It's my way of saying that it's nearly eleven, and you might be in a better mood if you ate something."

Lulu blinks pointedly down to the bar menu and orders a plate of shishito peppers and garlic parsley fries for the table to share, adding that the waitress should make sure to split that on the checks.

Calvin shifts beside me, moving closer.

"So, any other auditions on the horizon?" he asks her sweetly.

"Nothing new coming up. This was for a commercial for some electronics store, but apparently they wanted a fetus to play the part. Blah blah blah, just like all of them." She lifts her wineglass, draining it.

I can tell she's had a shit day; I've seen Lulu like this before. Normally I would walk over to her side of the table, put my arm around her, and tell her how amazing she is. Tonight, it's like watching her through a warped set of glasses; I'm not even remotely interested in placating her. She's being a complete asshole—not amazing in the slightest.

I take a sip of my own drink. "Where's Gene?"

"Working, I think. Who knows."

Calvin and I exchange a look.

"So what's going on with you two?" she asks, lifting her chin to us. "The show going well?"

"Other than the madness just now, it's brilliant," Calvin says, grinning. "I swear I sit down and the lights dim and it still doesn't feel real."

"I lose my shit every time I see him up there," I add. It comes out as a jumble of breathless words and Calvin laughs at me, leaning over to kiss my jaw.

As if on cue, a woman approaches, clutching a *Playbill*, and although Calvin initially looks mildly wary, she ends up asking—very politely, with a shaking voice—for an autograph. Calvin smiles at her, charming with his crinkly eyes, and she goes into full-on fangirl mode, asking for a selfie, a hug, practically offering to birth his firstborn. He reaches for me, his hand landing on my thigh, and the cold press of his wedding ring through my tights makes heat spread in a wave across every inch of my skin. I clench my thighs together; for crying out loud, I'm still sore from last night.

It's obvious to anyone watching that this still feels surreal for him, and I love witnessing him soak it up. How many of us in our lifetime get to experience this type of adulation? But across the table, Lulu is playing on her phone in dramatic boredom.

With the *Playbill* signed and selfie taken, Calvin looks at me in question before turning back to Lulu and offering, "I can get you tickets if you want to come?"

"Thanks, but no." She slides her phone back onto the tabletop. "I see enough of it every freaking place I go. Wasn't Ryan Gosling there the other night or something? People were wetting themselves all over my Twitter feed."

Calvin grins—it was a huge commotion and, honestly, a ton of fun backstage. "He was. He's a friend of Ramón's."

"Did you meet him?"

"I got to talk to him for a few minutes."

Lulu looks at me, and then back to him, clearly expecting more fanfare. "Did Holland lose her shit?" She nearly knocks her wineglass over. "I think she's seen *Blue Valentine* about five hundred times. I mean, it was nothing compared to the crush she had on you before you met, but—"

My heart stumbles in my chest and I quickly cut in. "Did Gene mention he was looking for another job? Jeff's friend is opening a—"

"I see you." Lulu wags a drunken finger in my direction. "I see what you're doing. You don't get to change the subject that quickly. Look at you two *now*. Don't you want him to know? You were *crazy* about him."

"I'm sorry, who are we talking about?" Calvin asks.

My pulse is running like I've just finished a marathon.

"We're talking about *you*." Lulu reaches over and taps his nose before he can dodge her. "I still remember the first day she saw you. She lost her goddamn *mind*. She even sent me a video of you playing at the subway station."

Calvin glances at me, confused. "From the night of the attack?"

She looks at him like he's dense. "No, like *waaaaaay* before. She sent me a video of you playing last summer and wouldn't shut up about it. Oh my God, she called you Jack!" She smacks the table, cackling to herself. "Do you remember Jack the Busker, Holland?" She turns back to him and leans her chin on her hand. "We used to give her so much shit about it."

I'm trying to get her attention, begging her with my eyes to stop talking, but she either doesn't see me or—more likely— doesn't care. I'm honestly wondering if it would be less awkward for me to pull the fire alarm or just knock the table over to shut her up.

"*Okay*, Lu. Why don't you let me have that?" I reach for her glass but she jerks it away and wine sloshes over the rim and down her arm.

"Are you kidding me?" she yells.

Heads turn. It's the height of the post-show crowd, and there's not an empty seat in the place, but Lulu's obnoxious drinking voice has risen to a level that can be heard even above the noise. "Do *not* pretend like you don't know what I'm talking about. You knew his *schedule*. You gave him a *fake name*. You didn't even need the subway but went to see him play!"

"Because he's talented," I hedge, my mind racing with a way to get out of this.

"You're telling me you married him because he's talented?" she asks, and then laughs, but it's choked off by a hiccup. "You're telling me you're *fucking* him because he's talented? You were obsessed. Why do you think Brian was so quick to suggest you marry him? It was a *joke*. Do you really think he was serious? I mean, that is *insane*." She leans back in her chair, staring at me with unfocused eyes. "But look, it all worked out. Now he's in your bed and—"

"That's enough, Lulu," Calvin says, pulling me back from the table. He's barely touched the beer in front of him. "Enough."

"What?" She raises her hands like she's innocent. "I'm not making any of this up."

I don't know what's happening, or why she's doing this. I feel like I don't even know her.

Standing, I reach for my purse and pull out my wallet. There are three twenties inside and I toss them down on the table. "I think we should go."

twenty-three

Calvin is quiet the entire walk home, hands in pockets, shoulders tucked up to his ears. We went from the terror of the chase, to the intimacy of escaping it together, to the disaster of Lulu and her big mouth. I don't even know how to reel this night back in.

There's nothing I can say. I did everything she said: I took subway trips I didn't need to take, and I watched him over and over, I sent her a video of him playing once and even took a picture of him at the Hole in the Hall. I essentially told him all of this during our interview, but then let him believe it was just a story I made up to cover for my stumble with Dougherty.

I'm nauseated. I felt so powerful and necessary as we were walking into the bar, and then Lulu made me sound so creepy. If I were Calvin I would definitely be silent on the walk home, too. It's just . . . what she said, and the way she said it, didn't *feel* true to me. I feel slandered.

As soon as we arrive at the apartment, I sense it like a storm rolling in; I know it's coming. Calvin isn't a complicated man, but he doesn't let things go unsaid, either.

He places his keys and wallet on the counter carefully, like he doesn't want them to make any noise, shake anything else loose. He toes off his shoes near the door, and whispers a quiet "Excuse me" when he steps past me to use the bathroom.

I want to vomit.

I take the time to put on pajamas, selecting my favorite frog tank top and pink polka dot shorts for courage. And then I sit on the bed, waiting.

We've spent nearly three dozen nights together in this room—what if, after this, he returns to the couch? Am I super weird? How would I feel if I found out he was essentially going out of his way to watch me for six months? How would I feel if he had video of me on his phone, and then offered to marry me to "help" me?

A throat clears, and I look up to see him standing in the doorway, shirtless. He unfastens his pants, pushing them down his hips and kicking them into the laundry basket. "Do I need to ask, or are you going to talk to me?"

"Ask what?"

His eyes turn up, meeting mine, and I can tell he's disappointed that I'm evading.

"Yeah," I say, chewing at my lip. "I know what you're talking about."

"Of course you do."

"Before I start, can I just say that Lulu was being terrible tonight? She made it sound different than it actually was."

He leans against the doorway, pulling off one sock. "What part did she have wrong?"

"She made it sound a little more *Fatal Attraction* than it actually was. I wasn't obsessed," I say lamely. "I just . . . had a thing for you."

"Had a thing for a stranger you called Jack? Videotaped him in public? Followed him to a bar where he—"

"I had *no* idea you were playing with that cover band," I interrupt, face hot. "That was a total coincidence."

"Holland, imagine if the roles were reversed." He's half-naked as usual, and for once I want to ask him to put on some goddamn clothes so I can concentrate. "Imagine if you found out that I had gone to where you worked, taken pictures of you, taken *video* of you and sent it to a friend. And then we coincidentally end up in a marriage of convenience?"

I shake my head and look at my hands in my lap. "Look, I know what you're saying, but I also know me and what my intentions were. I never intended to try to talk to you, or even make this into more."

When I look up at him, I find him studying me dubiously. He moves his hair out of his eyes with a quick shake of his head. "Yeah, but *I* didn't know you or your intentions. It washes things differently in hindsight."

The tiny seed of heat in my chest starts to burn brighter.

"I *admired* you," I say, feeling a little defensive now. "It was a private thing—for me. I wasn't being weird about it; I wasn't talking about you on Twitter or Facebook. I wasn't posting video of you on Snapchat. You played at the station—some of my favorite pieces—and it was *amazing*. You seemed too good to be true sometimes. I got caught up in that and sent a fifteen-second video to exactly one person. Are you saying it's a bad thing that I was so invested in you?"

He walks over, sitting on the corner of the bed with his back to me. "I'm not saying that. It ended up being fine. It's just odd." He lets out a heavy breath.

Fine? It ended up being *fine*?

I watch his shoulders rise and fall as he breathes, hating that I can't see his expression. "I thought we came into this the same—strangers—and you were helping Robert and I was helping me." He tosses his socks into the hamper. "But I feel like—" He shakes his head. "I don't know. Like you lied to me."

"Lied?"

"Yeah. Or manipulated me."

This hits a trigger beneath my ribs: the seed of heat turns into a flaming brick, and I reach my boiling point. "You've got to be kidding me."

He turns, meeting my eyes, but doesn't say anything.

"So what if I had a crush on you?" I ask. "Yeah, now I'm getting sex and some help paying rent—but I didn't plan that part. In fact, if I recall, I was so covert about my feelings that you had no idea I felt them. I had to endure the anger of Jeff and Robert, my brother Davis isn't sure how to even ask me about what we're doing, and my parents don't even know about this. Now Robert has the virtuoso he wanted, and you have the dream position in the most popular show on Broadway and sex at home, with your fake wife. You're seriously giving *me* shit right now?" I stand, walking to the bathroom to get my toothbrush.

He follows. "I just wish you had told me you had feelings."

"Is that what bothers you here?"

"That's part of it, yeah."

I turn to him, squeezing too much toothpaste on my brush, but I'm too angry and proud right now to do anything but shove it in my mouth. I immediately pull it out again.

"Look, you were coming to live here, and I didn't want you to think I had any expectations." I point the toothbrush at him. "I was doing this for Robert, yes, but also because I'd admired your music for so long, and I wanted it for *you*, even if I didn't know you."

I pause, and his eyes search mine, looking for some answer I'm not sure how to deliver. "I did tell you all of this in the interview with Dougherty," I remind him.

"Yeah, but then you let me think it was just a story."

"Right," I say, nodding. "Because you called it 'insane' that I would do that." I laugh dryly. "I like to think that it makes me *kind*. But here I am, doing shit for other people and getting treated like I'm monstrous somehow."

His jaw ticks and I can't figure out what's going on here. All I know is that I'm out of words, and I'm done explaining myself.

You let me think it was just a story.

But if he'd asked me whether it was true, I would have said yes.

I bend over the sink, brushing my teeth with the energy of a woman who wants to lift up the entire building and hurl it into the ocean. I can feel Calvin standing behind me, wordless, but eventually he turns. I can tell from his footfalls that he's walking to the living room, not the bedroom, and am a little heartbroken to realize that I feel relieved.

- - - -

I'm up at six, having slept like crap, but I must have slept *some*, because as soon as I open my eyes, I remember last night and a sense of dread falls like shade passing through a room. The last thing I want to do this morning is rehash everything, or feel the tension between me and my new favorite person, who is presently buried under blankets and sound asleep on the couch.

I dress quietly and slip out before Calvin wakes up.

It's been forever since I did my little routine of walking to the Fiftieth Street station, taking the train to get coffee at Madman, but I want to do it today. I want to walk in my old shoes, to try to remember that surety that this mission was critical, that I alone was connecting two universally vital dots by bringing Robert to Calvin.

The subway station is as busy as it always is, and there is no guitarist to greet me at the bottom of the stairs. There is, however, a sufficiently capable saxophonist, and I throw a five-dollar bill into his case. He stops playing to thank me.

So, he's here for the money, not to get lost in the music, and the honesty of that is so fucking refreshing. Calvin could have played his guitar alone, forever at Mark's apartment if it really was *only* about the music for him, but it isn't. It's also about the audience, about the adulation, about the income—so how can he be so fucking upset that he's receiving it? Sure—I should have told him at the outset that I'd been watching him at the station for some time, and admired his music. But his reaction to my crush was so overblown that it sours something inside me. I'm torn between staying away all day and rushing home to rip into him again.

And . . . I actually cling to this feeling, because I never get angry . . . and I forget how being angry can feel so good because it makes me feel *strong*. For the entire time I've known Calvin, I've felt like I haven't totally deserved having him in my apartment, in my life, in my bed. My anger is my new best friend, telling me I've deserved every second of the happiness I felt before this stupid fucking fight.

I press through the crowd and onto the train, hopping from station to station, listening to every busker I find. I'm on an unnamable mission, and it isn't until I'm on my fourth or fifth station that I realize I'm looking for someone as talented as Calvin.

But there's no one like him in any subway station in New York. I've heard music my whole life; I know there's no one like him anywhere. I knew it. I *always* knew it.

Calvin was right that by coming into this only as strangers, we were equals. But . . . are we no longer equals because I had feelings before he did?

Or is it that I have feelings and he doesn't? Does this answer my question about whether he's been playing me all along? Is banging me every day his way of keeping me loose, keeping me comfortable, keeping the government away?

Back up on the street, I get my coffee and walk for hours. I cover miles. By the time my stomach gnaws at me to eat, I realize I've left both my watch and my phone at the apartment and have no idea what time it is. There's a giddy thrill in knowing that I'm completely unreachable. I'm sure Calvin did just *fine* getting his grouchy ass up and fed. He can get himself to the theater later; I'm not going to bother going in. Contrary to the popular idiom, those T-shirts do, in fact, practically sell themselves.

- - - -

I show up unannounced at Jeff and Robert's apartment at five, when I know for sure Robert won't be there. For the first time in my relationship with my beloved Bobert, I feel a little disloyal, wanting to avoid him. I didn't feel this way even when I went behind his back and married Calvin, because I was so convinced that it was for Robert's own good. Obviously, Robert agrees with me about this now. He thinks Calvin walks on water, so I'm not sure how it would feel to hear him defend Calvin in all this.

Thankfully, I don't have to worry about that with Jeff.

Jeff answers the door in his work clothes, holding a stack of mail. His eyes widen in surprise. "Hey, you."

"Did you just get home?"

Stepping back, he waves me in. "Yeah. Aren't *you* working tonight?"

The familiar smell of sandalwood calms me almost instantly. "I'm going to call Brian and tell him I'm taking a personal day. Can I use your phone?"

"Sure." Jeff leans against the wall, watching me as I pick up the landline in their kitchen. "I guess this answers why you never replied to my text today."

A sudden panic about the interview barrels through me. "Oh shit. Did something—"

"No emergency." He seems to reconsider this. "I mean, at least I hope not? I'd texted a couple times because Calvin called me, looking for you."

"He called *you*?"

Well. That's something, at least. My anger dims, minutely. I give Jeff a grumpy look with my *I'll explain in one second* finger gesture, and then finish dialing Brian's number. Thank all that is holy—it goes to voicemail. "Brian, it's Holland. I'm unable to make it in tonight. If you need anything, call me at Robert and Jeff's." I hang up and immediately step into Jeff's arms.

He speaks into my hair. "I take it all is not well in Married Land?"

My "no" comes out muffled against his suit.

"Marriage is hard," he says.

"I think fake marriage might be harder."

He stills, and then hums sympathetically. "Let me change into comfy clothes, and then we can have a night in."

I make tea while he puts on University of Iowa Hawkeye pajama pants and a Yankees T-shirt, and we meet on their enormous, fluffy couch. Jeff sits, pulling one leg up so he can turn and face me. Only a single lamp is on in the room, and it gives his cheeks a hollow, gaunt look. Jeff has always been slender, but for the first time in my life, I think he's starting to look old. My heart breaks a little.

"Okay," he says. "Let's have it."

I take a bracing breath; there's no use warming up slowly to any of this: "Things with Calvin have been really good. We're actually . . . together."

My uncle laughs in mock-scandal. "*No.* What will the *ton* say about two married people having an affair together!" He leans in and whispers, "We had a hunch."

I tilt my eyes skyward and ignore his teasing. "So, last night, we were mobbed outside the theater, and it was so surreal. Afterward, we had this moment—this super-intense moment that felt really grounding—where I felt like we were in this together. I felt so protective, and he was so grateful, and it was just . . ."

"Loving," Jeff finishes, with a question in his voice.

"Yeah . . . But then we went to meet Lulu at Dutch Fred's"—Jeff groans knowingly—"and she got really drunk— per usual, I guess—and told Calvin how I used to basically stalk him."

Jeff pauses, eyes narrowing. His voice goes low like it does when he's turning more protective animal than uncle. "You had a crush on him, and were justifiably infatuated—in part because of his talent."

"Well, she put on a pretty great show and made me sound super creepy. She told him what I used to call him, how I'd go see him play, how I knew his schedule. It wasn't just that she was being a dick, she completely shattered this really great moment we were having, and I feel like we went back to being strangers."

He runs a hand down his face.

"So we got home," I continue, "and Calvin wanted to talk about it—"

"Which is good," he gently interrupts with a hand on my arm.

"Right, it was good, but not the way he did it. I got pretty pissed." I look at him and explain how the conversation went, how Calvin made it sound like I'm getting the most out of this arrangement, how he feels *lied* to.

"I hit a wall," I say. "I did this for Robert, and for him—and maybe also for me—but why is that bad?" I stand up, walking across the room and back. "It's not like I *expected* this marriage to turn real. It's not like I put a video camera in the bookcase and took footage of him sleeping and stole his underwear."

"Of course not, honey," he says. "You have an incredible ear for music, and of the tens of thousands of people who probably heard him, only you were able to connect him to Robert—to make this *happen*."

"But last night, the way he was talking about it, just made me feel so gross—just when I had accomplished something, when I was feeling good about having a voice and protecting Calvin like I did. I have nothing going for me," I say, squeezing my eyes closed. "Nothing except you guys, and your support and hopes for me. I'm not Calvin. I'm not Robert. I'm not you."

"You're right," Jeff says, laughing. "You aren't a buttoned-up financial analyst."

"You may not always love your job, but you're good at it— and you found a hobby that you love doing." I pull my shoulders up, feeling tense everywhere. "I have no idea what I want to do. I want to write and read and talk about books with people. I want to listen to music, and go out to dinner, and just *live*."

"That *is* a life," he insists. "That is a *good* life."

"But I have to be able to support myself, too. I have all these things I wanted to do, and I haven't done any of them."

"I didn't find pottery until I was fifty," Jeff reminds me. "Honey, you are only twenty-five. You don't need to have it all figured out."

I fall back down on the couch, covering my face with my hands. "But shouldn't I have some of it figured out?"

He places a large hand on my knee. "That perception is *only* coming from you."

"Last night, it was coming from Lulu and then Calvin." I drop my hands. "I love you guys, but I have to take your sentiment with a grain of salt. You're biologically and/or legally obligated to love me."

Jeff leans in, pressing a kiss to my hair. "Hollsy, think of it this way: If I compared myself to Robert when we first met, I would constantly feel behind. He was a musical prodigy. I was a waiter, trying to figure out if I had the grades to get into the mediocre MBA programs in my area." He smiles at me. "But I knew I wanted to be with him, and he wanted to be with me, too, and also knew what he wanted to do with his life. So, we compromised. He took the job in Des Moines, and it was my responsibility to get a job that would make enough money for what we needed, and that I enjoyed *enough*. I didn't have to love it, but it didn't matter whether I did, either, because I had *him*. I kept trying new things, too, and eventually discovered pottery. It's fun, of course, but the most important part is that I didn't feel like my job had to be my everything."

This is what I have to keep reminding myself. Sometimes

a job can just be a job. We aren't all going to win the rat race.

"I know."

"You know I didn't approve of your marriage," he says quietly, and guilt floods my bloodstream. "You didn't know each other, and your feelings being what they were, I worried you would get hurt."

I groan into a pillow, but Jeff pulls it away.

"I'm not chastising you. Listen. All of that was true, but I also didn't expect things to turn romantic between the two of you. Seeing you two lately is wonderful for us."

"I'm not sure it's real, though." I pull at my lower lip, working not to cry. After all the walking and righteous anger, not only am I physically exhausted, but the softer emotions are starting to rise to the surface. The thought that Calvin has been toying with me all this time is painful. It was easy to push the worry away when he was kissing me, when he was smiling at me. "Maybe it's just a game."

"I've seen you together, and I know men. It would be very surprising if he was faking that level of absorption. He called me twice, Hollsy. He called Robert, too. He didn't sound like he was playing a game."

I press my hands to my face. "But he needs things to be okay with us because he needs to stay here. I'm not sure how to trust anything he does."

"Well, that's *one* of the reasons—"

"I know. I know."

"But for the sake of optimism, let's assume that he is genuine," Jeff says. "If things work out between the two of you, Calvin is lucky because he has a job he loves and he has *you*.

This gives you room to find yourself, and figure out what you want your life to look like. It doesn't have to look like mine, or his, or Robert's."

"I know."

"And it doesn't have to look right now the way you want it to look in ten years."

"But I think that's what scares me the most," I tell him. "I'm terrified it will look the same in ten years—for me. But for Calvin? He will have moved on, or moved up, or moved away."

"You don't know that. You have no way of knowing. All you can do is forge *your* path." Jeff stands up, taking his empty teacup to the kitchen. "Come on. Let's order some food."

- - - -

I fall asleep like a rock in the guest room, sleeping so soundly that when Robert shakes me gently, I startle-snort awake, arms flailing wildly, and nearly knock the cordless phone out of his hand.

"Call for you," he says. He puts the phone in my palm, adding in a growl, "Your guy played like shit last night."

Standing, he leaves the room and closes the door behind him with a quiet click.

I stare at the phone, blinking into clarity. I don't have to say anything to know it's Calvin. And he played like shit last night?

Lifting the phone to my ear, I give a hoarse, "Hey."

His voice sounds all sleepy and deep. "Hey." I can feel the

resonance of it as if he'd rolled over and spoken into my neck. "I hope it's okay that I'm calling this number."

Goose bumps break out along my arms. "Of course. My phone is at the apartment."

His laugh is a hollow sound. "Yeah, I know."

I stare up at the ceiling, waiting for the words to pop into my head. My anger feels like a next-day campfire—cooled off to only a dusty smolder.

"I was hoping you'd show up last night," he says quietly. "At the theater."

"I was upset."

He inhales slowly, and lets the breath out in a groan. "Then I was hoping you might sneak in later, after I fell asleep."

"I slept at Robert and Jeff's."

"I assumed that's where you were when I came into the bedroom this morning to climb into bed an' apologize," he says, growly and soft, "but y'were still gone."

He wants to apologize? I squeeze my eyes closed at the desire I feel to have his warm body next to me in bed.

"D'you think you might come home today?" He takes another deep inhale, and when he speaks, I can tell he's stretching. "This isn't right, *mo stóirín*. I don't like this."

"I don't like it, either," I say quietly, wondering whether Jeff and Robert can hear me out in the living room. "But you made me feel shitty, like I'd done something wrong. I don't think I did."

"I know. Shite"—he exhales through his nose—"I didn't handle this right. Last night I was miserable over it. I played horribly."

"Yeah, I can imagine how stressful it would be to think you

might have to leave the country if things don't work out with us." I wince as soon as I've said it.

It's a long few seconds before he speaks again, and his accent seems so strong across the line. "It isn't like that. Do you really think I'd play you that way?"

I squeeze my eyes closed at the gentle lilt to his words.

T'isnt like dat. D'ye really tink I'd play ye dat way?

"I don't know."

"Would you prefer I come there? What do you want?"

In truth, I want to go home, climb in between the sheets with him, and feel that heavy warmth all around me as he pulls me close. I want the vibration of his voice on my neck, my shoulder, my breasts, and the way that every bit of light is blocked out for a moment when he climbs on top of me. But I also want this spark of strength I feel right now. I woke up in some ways yesterday, and it still doesn't feel totally defined, but I don't want it to evaporate before I can name it.

"I want to tell you I'm sorry," he says, voice a low burr. "Come home and kick me in the teeth if you need to, but then kiss me."

- - - -

The living room is empty when I walk inside, dropping my keys on the counter and hanging my coat over the back of the chair. The bathroom door is open—he's not in there, either. The apartment feels oddly still; there's no rattle of the radiator or clinking of dishes being washed. It feels like I've been gone a week, instead of twenty-four hours.

I find Calvin in my bed, leaning against the headboard and staring at the doorway.

His expression relaxes immediately when he sees me. "Hey."

Kicking off my shoes, I give him a little smile and sit on the edge of the bed, but he pulls back a corner of the covers, patting the mattress. "Come here. We can talk in here."

It's a hard offer to refuse. I tug down my running pants and pull off my sweatshirt before burrowing under the sheets. I'm immediately hit with the solid heat of his chest and crawl into his arms; he's completely naked, and somehow feels warmer than the sun. Calvin slides a hand up my back, unfastening my bra and pulling it away to toss it somewhere over his shoulder. He lets out a quiet groan, and a tiny thrill winds through me that he needed to feel skin on skin as immediately as I did.

"I'm sorry." He sucks his lower lip into his mouth and stares into my eyes. "It wasn't fair, what I said. I think I was just embarrassed that I didn't realize you'd been honest at the immigration office. Or, maybe frustrated that all that time I'd wanted you, and you were pretending not to want me. It seemed so easy. I think I felt confused."

I smile at this and it unlocks his own grin; he looks relieved.

"I'm not sure I totally trust why you're doing this." I press a hand to his chest. He looks down and shakes his head a little; he doesn't know what I mean. "You could stay in the apartment and have the job without having sex with me, you know."

His eyes fall closed and he lets out a little "Ahhhh," as if I've just confirmed something for him.

"We could be convincing without this," I say quietly. "But now that you know I had a thing for you before we met, I'm not comfortable doing *this* without knowing where you stand. It feels really unbalanced."

His eyes flicker back and forth between mine. "My desire for you as a lover is *entirely* separate from my desire for the job you helped me find."

I struggle to speak past the glow these words trigger in me. "Really? Because as you said yourself, it would be incredibly shitty of you to play me like that."

He leans down, close enough to kiss me, but stops just shy. "Really. Of course my feelings are influenced by your understanding of music. Your opinion matters more to me than even Robert's, or Ramón's. But that isn't about the job, that's because music is part of you, too."

I move in, resting my lips on his, and he groans, rolling over me, bringing a hand up to cup my jaw. Tension melts everywhere inside, and I rock into him when he settles between my thighs.

Making up is . . . pretty fun.

Calvin pulls back slightly, grinning down at me. "Six months before we met, huh?"

"At least," I say, laughing and blushing. "It was a pretty epic crush."

I slide my hands around his shoulders and then into his hair as he kisses lower, to my breasts, and my stomach, and then beneath the covers, where he kisses one thigh and then the other, and then sweeps his tongue across me.

Wanting to watch, I push the covers away, and he looks

up, smiling into another kiss. He teases, pointing his tongue, nipping—almost as if he's *performing* for me.

"I know what you're thinking," I whisper.

A long, soft suck and then: "What's that?"

"And the answer is yes, I imagined you doing this before I met you."

He pulls back a little, expression heating. "Imagined me kissing you here?"

I nod, and a deep ache builds just watching him watching me.

"Would you touch yourself?"

"Sometimes."

He glides a finger over me, up and down, and then pushes it inside. "You're getting wet just telling me about it."

I dig a hand into his hair. "I'm not going to apologize for fantasizing about you."

"I would fucking hope not." He watches what he's doing. "I don't want you to stop fantasizing, either."

"What do you fantasize about?"

He closes his eyes and bends to lick me, thinking. Pulling back, he says, "A lot of things," and I feel the heat of his breath against me.

A lot of tings.

I tug at his arm, and he climbs back up my body, bending to kiss me with an open, hungry mouth.

Pulling his hand over my breast, I say, "Tell me."

He squeezes, and then bends, sucking. "I think about saying some filthy things to you while we're on the couch. I like when you're facing me, so I can lick you how you like it."

Oh. My blood heats and I arch into his mouth.

"I think about having you near the window and letting those paparazzi down on the street watch us. I get a little kick out of imagining *those* pictures on Twitter."

I reach down, wrapping my hand around him, and he groans before coming back up to kiss me.

"I think about how you look when you put me in your mouth. How fast I come when you do that." He slides his hand between us, pushing two fingers into me, and we start to move, his words speeding up. "I think about being somewhere with you, and you do that—you go down on me and no one knows."

"Like at the theater?"

"Or anywhere," he says, breath hot on my cheek. He grunts, fucking my hand, so close to where I want him, and I guide him there, nudging his own hand away from me. He slides in bare, so deep, and I cry out before he swallows the sound.

We haven't done this before . . . we need to put on a condom.

"I think about *this*," he whispers, "just like this. Oh, Christ, it feels good."

It does, and so neither of us stops it. It's so easy to keep moving, to fall into that rolling rhythm; in the past weeks he's figured out what I need and starts there: deep, pressing, immediately. My hands roam the skin on his back, down over his ass, his thighs, as far down as I can reach.

He must know he's forgiven because he doesn't talk anymore, doesn't check in with me to be sure I'm okay, and this is something I adore most about him. I think he trusts that if I didn't want this right now, I would tell him. He isn't going to let something go unsaid.

But even so, as he moves in these perfect circles over me, another shadow steps into view. I wonder what it is we're fixing here, and to what end? I've already established that we don't need to be intimate for him to stay here. And we certainly don't need to be in love. But he kisses me like it's love, and as he pushes faster into me, he sounds like a man overcome with love, and when he rolls so I'm on top of him, he watches me with something that looks a lot like love in his eyes.

But how would I really know?

"Why did you stop?" he asks, cupping my hips. "Is it okay?"

His chest has a faint sheen of sweat—from exertion, from the heat of our bodies moving together—and I press my palm to it; his heart is racing. I search his face. His eyes are clear, maybe a little worried.

"It's good."

I am so bad at asking for what I want.

"Did I hurt you?" he whispers.

Shaking my head, I say, "No."

He sits up beneath me and wraps his arms around my waist, looking up at my face. "What are you thinking? What can I say to make this okay?"

"I guess I'm wondering what we're doing."

He gives me a wicked, cheeky smile. "I thought we were busy making love."

"Is that what this is?" I honestly have never felt this before, so I don't even know what to call it. But I'm not sure I can do this and keep myself from falling in love with him.

He kisses my chin. "Does it feel like something else to you?"

"I think it's starting to feel like that to me, but I don't actually know." I press my mouth to his and let him deepen it, before pulling away the tiniest bit. "It feels like we should make sure we're on the same page after"—he kisses me—"what happened with Lulu and—"

He interrupts me with another kiss. "And the fact that we're already married?" he asks. His hand moves up my back and into my hair.

"Yeah, exactly. We've talked about logistics and backstory and fantasy, but we haven't really talked about feelings."

"You were gone all day yesterday. I woke up this morning and you still weren't here." He tilts his head, sucking on my neck. "I thought I fucked it up with you, and I honestly have never felt so panicked in my life."

"The initial plan was a year," I whisper.

"I say to hell with the initial plan."

"It's more complicated than just having a new girlfriend. We took vows."

Calvin grins up at me. "I'm aware."

"Doesn't that paradoxically complicate the new plan?"

"How am I supposed to know?" He laughs into my shoulder and bites me gently. "I've never done this before. I just know I'm falling for the girl I married."

twenty-four

Calvin hands me my buzzing phone. "Lulu again."

I put it facedown on the coffee table and turn back to my laptop. For the first time in ages, I woke up with words in my head, and I'm determined to get them down before they fade back into fog.

He lies behind me on the couch. "Aren't you going to call her?"

"Not right now."

I can feel him reading over my shoulder. "What is this?"

"I don't even know, actually." I'm so tempted to cover it up, to hide the words by closing my screen because it feels like a bare tree trunk—all naked and vulnerable to the elements. Instead, I pretend my hands are glued to the keyboard. I've listened to Calvin stumble through a new run of notes or work out a new composition a hundred times already, and he's never shy. Why should I be?

"For a book?" he asks. He knows how long this has eluded me, what having that spark of inspiration has to mean.

"No. Maybe? I'm not sure." I read back through the notes I've made, almost tentative, careful not to chase off the spark. I can't stop thinking about how it felt to roam the city yesterday in search of a talent like his. I can't stop thinking about how it feels to listen to him and Ramón play together. "I just had this thought in my head, about how we met and where you are now, and how it feels to have heard you in both places."

His hand runs over my shoulder and into my shirt, resting at the swell above my heart. "I like the look on your face right now. So intense."

I miss writing. I wrote endless short stories during college and while getting my master's. I had to write every day or I felt like a clogged drain, full of words. The day I got my degree and turned to face the world as a person no longer under the protective umbrella of school, it seemed like all the ideas dried up.

And that's been true since I started working at the theater. After talking to Robert and Jeff, I wonder if it's because I'm surrounded by people who are brilliant in a way I'm not, and it leaves me feeling ordinary by comparison.

But this . . . writing about how it feels to listen to music, to have found him—it almost feels like I'm writing a description of how my organs work together, what keeps me breathing. I don't think I've ever felt this before.

His hand slips lower still, toying with my nipple, and his mouth comes to my neck, warm and biting. "Can I do this while you write?"

I'm still tender from the second round of makeup sex we had only an hour ago, but when his fingertips trap the peak of my breast in a gentle pinch, my whole body hums. "I'm not sure

I could focus. It'd be like me putting my mouth on you while you play."

His laugh is a low vibration against my skin. "We should try that later."

I turn to capture his mouth in a kiss. "I'm almost done."

Calvin retreats a little, moving his hand back up and returning his mouth to the back of my neck, and although I worried this distraction would chase away my muse, the words seem stronger, if anything. I remember this feeling—the thrill of being so full of something and having it come out with such clarity. My fingers fly over the keyboard and I ignore the typos for now, ignore the way I see him following my thoughts on the screen, ignore everything.

The creativity is back, and the knowledge that it's back because I'm happy propels me forward in this positive feedback loop that just keeps sending more and more words from my brain to my fingers.

My phone buzzes again, and Calvin reaches for it, turning off the vibration.

And then it lights up again, and again, ringing. I catch the name *Lulu* on the screen, and my writing mojo is still flimsy enough that the anxiety over dealing with her punctures a tiny hole in it.

"She's called ten times already today," he says. "She called a million times yesterday, too."

I growl at the sight of the phone lighting up with another voicemail.

"I bet she's violently hungover even two days later." He rests his chin on my shoulder. "Do you want me to put your phone in the other room?"

I want to say yes. I want to return to what I was doing, and have him return to peppering kisses along my neck and shoulders, but in truth, the core of the idea is laid out on this page in front of me, and I know that the niggling awareness of Lulu's panic is going to spread if I don't call her back.

I'm angry, yes, but I'm not punitive.

I drop my hand onto my phone and pick it up, sighing. "Let me just get this over with."

The call doesn't even seem to ring through before she's answering. "*Holllllls. I am an asshole.*"

"You are."

"Dude. I am so sorry. I am so, so sorry."

The thing is, I know she's genuinely mortified about her behavior the other night. Lulu is her own worst enemy. Drunk Lulu is a brutal alter ego and a burden she has to carry as long as she lets herself get wasted like that.

"I don't even know what to say," I tell her, rubbing my eyes. I feel gross all over again just thinking about it, and part of me wishes I hadn't called.

"Are you guys okay?"

"We are now. We talked it out this morning."

"This morning?" She groans.

"I stayed at Jeff and Robert's last night."

She makes a little squeaking sound of terror. "Holls. Was Calvin pissed?"

"What do you think?"

"Were you?"

I bark out an irritated laugh. "Lulu, be serious. You made me sound like a total freak."

Calvin leans forward when I say this, resting his lips on the side of my neck. I reach back with my free hand, sliding my fingers into his hair.

"What can I do?" she whines.

The simple fact is that something was damaged that night—things have been chipped away for a few weeks now—and I'm not sure we can go back to the way things were. I know Calvin can hear her, too, and so I look over my shoulder at him. He shrugs.

"Anything," she says. "I want to make it up to you."

"Don't be rude and obnoxious with us anymore."

She lets out a hoarse laugh; I can practically hear the hangover in it. "I know. I think I'm just thrown by this marriage thing. You used to be my person."

It's true. I was there whenever she needed someone to go to a show with, a bar, a concert. But I was also her fallback when she didn't have a steady plus-one for her Groupon adventures, and it's been our dynamic ever since I can remember: I've *always* been there for Lulu.

"Things with Calvin are good," I say quietly. "I get why it would be weird for you that I'm not totally, one hundred percent available anymore, but I'm really happy, and I feel like you're not happy for me."

He pulls me back to the couch with a warm arm wrapped around my chest, palm to my breast.

"I totally get what you're saying," she says. It's painful to hear her grovel; I've never made her do it before. "I want you to see me being supportive! I swear I can."

"Well . . ." I say, and laugh. I can feel Calvin's smile against my neck.

"Maybe I can book you a romantic dinner at Blue Hill?"

This trips an idea in me, and I lean forward, thinking. Calvin's birthday is in a few weeks, and I've already planned for his mom and sister to fly out and surprise him, but Blue Hill is a great restaurant, and Lulu could get us a great table, for sure. Something a little more private to celebrate his birthday wouldn't hurt, would it?

- - - -

I stand in front of a table at Blue Hill, Lulu at my side. After hugging me for a solid five minutes and promising to never be such a jerk again, she took me to the back of the restaurant and showed me the site she had in mind for my plan—my crazy, crazy plan.

The booth is in the deepest corner; it's a table big enough to seat at least four, but she's promised to keep it free just for us. Tilting my head, I check to see how much floor is visible. The top cloth comes down only about a foot from the table, but the lower one nearly sweeps the floor.

"You're sure it would work?" I press my fist to my diaphragm, willing my nerves to chill. The dinner in question is still two weeks away, but I feel like Calvin is about to walk in here any second.

All around us, Lulu's fellow waitstaff carry trays of flatware and napkins, setting tables, completely oblivious to our little plan.

She bounces a little beside me. "Totally sure."

My heart beats my blood into a frenzy. I've never done anything this insane.

Well, except marrying a stranger. And then lying about it to a government official.

"Are you really going to do it?" she asks, thrilled. "This is the best idea, ever."

I swallow the panic in my throat. If *Lulu* thinks it's a good idea, I've definitely lost my mind. "I'm going to do it."

- - - -

Two weeks and one day later, I'm back at Blue Hill, at exactly 4:50 in the afternoon. Dinner service begins at five, Calvin will be here at six, and this gives me plenty of time before the crowds roll in.

I brought a book and my phone, and am wearing a dress whose manufacturer has assured me it is wrinkle free. Now I have to wait.

Every second leading up to now, it seemed like a *fantastic* idea. It was daring, and adventurous, and something we'd remember forever. Lulu will get Calvin to the table, under the assumption that he's still waiting for me to arrive, and boom, surprise of a lifetime. It's his birthday in three days, and what better way to celebrate turning twenty-eight than with some surprise oral sex in a fancy restaurant?

I was confident right up until the moment Lulu led me to where I'd be hiding. But now that I'm under here, hearing diners come in and be seated only feet away, feeling mildly uncertain about the cleanliness of the underside of the table, hoping that nobody can see my feet and that this is what Calvin meant when he said he thinks about doing this somewhere while nobody knows . . . this seems like a pretty insane idea. And by insane, I mean *terrible*. It was one thing to imagine this, quite another attempting to carry it out.

The problem is . . . I'm stuck.

I pull my book from my bag, and realize it's too dark to read. I don't want to risk the light from my phone bleeding out through the tablecloth, so I don't use that, either.

Time inches forward. Food smells seem to seep beneath the table and get trapped here. I'm sure that under normal circumstances it would smell amazing, but I'm really *not* this person—a sexually adventurous law breaker—so my appetite has vanished and apprehension now seems to live permanently in my throat.

Lulu's signal that Calvin is here is a knock on the tabletop as she passes on her way to greet him, and when it comes— after I've been sitting here for seven years—it is a single sharp rap without any other warning. I startle upright—well, not really, because my legs are asleep—nearly breathless with an indescribable mixture of relief and nerves. But I hear feet returning, and another more tentative knock on the table just above my head.

"She's going to be so surprised to see *all three of you!*" Lulu yells.

What?

"It's her birthday, too," Calvin says. "Well, almost."

And then I hear it: Robert's deep rumbling laugh.

My stomach drops through the floor. Oh, fuck.

Oh fuckfuckfuck.

I can barely see anything—only the shadows of several pairs of shoes.

"Calvin, why don't you sit on *this side over here* so she can see you when she walks in?" Lulu says, knocking a hand on the right side of the table.

I quickly scurry over there. My legs are pins and needles and I am going to vomit all over this place.

Calvin slides in, colliding with my shoulder. I muffle a gasp and he lets out a surprised "Oh my Christ!" before Lulu jumps in.

"Good!" she cries, voice shrill, and I can imagine her distracting him, giving him a meaningful look and miming my location like an insane person, when she says, *"Now you'll see her when she comes in."*

"Oh," he says, on a quiet exhale. *"Ohhhh."* His hand grapples beneath the table, finding my shoulder, my face. And then I hear him let out a quiet laugh of disbelief and a whispered "What in the world . . . ?"

"Robert and Jeff," Lulu calls, loud enough for me to hear, "let me take your coats."

There's some commotion and then Calvin bends down, his voice suddenly close. "What in the bloody hell are you doing?"

"I was going to surprise you with a blow job!" I whisper-yell.

"Oh my fuck. *I* was going to surprise—*heeeeey.*" He sits back up, and spreads his legs a little so I can shimmy closer as Robert and Jeff slide into the booth.

Robert's knee is less than six inches from my arm. Oh my God, this is a disaster. Why didn't Lulu take them on a tour of the . . . room or something? Why didn't she seat them somewhere else?

The only saving grace here is the enormous booth. I curl my knees up, leaning into Calvin's hand when he slides it reassuringly beneath the table. As carefully as I can, I pull my phone out, quickly dim my screen, and open my texts.

Lulu has already texted me.

> What the fuuuuuuuuuuck?

> Why did you seat them???

> There aren't other tables, and Calvin knew you'd made a reservation. Fuck I screwed up. I'VE NEVER DONE THIS SORT OF THING BEFORE AND I PANICKED

> WHAT AM I GOING TO DO???

It's hot under here and I'm starting to feel a little dizzy— am I just rebreathing the same air and possibly suffocating?

> Just climb out, what are they going to say?

I close my eyes, banging my head silently against Calvin's knee.

"Where is she?" Robert asks, and within a few seconds, another text pops up on my screen from him.

> Where are you?

> Running late. Go ahead and order.

"She said she's running late," Robert tells them. "Should we order for her?"

"I imagine she'd like the venison sausage," Calvin says. I pinch his leg and he coughs, reaching down and grabbing my boob.

"She doesn't like venison," Jeff mutters absently.

"No," Robert argues, "it's elk she doesn't like."

"I'll ask her," Calvin says, and soon another text pops up on my screen.

> Would you like the venison or the grass-fed lamb? Also, I am going to fuck you so hard later. You are a hero to men for even thinking of doing this.

> The lamb. Should I just come out?

> I think that would be bloody fantastic

> Should I warn them?

Above the table, Calvin laughs.

"What?" Jeff asks. I imagine him looking up from the menu, lowering his reading glasses and gazing innocently at Calvin across the table.

"I think you'll see in a minute." I can hear his grin when he puts the saucy emphasis on *tink*.

Jeff's legs twist slightly, as if he's turning to look behind him at the door to the street. "Is she here?"

I sigh, texting him and Robert in a shared window.

> I'm already here.

> Where? I don't see you. We're in the back booth.

Fuck.
Fuck.

> I'm under the table.

"What the hell?" Jeff bends, lifting the tablecloth. His eyes go saucer-wide when he sees me, and Calvin bursts out laughing.

With a groan, I climb out, sliding onto the curved booth between Robert and Calvin. "I was going to surprise him! I didn't know you'd be coming along."

"Surprise—? Oh *my God.*" Jeff bends, putting his forehead to his palm. "Holland."

I hold up my hand and stare with great intensity at the menu. "I don't ever want to discuss this again."

– – – –

"I should honestly never try to do something sexy and impulsive."

Calvin pulls me down onto the bed, digging tickling fingers into my sides. "I will never forget this."

"Blow job fail."

"It's a very good reason for a blow job to fail. I would have had a hard time performing, I fear."

I groan. "I can't even contemplate that."

He laughs into my stomach, kissing as he pushes up my shirt. "It was a nice thought for a birthday gift."

"There are more surprises to come."

And no matter how hard he tries to get the secret out of me—no matter how much he makes good on the promise to fuck me hard in gratitude—I hold strong.

twenty-five

I remember coming to New York for the first time at sixteen to visit Robert and Jeff. I landed at the airport, and although Jeff had planned to meet me at JFK, he was held up with some work emergency, and instead texted me directions to the AirTrain, and then the subway, and then the walk to their apartment, where he would meet me.

It sounded simple, but that was before I had the true scale of New York bearing down on my Des Moines naiveté. It wasn't just the number of people and the number of signs, it was the noise. I felt like a bubble trying to push my way to the top of a carbonated bottle.

And even though New York seems almost comically easy to navigate now, I remember that feeling of complete disorientation as I head out of the apartment. I've fooled Calvin into thinking I have a gynecological exam in some mysterious region of Manhattan, and, no, I do not need him to accompany me—because really I am going to meet his mother and sister at the airport.

Nerves are a funny thing. I thought I was nervous at our wedding. And then, no, I realized that had nothing on the jitters of his first rehearsal. But that was swallowed whole by the whale shark of my restlessness during the immigration interview, and—later—on the Night of the Failed Birthday Blow Job. All of that feels like a tiny dot on the horizon compared to my anxiety today.

Despite our many texts, Brigid and I have never spoken. And after our plan to bring her and Marina out here took root, our interactions became pretty transactional, in part because I warned her that Calvin is highly casual about phone privacy—both mine and his. He'll have me read emails to him while he plays, or answer a text if his hands are full unloading groceries. And although I don't think he ever intends to be nosy, he'll often inform me when Lulu or Robert or Jeff has texted or called, asking me if I want him to read it aloud. And usually, why not? I have nothing to hide.

Except this visit, which we are all determined to keep a surprise.

I admit I'm nervous as hell. I'm meeting my mother-in-law. I'm meeting my sister-in-law. These people are technically family, and what if they take one look at me and I'm nothing like what they'd hoped for him?

Calvin is so open and easy to talk to; normally I would let loose all my thoughts about this visit with him. Obviously, that's not really possible here. And I can't trust Lulu to keep her trap shut, Robert is composing a new show with a writer friend of his and is completely unavailable, and Jeff has listened to my concerns but what can he say? *Don't worry, you're perfect?*

What does Calvin's family know about me? What has he told them?

I'm so distracted wondering what they'll expect, what they'll assume, what they'll want to see in his wife—that when a subway car jerks along a bend I make a rookie mistake and lose my footing, sliding roughly into the door.

A man helps me, pulling me upright again. "Hold on to the bar here, honey."

It is on the tip of my tongue to tell him that I live here, and I'm just nervous about meeting my in-laws, but he doesn't fucking care—and neither do my thoughts, which are back on a wild bender, buzzing around.

I wait outside of international arrivals, hoping I'll recognize the two women I've seen only in photographs. From what I can tell, of all Calvin's siblings, Brigid looks the most like him, and it's true in person, too—the second she walks around the bend into the terminal, I know it's her. She has the same thick, light brown hair, the same olive skin, the same crinkly-eyed smile when she sees me. Marina is right behind her, and cries out when she follows where Brigid points in my direction, clapping a hand over her mouth.

They run, throwing their arms around me, and I feel the moment Marina breaks down and starts crying.

"Aw, Mum." Brigid laughs as she pulls her mom into a hug. "We've just been so excited," she explains over the top of Marina's head. "We haven't seen Calvin in four years."

Marina is tiny but has the appearance of being unmovable and ageless. "You have no idea," she says, pulling away and wiping her eyes. "And we've wanted to meet you for ages.

We were excited thinking the two of you might come home at Christmas, and then it fell through."

What a curious thing to say. I smile, returning their individual hugs and guiding them out of the terminal with a stunned numbness.

Does she mean this upcoming Christmas? It didn't sound like that.

I'm trying to answer their questions and ask my own, but her words are pinging around in my ears, unwilling to move aside and let other things in.

We make small talk, about the weather, about the flight, about the food that was served, but in the background, the high-pitched voice needles me.

She's wanted to meet me for *ages*? It's April 8; I met Calvin officially just over three months ago.

We load up their bags into a cab. "Forty-Seventh and Eighth," I tell the driver.

We pull away from the curb, and Marina takes my hand. "You look different in your recent photos than the early ones we got."

The early ones?

My stomach tightens again. "I do?"

"Your hair's lighter than it was when you first met in school."

Something is very, very wrong . . .

I pat my hair, plucking a lie from the chaos of my brain. "Yeah, I lightened it a little since then."

I have never colored my hair.

"Amanda?" Brigid says. "Amanda." She reaches around her mother in the middle seat and taps my arm. "Amanda, love, is that the Empire State Building?"

She means me.

She's talking to *me*.

In all of our texts, not once did she ever need to use my name. She doesn't know me as Holland. Apparently she knows me as Amanda.

Who the fuck is Amanda?

I am worried I'm going to lose my breakfast in the back of this taxi. "Yes, that, um . . ." I nod to where she's looking. "That's it, over there."

- - - -

The refrain I put on a loop in my head is to not assume anything until I've spoken to Calvin. My first Hail Mary was hoping I picked up the wrong Irish family from the airport, but when they started rattling on in the taxi about being so proud of Calvin, and unable to believe that he was really playing with the orchestra for *Possessed*, I was pretty sure that wasn't the case.

Don't assume anything, I tell myself, walking up to the apartment building. *Don't freak out.*

"He's here?" Brigid asks in an excited whisper. "He's upstairs, in your flat?"

"He should be," I tell her over my shoulder. "He doesn't head to the theater until around five."

Behind me, Marina lets out a quiet sob. "I cannot believe we are going to see him play."

That's right . . . Robert got them front-row tickets for tonight's show.

Dread has settled as a brick in my stomach, and I can't

even find the enthusiasm to turn and smile at her. "It's a stunning performance," I say over my shoulder. "He's going to be so happy you're there."

"He has no idea!" Brigid squeals.

A dark laugh rips through my thoughts. *He has no idea— apparently none of us has any idea what we're in for.*

I fit the key in the lock with a shaking hand. Inside, we can hear Calvin strumming his guitar, absently playing "Lost to Me," and the song performs the same silent seduction on me that it always does.

But then Brigid presses up against me, and I pray to the benevolent gods of everything that whatever this lie is, it doesn't ruin us . . . if there is or was ever an *us*.

The door has barely swung open before Brigid bursts past me, screaming, "SURPRISE!"

Calvin shoots up, dropping his guitar in shock. He lets out a choking *"Bridge?"* and then bursts into tears as his sister launches herself into his arms. He sees his mom behind her and a sob tears out of him as he loosens one arm to pull her into the tangle.

I hover near the back, feeling the sting of tears across my eyes, too, because this scene is wonderful and they're all sobbing and I love him

I love him

I love him

and this reunion is truly one of the most genuine displays of joy I've ever witnessed.

"How did you manage this?" he asks, his voice muffled by his mother's coat.

"Amanda," she cries, squeezing him tighter. "Your sweet Amanda and Brigid arranged the whole thing!"

Calvin looks up, sobering as his eyes meet mine across the room.

- - - -

I put on a pot of water for some tea and make myself busy in the kitchen while they take a few minutes to get caught up. My movements feel robotic, my pulse is paradoxically slow.

Why did he give Brigid my number?

What was he thinking?

And how did we manage to never use *names* for crying out loud? How did she never ask me why we were in touch now—rather than years ago when we supposedly first got married?

She won't get too personal, he'd said.

It's the McLoughlin way.

Would Calvin have *told* her not to ask?

The deception of that possibility feels cutting.

"When did you get in?" he asks them.

"Just now," Marina tells him. "Amanda met us at the airport, we took a car here."

I feel him glance across the room into the kitchen. "She said she had a doctor's appointment."

"Oh, she fooled *you!*" Brigid laughs, and I hear the sound of them groaning happily in another embrace.

"Are you tired?" he asks, and I note how thick his accent becomes around them.

"Exhausted," his mother says. "We didn't sleep on the plane."

Calvin is quiet for a few breaths, and then says quietly, "We could make up the bed here for you to rest a bit."

"Not at all, Callie," Marina says to her son. "We're staying at the Sheraton."

"Let's get you checked in, then. You can have a lie-down."

"Amanda's uncle got us tickets to see you tonight."

"Oh, he did?" His voice is so tight. "Wonderful. Thank you, love," he calls out to me.

I try to reply with as much natural brightness as I can muster: "Of course, Callie!"

"Come on, then," he murmurs to them, "let's get you sorted."

He moves them toward the door before ducking into the kitchen and putting his arms around me in a show of gratitude. "Thank you for this," he says.

"Are you kidding?" I give him a bright smile, knowing they're listening and hoping they can hear it in my voice. "I'm so happy for you. That was so sweet, I started crying, too."

He pulls back, kissing my temple, and looks at me; I can feel how flat my expression is. A book's worth of words is communicated in our eyes.

"I'm going to take them to their hotel to get checked in," he says.

Nodding stiffly, I say, "Okay."

Calvin leans in, lips pressed to my cheek. "I'll explain everything later, please don't leave."

I don't say anything.

His lips come right up against my ear. "I'm so sorry, *mo stóirín*."

So many times I've felt his kiss there, and in the rearview mirror, every one of them now seems suspect.

"Don't leave," he repeats.

Unable to stop it, I feel a fat tear roll down my cheek. "Okay."

- - - -

Calvin returns an hour later, alone. He walks in, shuts the door, and then leans against it, closing his eyes.

I watch from the sofa, still nauseated, waiting to see how this is all going to unfold. In a weird way, I feel like I've been cheated on, and I know that sentiment isn't quite right, but the betrayal is sharp like that: bewilderment with a side of inexplicable shame.

"I was going to tell you this whole story," he says, straightening and walking toward me with wary eyes. "I didn't think it would come out this way."

"I'm just sitting here reeling in the irony that a few weeks ago you were so upset I didn't admit I had feelings for you before we knew each other. Meanwhile, you've been married for years to a woman named *Amanda*?"

"It's a lie." He sits beside me, reaching to put his hand on my thigh before he seems to think better of it.

"But *is* there someone named Amanda?"

"She's my ex-girlfriend."

Inside, my heart seems to flip over and twist, and I remember. "Oh."

"I mentioned her when we first . . . were married."

"The bossy one."

He laughs, but it isn't a joyful sound. "Right."

I don't even know if I need him to tell me more, because the story unfolds so obviously in front of me. His words fade in and out, close on the heels of my own spiraling understanding: "I haven't spoken to her since we broke up. We were together only six months or so. It was so good when we first met . . . I was young, and stupid. After only a week I told my family that I was going to marry her, and stay in the States. Things went off the rails, but I didn't bother to tell them. Didn't want them to worry, and it got to a point where it was easier to lie."

I nod, staring at my hands folded in my lap.

"I sent them a photo of us—of me with Amanda—and told them we'd been married at City Hall." He pauses, wincing. "But . . . this was after I'd ended things with her. Before then, Mam kept threatening to bring me home. Dad was sure I'd never make anything of myself here. Since then, they've not worried so much. I sent money home, wrote letters. I think they've been really proud."

"*You* were proud, you mean," I say quietly. "You were too proud, and you lied."

"I suppose." He takes my hand and I let him. I'm sort of torn between understanding and fury. Of course I get why he would lie about this, but he lied to the people he loved, he lied to *me*. After our first fight, we were honest about everything; all of this has felt so genuine that it's shattering to think it isn't quite real.

"They said I looked different from the earlier photos."

He nods. "That's the silver lining. I suppose it will make it all easier because you look like her."

I pull my hand from his and stand.

The silver lining, like it turned out to be convenient that the girl who found him at the subway looked like the girl he had pretended to marry. It fits into a perfect narrative he created. I want to scream.

I feel like the trust we've built in the past few weeks has been hurled against the wall.

"'*Will* make it easier'? You're asking me to play along . . . ?" I try it out in my head and, if possible, the hurt deepens. I can almost understand lying to his family for all these years out of a desire to protect them—after all, I haven't told my parents, either. But I imagine spending the rest of the week responding to someone else's name with a smile. Obviously it's a temporary solution, but I guess the problem is that I didn't think *I* was temporary anymore. If he wants to do away with our initial year plan, then isn't it better for us to tell them the truth now?

I'm in this same spot again, playing a secondary role in Calvin's life story. The role of Amanda.

His eyes track me as I move around the sofa. "It's only a few days," he says softly.

My heart is a deflating balloon. He's fine with his family continuing to think I'm someone else? Isn't he proud of me? Of what we've built together? Doesn't that outweigh the shame in having to admit his lie?

I'm saved from replying when his phone rings, and use the excuse to walk into the bedroom to get some space, and some air.

The call lasts for only a second because when I look up, he's in the doorway, moving toward me. With a finger under my chin, he tilts my face up.

"Hey," he says, face softening when I meet his eyes. "I don't think I'm doing this right."

I nod, fixing my gaze on his jawline, his lips, the bob of his Adam's apple when he swallows. "Things lined up strangely, that's all." He leans forward, kissing me once. "It doesn't change me and you."

I have no idea what to say to this; it feels like this changes everything. I don't even get my own name here.

"I want to talk more, but I need to run downstairs. A messenger dropped something off and I need to sign for it. We'll finish this when I'm back, okay?"

"Okay."

"I love you, Holland."

He's said it. He's said it for the first time, and I feel numb. "Okay."

"Okay," he repeats, and with another brush of his lips against mine, he's out the door.

He's gone less than five minutes, and when the door opens again, I know right away that something's wrong. He's staring in shock at the paper in his hands.

"What is it?"

His eyes jump to the top again. "It's from immigration."

A trapdoor opens and my stomach plummets. We've been expecting a letter—the official notification of his green card contingency details—but judging by the look on his face, it isn't that letter.

Reaching up, he runs a hand over his mouth and in a hoarse voice adds, "They want us to come in for another interview."

"Does it say why?" I move to his side to read over his shoulder.

Calvin shakes his head and hands me the letter. I scan the words, trying to make sense of them, to find some piece of information hidden in the handful of vague sentences.

In regards to your interview dated . . .

Further clarification . . .

My mind spins back to that drab gray office, and I'm trying to find some memory that might help explain what we did wrong. Calvin paces the living room.

Dropping the papers on the counter, I head straight to where my phone is charging on the bedside table, and press the tiny photo next to Jeff's name. It only rings once before someone picks up.

"Hey, kiddo," Robert says, answering his husband's phone. "We thought you might call."

"Calvin got a letter from—" I stop, processing what he said. "What?"

"Jeff woke up to a text from Sam Dougherty." I imagine him standing in their cozy kitchen, having a lazy morning and his second cup of coffee. "He's on the phone with him now."

I'm not sure if I feel better or worse that Dougherty thought to contact Jeff about whatever is going on.

"Can you hear what he's saying?" I ask. There's a pause and I can hear the faint murmur of Jeff's voice in the background. I chew on my fingernail, waiting for an answer.

"It looks like he's hanging up, so hold on a second and you can ask him yourself."

"Okay," I whisper. Calvin appears in the doorway. The living room curtains are open, and with the sunlight streaming into the apartment behind him I can barely make out his face.

But I can easily identify the rigid line of his shoulders and the tight clench of his hands at his sides.

"Hey, Hollsy," Jeff says, startling me back to the call.

"I'm here. Dougherty texted you?"

"Yeah, early this morning. He said he needs you to come back in for a few more questions. Both of you."

"Did they say what kind of questions?"

"He didn't want to get into it, but didn't sound all that concerned." I want to curl in on myself in a paralyzing combination of anxiety and relief. "Now, Holland, listen. I'm sure this will be fine. They're just doing their jobs and clarifying a few things, making sure everything's on the up-and-up. Things are good between you and Calvin, so there's nothing to lie about. It *is* a real marriage."

I look up to where my husband is quietly listening to my end of the conversation, and quickly divert my eyes. "Right."

"I know the letter said to call for an appointment," Jeff says, and there's the shuffling of paper. "But Sam's moved some things around and can get you in at noon today. Can you guys make that work?"

"We'll make it work," I say. "Noon."

We end the call, and the resulting silence feels oppressive. In unison, we glance to the clock on my bedside table: it's eleven.

Calvin turns away, muttering, "Right."

I watch him move to the door, pull his phone from his coat on the hook, and bend his head, dialing. The muscles beneath his shirt shift as he lifts his arm to place the phone by his ear. I have an acute memory of those muscles moving beneath my hands only this morning, with the sun barely filtering in through our bedroom window.

I really should look away, but I don't know how much longer I'll get to enjoy this view.

"Mam." His voice is quiet. "Yeah, good, good." A pause. "Right, so Amanda and I need to hop over to a meeting at noon." Another pause, during which my heart bleeds into my stomach. "All's good, but we're not going to make lunch." He goes quiet, nodding. "Sure. Sure. That's fine. We'll meet you outside the theater at half four."

I watch him lower his phone and end the call. The name *Amanda* was a stone skipped across a lake; the ripples from it spread out across the room.

Calvin turns to look over his shoulder at me. He looks resigned, like he clearly doesn't know where to start fixing this. Given the meeting we have less than an hour from now, I'm wondering whether we'll even get the chance.

"Is there anything you want to take with you?" I ask him, hedging.

He startles a little. "You think it's *that* kind of meeting?"

I shrug, helpless. "Calvin, I have no idea."

Panic animates him, and he moves back over for his guitar, hurriedly bending and shoving a bunch of documents and letters into a messenger bag. And what if he doesn't come back here with me? What if he gets put on a plane? The prospect seems nearly preposterous, with his mother and sister finally only a mile or so away in a hotel.

I feel like I can't quite catch my breath in this madcap circus between us. We've gone from strangers to spouses to friends to lovers, and now are spiraling in this no-man's-land of awkward. Amanda is still a shadow on the wall, and here we are, defending our marriage to the government, again—and this time it feels real.

He loops his bag across his chest, picks up his guitar, and meets me at the door, expression somber. "I hate how this has turned."

I can't help it; I laugh. The sentiment is sweet, but so unbelievably obvious.

"It's funny?" he asks quietly.

"It's just . . ." I look up at him, and for the span of three tight breaths, it all reels through my head: his first small smile at the station, the easy comfort of our first lunch together, the vibrator in the couch, the first interview, the drunken blur of his body on mine and then the clarity of making love with him again, and again, every day for weeks. I swear I know him but then there's *Amanda*, and another interview, and I realize with startling horror that I am a complete disaster of an adult. "It's just a lot."

- - - -

I don't trust any of the sweet gestures right now. I don't trust his hand reaching for mine on the C train, or his reassuring chatter as we walk the three blocks to the federal building. I don't trust the tenderness in his eyes when he bends outside, cupping my jaw in his hand and whispering right up against my ear, "I want to fix all of this. Let me fix all of this."

Obviously, he has the most to lose here—at least on face value, because it's impossible to assess the damage this is doing to me emotionally. He has his work permit, his dream job, a pretty sweet apartment in walking distance to work, and a wife who conveniently looks a lot like the woman he's been pretending to be married to for the past four years. *Of course* he wants to fix this. I only have this blossoming joy in my heart that I've felt waking up beside Calvin McLoughlin for the past several months.

Not to be melodramatic, but who needs love?

So I don't bother to answer him, and instead turn into the building. Through the security screening we go, up the elevator, down the marble hallway, and into the immigration suite. Calvin gestures for me to sit, and then lowers himself into the chair beside me in the waiting area, pulling out his phone. I watch as he turns on the screen . . . and reads a text from someone named Natalie.

I can't help it. I'm already a bare wire, exposed. "Natalie?"

He doesn't even try to hide it. He tilts his phone so I can read the text there.

Hey you! Checking in to see if you're free?

When I look up, he reminds me unnecessarily, "She's the girl I was meant to go on a date with that night at dinner with you and the uncles."

What the fuck?

Heat rises like steam to my face. "She's *still* texting you?"

He drops his head into his hands. "We haven't talked since. I guess she's just following up on what I said."

"What you *said*? We were married when you spoke to her. What did you say? 'Check back in four months for a rain check on that date'? What the hell, Calvin? What have you been doing with me?"

He begins to argue, but Dougherty has materialized a few feet away, and we stand in a burst, as if saluting.

How long has he been there? Did he hear us? Oh my God, we are idiots.

"Hey there," Dougherty says. "Come on back."

With a small, encouraging smile, he turns and we follow. It feels so familiar—the walk to his office, the gray view out his window, the tight ball of anxiety in my stomach—but I'm also struck by how different it is, how much more we know now. Our first interview was a naive shot into the dark, with fingers crossed. Now we're walking across the room, dragging all this emotional and marital baggage behind us. Even if we make it out of this meeting intact, how long will we stay that way?

Do I want to be married to someone who's been keeping a Natalie on the back burner?

Do I want to be married to someone who may have married me only for this job, and because I looked like someone named Amanda?

Dougherty tells us to sit and closes the door behind us before rounding his desk. In front of him are three stacks of papers, and to the right is a thick file I can only assume is ours.

"I'm going to lay it out straight up," he says, scratching an eyebrow. He doesn't look pleased. "After your first interview, I'm required to do an audit of the documentation to create my report."

We both nod.

"At first blush, your story was pretty clear-cut. You met at the subway station, went on a date, fell in love."

Calvin and I nod again.

But it's like I know what's coming, and I can't breathe.

"Something jumped out at me." He pulls a sheet off the top of the middle pile, and reads it quietly for a few seconds. "The police report. Holland, here it is, dated January ninth. You were assaulted at the Fiftieth Street station. You claimed there was an unnamed musician in the station as a witness to your injury, correct?"

There it is.

I swallow before speaking. "That's right."

"Now, you also mentioned that Calvin used to play sometimes. Wasn't the assault at the station where you used to play, Calvin?"

"That's right, sir." And before I can catch his eye, give him a tiny shake of my head—he adds, "That's how it all began."

But then he pulls back in a jerky motion, turning to me. "Wait."

I watch as understanding dawns.

"No," he says. "I wasn't there that night, right?"

Silence blankets the room.

"You don't remember whether you were present when your girlfriend at the time was assaulted?"

Calvin closes his eyes, slumping. "I was there."

Slowly, Dougherty slides the paper onto his desk and leans back, rubbing his eyes.

Neither of us says a thing. We both know we're busted.

We told Dougherty we met six months before we got married. If Calvin was at the station when I got injured in January, he would undoubtedly be named in the police report as a witness—the victim's boyfriend.

"Okay, so I was right. The timelines don't match up," Dougherty says quietly, resting his elbows on his desk and meeting
our eyes in turn. "See, I do the first audit, but there's always a
second, independent assessment of the docs. Sometimes they'll
skim the paperwork, but sometimes they're really thorough."
He leans back again, studying us. "Normally, I would reject this
outright and not even bother to bring you in, but I like you, and
Jeff is a good friend. Unfortunately, this is easy to catch, because
I have that Calvin played at that station, and you were assaulted
at that station. If Calvin was there the night you were assaulted,
then why didn't he come forward with information, and why
isn't he explicitly named? I don't want to get caught in a situation
where I've pushed through an obviously fraudulent marriage."

"It isn't, though," Calvin says, sliding forward in his seat. "We
may have . . . stretched a few details, but it's a *love* marriage."

A thick knot of emotion takes up residence in my throat.
Dougherty looks at me, and I nod. He probably assumes my
watery eyes are tears of intense agreement rather than heartache because I'm not even sure whether Calvin is telling the
truth or is just a really, really good liar.

"On a personal note, I'm glad to hear that," he says, "but
it's pretty immaterial here." He sweeps his hand over our files.
"This doesn't look great."

Beside me, Calvin leans back heavily in his chair, covering
his face with his hands.

"Before you panic," Dougherty continues, "I have come
up with a solution." He pulls the pile of papers from the left
side of his desk and pushes them toward Calvin. "When Jeff
approached me initially, I advised him off the record that you'd

be unlikely to qualify for an EB-1A green card, or O-1B visa, because of the length of your illegal tenure in the U.S."

"Right," I say. "Jeff said those are really competitive and Calvin wouldn't qualify because he'd broken the law."

Dougherty nods. "But given the current change in circumstance—specifically that Calvin is arguably one of the brightest stars on Broadway at the moment—I say we can easily make the case for national or even international acclaim and apply for a visa for Persons with Extraordinary Ability."

Calvin sits forward, eyes red, and finally takes a look at the papers. "So we'd do this sort of visa instead of the green card?"

Dougherty nods. "Whether you stay married is up to you, but I worry about the red flags there. I *know* we can put an O-1B through now."

The sun can't decide what it wants to do; it fights behind clouds, and even when it's free and exposed, it seems to beam weakly down on us. Outside the building, Calvin and I huddle in our coats. I want to look up to the cold spring sky and laugh my face off. All of this was moot—the wedding, the information sharing, the checking account, the utility bills. Even the emotional entanglement. We were all so naive.

"This is what happens when you put a bunch of artists in charge of a legal decision," I mumble.

"I'll fill these out later and send them in first thing tomorrow," he says, and nods down to the forms clutched to his chest. "Holy Christ, I'm glad this doesn't affect us."

It's like we've walked out of a movie theater thinking we were together only to realize we watched two different shows. "This," I say, pointing between us, "is *totally* moot. You get that, right?"

He reacts like I've shoved him, shifting a step back. "Is that what you're taking away from the meeting?"

"That we don't need to be married?" I say, laughing harshly. "Yeah. That's what I'm taking away."

What a mess this is. I want to go back in time—two weeks, that would be perfect. And I want to find a way to get him to tell me about Amanda, and explain it in a way where his explanations don't sound convenient and shady. I want it to happen before I meet his family, before I realize that I could be Holland, or Amanda, or Natalie, or anybody—that Calvin just needed a warm American citizen in his bed.

But does that time exist? I'm not sure there would have been a way for him to tell me about Amanda and our convenient similarity without it sounding like utter bullshit if he said in the next breath, *But I do love you.*

He stares off down the street, squinting. "My takeaway was a bit different."

"Which is?"

"That we're free to just be *together* now." He turns back to me. "That this marriage can exist without the odd pressures of obligation."

Defeat is a weight, pulling my heart low. "I like the idea of that, but two hours ago I found out I'm just a convenient doppelgänger. Even without the obligation of the green card, we still have *that* to address."

He growls, tugging at his hair. "The Amanda thing isn't relevant here. It's not relevant between *us*—it was just a way to keep my family from worrying!"

His defensiveness stokes a fire in me. "Then why didn't you tell *me*?"

"Because it sounds terrible," he says, laughing incredulously.

"It *is* terrible."

Calvin tilts his face up to the sky, his jaw tight with frustration. "You know, I think you need to back off me a little here. Your parents still don't even know I exist."

"You're right." I nod. "But I never lied to you about it. I planned to tell them everything. The emotions that happened between us were unexpected, and I figured I had time to tell them before I took you home. I was just swept up in it."

"As was I."

"Yeah, but I only need to tell them that I fell in love with someone. Your family has been carrying around a photo of a woman they think is your wife—a photo you sent them, by the way—and have explained away the differences between us because they think I've lost a little weight and that I've done something to my hair. Is that why you always want me to wear it up?"

He looks furious. "No! I want you to wear it up because *I like it up*."

"You've been lying to me about all of it this entire time, and would have been happy for me to go along with it."

"Not everything here was a lie, Holland." The wind whips his jacket collar against his neck. "I think we can both admit that what happened between us in bed wasn't a fraud."

He's right, and inside, I am a simmering pot of feelings. Without question, I'm in love with him, and can so acutely remember the bliss of making love to him in the middle of last night that it makes my jaw clench with need. But I'm mad at myself for thinking this fucked-up situation was what I deserved. What happened between us *in bed* was the truth, but what about outside of that? I can't even trust my internal compass of emotion anymore. *Is this love?*

"I know the *sex* wasn't a fraud," I say, and meet his eyes in time to catch his tiny wince. "But I don't know how to believe you want more than that when you stood there and asked me to let them call me Amanda. That doesn't scream long term."

"Holland, I—"

"I need some time to think. Maybe I'll call my family tonight and talk it out."

"The show is tonight, love. Mam and Bridge—"

"You can't honestly expect me to come along, can you?"

His expression crashes and he steps forward, holding my arm in his free hand. "Holland, this is all shite, I get that. But I'll talk to them, I'll explain. We'll fix this."

I know I'm going to hate that I say it, but I can't seem to hold the words back: "We don't *need* to fix it anymore. You're free."

The wind chooses this moment to burst past us, propelling us apart. It's the perfect moment for the perfect metaphor.

Calvin searches my eyes for a few more seconds and then looks away. "All right. I'll come round later to gather my things."

twenty-six

I've done a lot of crazy things in the last four months, but calling Brian and quitting before tonight's performance might be the craziest. I couldn't tell if he was speechless from glee or shock, but his silence on the other end allowed me to get the words out, even as my own realization that I was quitting rather than just calling in sick unfolded over the phone:

I'm not coming in tonight.

Actually, I really need to find something else to do.

I'm not happy working there anymore.

I think . . . I'm quitting.

Jeff and Robert I have to tell in person—I owe them that courtesy after everything they did to get me the job in the first place. But Lulu—bless her heart—replied with a string of hearts and eggplants and smiley faces and rocker-hand emojis before typing the actual words It's about fucking time. Within ten minutes she sent me a list of restaurants where I should apply.

So while the fire of mania and heartache and terror and regret still burns me up inside, I update my résumé, planning to take it to a dozen places this week.

I worked at the dining hall when I was at Yale—that's about the extent of my food industry experience. But I'm hoping that my days at the Levin-Gladstone will cash out here, because it is hard as hell to get a job there, and *archivist and customer relations* looks pretty bad-ass on paper. I get now that what Robert gave me wasn't a great job, but a great investment.

And then I come home and open my article on Calvin, and the production, and my hunt for talent in New York, trying to Rumpelstiltskin my black angst into golden prose and do everything I can to avoid thinking about how it's going to feel when Calvin gets home and I realize we're really over.

- - - -

I'm hammering away at my keyboard, high on word count and two glasses of wine, but my righteous resolve melts when Calvin walks into the apartment and hangs his coat up on the hook.

He stands by the door, expression somber, and then pulls in a deep breath, stepping into the room.

Taking a perch on the corner of the coffee table, he says quietly, "You weren't even out in the lobby." He looks exhausted: blue circles bloom beneath bloodshot eyes, and his normally smiling mouth is a grim, flat line.

I slide my laptop onto the table beside him. "I called Brian and quit."

He doesn't seem at all surprised by this. He just nods, staring down at his interlaced hands. Seeing his wedding band glint in the lamplight is enough to suck the air from my lungs.

"Where are your mom and sister?" I ask. A glance at the clock shows me that it's well past midnight; the show ended at least two hours ago.

"Back at the hotel."

"Did they have fun?"

He nods but doesn't answer aloud.

"I'm sure they were so proud of you."

"I think so," he says.

I tink so.

This is nothing like my breakup with Bradley, where it felt like all we had to do was put a lid on a box. Right now, my heart *hurts*. It's squeezing and squeezing and squeezing, trying to keep me moving through this moment where I'm pretty sure I've decided that in order to get myself back, I'll be losing him.

"I told them about Amanda." He scratches at a fleck of white on his black dress trousers. "They're peeved. They'll get over it."

I don't know what to say to this. All that comes out is a sympathetic hum.

Calvin looks up at me. "Will you?"

"Get over it?"

He nods.

"Maybe," I tell him, "but not right away. I mean, I think I understand why you lied to them—you didn't want them to worry about you out here. But then you didn't tell me, either, and it all just seems very . . . convenient. I had a hard time trusting that this was real at the beginning, and it doesn't exactly help that you wanted me to lie about my name to your family."

"I'll explain whatever you need me to," he says. "I did a shite job explaining this—I was panicked. I realize it all looks so bad from where you're sitting."

"Yeah." I look up at him. "And although we can hash out the Amanda thing, I'm not sure you can explain away Natalie."

He leans forward, taking both of my hands in his. "There is nothing happening with Natalie. When she called at the restaurant, I told her I was starting a new relationship. *That's* what I said. I didn't give her an expiration date." He bends, kissing my knuckles. "It was cowardly to not tell my parents about Amanda. Plain and simple. And yeah, I married you at first to stay here but my love for you isn't a lie. It was shite to expect you to lie with me. I just . . ." He shakes his head, and looks to the window. "In the moment, it was all a swarm in my head. I'm so sorry, but I'm here now, and I'll do whatever you need me to do to fix this between us."

I study his face. His smooth skin, dancing green eyes, the full mouth I've kissed thousands of times. He looks positively miserable, and I don't even know what to say.

"I fucked this up," he whispers, and his eyes fall closed. "I really fucked it up."

God.

This hurts.

I hate this,

I hate it. I hate it.

When he opens his eyes again and looks at me, I don't

want him to leave, but I know I'm going to make him go. We are such a mess.

"Well, anyway, I told you I'd come back later and get my things," he says, trailing off.

I try to swallow around the clog in my throat, my chest, my gut. "Yeah."

"Do you want me to go?"

"I don't *want* you to, no. But right now I need you to."

He directs his next quiet question to the floor: "Do you want to stay married?"

My heart screams *yes*. Most of my body, in fact, screams *yes, yes, yes*. But a tiny fragment inside, a spark that's turned into an ember, whispers *no*. I know we could talk through Amanda, or Natalie, or all the secrets we've kept from our families, the way we talked through Lulu's Insane Stalker accusations. But in the grand scheme of life, those are all small things, and the big things need to happen with a clean slate. Before this, I had nothing going on in my life. This man was presented as an option, and I was willing to marry him just to have something to do, some victory to claim.

My willingness to jump into a fake marriage seems depressing in hindsight. The fact that he lied to me feels terrible. The fact that—over and over again—I'm not sure whether or not I can trust his feelings to be genuine is gutting.

But the worst feeling is the deep confusion inside me about *why* he would love me at all; I feel stale and tiresome. No matter what my uncles say, Calvin and I aren't Robert and Jeff—we didn't start out with clear intentions and unequivocal declarations of love. I can't be the Jeff, working on the sidelines while Calvin takes off like a comet. I need to fill my life with accomplishments I create, not just witness.

"I love you," I tell him earnestly, and swallow a few times so I don't cry when I get through the rest of it. It's the first time *I've* said it. In every book I've ever read where the protagonist does what I'm about to do, I hate it, I yell at the pages . . . but I get it now. "And part of me really does want to stay married and work through this, and have the unexpected perfect ending. But I've been really good at letting other people take care of me, and making my decisions based on what other people need. I've been scared of figuring out my own shit, or trying something and failing. And now I'm sitting here thinking, '*I* wouldn't even be in love with me. How can I believe him when he says he is?'"

Calvin moves to interrupt me, but stops when I hold up a hand. I know he wants to reassure me that he honestly loves me, but he's only alluded to the fact that we should know we're in love because of how good the sex is.

"We could work on us, but I'm not happy with me right now. I want to *do* something, not just watch you do everything."

He stares at me, murmuring, "I get that."

Of course he does; he's got music, and he's put that first nearly his entire life. He was a complete mess in how he handled this, but now, looking at him—he's got it all figured out.

Calvin moves his gaze over my face—my forehead, cheeks, nose, mouth, chin, and last, my eyes—before slowly leaning forward and pressing his mouth to mine. "Okay."

I smile quizzically once he's pulled back. "Okay?"

"I can wait."

twenty-seven

I suppose I should be grateful for the truth in the saying *Sometimes when one thing falls apart, other things fall into place*. After all, without the meltdown of my relationship that afternoon outside the federal building, I would never have left the theater. Without leaving the theater, I would never have gotten a waitressing job two days later at Friedman's in Hell's Kitchen, where I work three afternoon shifts and three nights a week. Without the restaurant job, I wouldn't have my days free to write. And without writing, I wouldn't have what feels like a tree taking root inside me, growing up and invisibly out of every pore.

My scramble of ideas about growing up in the symphony hall, subway buskers, and the glitter and brass of Broadway turns from a journal of jumbled words . . . into an essay.

It seems so obvious now: *Write about music, you dummy.*

I forgot the joy of seeing words coming out of my hands before they've even come into my head. When I close my eyes and type,

I see Calvin's hands moving over the neck of the guitar; hear the clatter of change falling dissonantly into his guitar case down at the station, and remember how he barely registered the ocean of people crashing in waves all around him on the subway platform.

For a couple of weeks, I try to keep moving: waitressing, word count, running in Central Park at least once a day. In part, it's the rush of accomplishment and seeing my body shed the extra pounds, creating definition where there used to be none. But also, every time I slow down and sit on the couch, or lie in bed and stare at the ceiling, I'm miserable. The old standby habit of distracting myself online is impossible. I see photos of Calvin everywhere on Twitter and Facebook. On buses and at the subway station. Discarded *Playbills* litter the street.

He's texted a few times—once because he forgot some sheet music here, and he picked it up when I wasn't home. On four other occasions, he's texted to check in, and each time I answered the question directly, no more:

> How are you surviving this first week apart?

> I'm trying.

> I sent you six months' worth of rent. Did you get it?

> Yes, I got your check, thank you.

I haven't seen you at the theater in weeks.
Where are you working?

I got a new job. I'm working at Friedman's.

Will you have dinner with me on Monday?

I'm sorry, I can't. I work Monday nights.

This last one was sent only four days ago, and it wasn't a lie—I do work Mondays. But my new manager is nice, and likes that I work hard and don't complain; I'm sure I could have asked to swap nights with someone. The thing is, there isn't anything particularly romantic in Calvin's messages; as ever, my problem is that I have no idea how to read him. I worry that if we start talking more, this new, improved version of Holland will fall apart, because I'll want him back more than I'll want her to stay.

I do give myself a few minutes every day to think about him; I'm not completely dead inside, and I don't have that kind of self-control anyway: Sony Music rerecorded the soundtrack with Ramón and Calvin.

It is glorious.

When the afternoon lunch crowd is slow, I'll ask the head chef, José, to put the soundtrack on in the kitchen. I'll go to the dark corner with a glass of ice water and press it to my forehead while I listen to "Lost to Me." The sound of Calvin's guitar—

the hopeful opening chords that surge into an anxious, feverish rhythm later in the song—seems to reverberate inside my skull.

I know how those notes sound when they're coming from across the room, from across the *bed*. I know how they sound hummed contentedly into my ear with the warm curl of his body all along my back. I flush hot with the need to cry, and roll the cold glass along my forehead—back, and forth, and back, and forth—and try instead to think about my essay and my new job. Emotion takes over in a different way; loss is tinged with pride, and I can go back out and wait my tables and earn enough to pay my rent all on my own for the first time in my life.

- - - -

At one in the afternoon on a Wednesday, I finish the essay.

The cursor blinks at me, both patient and expectant. But there are no more words for this particular story. I haven't gone back and read it in its entirety, but when I do, I realize that it's more than just about music—it's about Calvin specifically, and my own journey after meeting him, and how pure, sublime talent transcends everything else, no matter where you find it. It's about how the clatter of trains and sour smells of the station dissolved away when he played, and the way the audience similarly disappears now when he's onstage. It's about the pride in having discovered someone and done something to make sure his talent didn't stay hidden forever.

It's a love letter—there's no hiding that—but the oddest thing is that I'm pretty sure it's a love letter to myself.

– – –

Like firing a homemade rocket into the sky and hoping it reaches Jupiter, I send my essay off to the *New Yorker*. In fact, I laugh when I put a stamp on it because the idea that I could be published there is hilarious—but what do I have to lose? I've never been published anywhere close to this level of prestige. It's easy to imagine an editor—a man so cerebral he cares nothing about appearances, has tea stains on papers all over his desk, and uses words like *hiraeth*, *sonorous*, and *denouement* in casual conversation—opening my submission and tossing it with a dismissive groan over his shoulder, where it lands in a pile of other delusionally ambitious essays. I say a quietly sarcastic "Go get 'em, tiger!" when I drop it in the mailbox.

But then, three weeks later, I think I stop breathing for a full ten minutes when I receive a letter saying that it's been accepted.

I walk around my apartment, holding the editorial letter, rereading it out loud. I want to call Jeff and Robert, of course, but I have to push past the Calvin cobwebs in my thoughts to get there. This article is about *us*, and not only do I need to get his permission to publish it, I want him to read it, simply because I want him to *see*.

To see *me*.

But strangely, I think he always has. And calling him after five weeks of silence is easier said than done.

I go for a quick run to work through my excited/nervous energy.

I call Davis, who makes me deaf in my left ear with his enthusiasm.

I take a shower, and make a sandwich, and do some laundry.

Step up, Hollsy, Jeff says in my head.

When I look at the clock, it's only three. I haven't wasted the entire day, and I can't procrastinate any longer: Calvin should be free.

The phone rings once, twice, and he picks up halfway through the third.

"Holland?"

The sound of his voice on the phone sends static along my skin, a low-frequency hum of nostalgia and want.

"Hey," I say, biting my bottom lip so I don't grin like an idiot. It is so good to hear him.

"*Hey.*" I can hear the smiling lean to the word, can practically imagine how he's flipped his hair out of his eyes, how his happiness reaches every part of his face. "This is a nice surprise."

"I have some good news."

"Yeah?"

I nod, swallowing down my nerves and looking again for confirmation at the letter in my hands. "I wrote an essay about . . ." I don't even know how to describe it, really. "About you? And me. Music and New York. I don't even know . . ."

"Th' one you were working on before . . . ?"

Before we split.

"Yeah. That one."

He waits for more, finally prompting, "And?"

"And . . . I sent it off to the *New Yorker.*" I bite back a grin. "They accepted it."

He pauses, and I hear his breath come out in a gust. "*No way.*"

"Yes way!"

"Holy shite!" He laughs, and the sound of it punches me right in the face. I miss him so much. "This is amazing, *mo stóirín!*"

His old nickname for me. There it is, and my heart goes boom.

"Do you want to read it?"

He laughs. "Is that a serious question?"

"I can trade shifts with someone on Monday, if you wanted to have dinner?"

Dinner, with Calvin, and this glow inside me that feels right for the first time in ages.

"Tell me where," he says, "and I'll be there."

– – – –

"You're finally going to let us read it?"

It's the first thing Jeff says when he opens the door Monday afternoon and sees me standing there, holding a large manila envelope containing the editorial letter and a printed copy of my essay.

"It's even better than that," I tell him, waving the envelope enticingly. I'm nearly drunk with glee. "Where's Bobert?"

"In the kitchen." Jeff grimaces in warning. "Come help."

Once inside, I register that the air smells suspiciously of Robert's cooking—a mixture of burnt bread and scalded tomato sauce. "Honey, come in here, I think I messed up the pasta."

Although he also calls Jeff "honey," I know for a fact he's speaking to me. I slide the envelope onto the entryway table, pointing at Jeff. "Paws off. I have news."

He holds his hands up in surrender, promising not to peek, and I meet Robert in the kitchen.

"You knew I was coming," I tell him as he sits down at the kitchen table with a glass of red wine, surrendering responsibility. "Why didn't you just wait for me to get here?"

"I was trying to surprise you with lunch."

He's adorable. I survey the meal: it's really just pasta and sauce.

"Just dump it," he says. "It's scalded."

I give him a sympathetic smile, and with one tilt of the pan over the trash, it's handled. Robert orders Vietnamese delivery, Jeff brings the envelope into the kitchen, and it sits there on the table, silently throbbing.

We start off with a little bit of small talk, though every few seconds I can see them glancing down to the table.

"How are things?" I ask.

"Brian really stepped in it last week," Robert says. I'm already feeling high from the impending dinner with Calvin, and the news that Brian fucked up somehow makes me feel plastered with thrill. "He got into a screaming match with a woman who was wandering around the lobby before a show, and she turned out to be some foreign diplomat's wife, who was getting a tour and lost her way coming back from the bathroom."

I wince; my happiness is tempered somewhat by the realization that the confrontation probably turned into a big mess for Robert and Michael. "Oof. Sorry."

Robert shrugs. "Calvin seems a *tiny* bit more alive these last few days." He says this carefully, knowing he's just dropped a live bomb in the room. "Ramón got engaged, so the cast threw a big party for him last week."

I know I should feel glad that Calvin looks more alive, but in a totally selfish sense it was a relief that he wasn't bouncing around, happy-as-ever Calvin without me this past month. And on top of that, to realize that I've missed what was probably a really fun party . . . this update bums me out. Basically, I am a jerk.

Jeff sees this written plainly all over my face, and laughs, but not unkindly. "You know, Hollsy, you could take him back anytime you want."

"I'm not sure about that," I say. For as excited as I am to see him tonight, I'm still not sure that we're in the same place emotionally. I've had so much time in my own head—on my runs, in the bustle of waiting tables—to understand how things got so intense between us so quickly, and how it could still happen even if he didn't love me the way he thought he did. Joining *Possessed* was emotional for him; the relief of being here legally was emotional. Gratitude can be deceptively deep sometimes. This time apart has sucked, but it's likely been a good barometer of how genuine our feelings are.

I know mine are real. I hope his are, too.

My stomach ties itself into a knot.

"Seems to me you were the one who ended things," Jeff reminds me.

"I was, but I think it was good for him to have some distance." I take a deep breath. "We're having dinner tonight, so . . . we'll see."

Robert grins widely at this, reaching across the table to squeeze my hand. "We're so proud of you, Buttercup."

"Thanks, guys." I look up at them, wondering whether I need to thank them more exhaustively—for raising me, for bringing me here, for propping me up, and for shepherding me through the crazy decisions I've made this year. But one look at them tells me they already know how grateful I am for them. So I just say quietly, "Thanks for everything. I can't even imagine not having you."

"You're the child we never had," Robert says simply. "You're our pride and joy."

We need to move into this essay business or I am going to end up an emotional puddle in their dining room.

"So, I had a bit of an epiphany a little over a month ago," I tell them, drumming my fingers on the table. "It feels so obvious now, but I think being with Calvin really pushed me to realize it."

They both blink expectantly at me.

I slide the envelope across the table.

Robert opens it, and claps his hand to his mouth as soon as he sees the letter from the *New Yorker* on top. Jeff shouts before he launches himself out of his chair and picks me up out of mine, holding me a foot above the floor.

After the screams and exclamations and several rounds of reading the letter out loud, we quiet down enough to sit, and for them to begin to read the essay itself through their proud tears.

Robert's expression sobers and turns heart-achingly tender when he realizes that this essay is, in part, about his influence on my life, and my future. Although I've incorporated the editorial notes that were suggested in the letter—and I know they've made the overall theme stronger—it's still scary to hand this over to him. I write like I know what I'm talking about in the musical sense, and now that he has the essay in his hands, I'm suddenly terrified he's going to tell me all the ways I got things wrong when speaking about pitch, and composition, and raw musical talent.

I see his eyes flicker back over the same sentence a few times, and try to guess what section he's reading. My nerves are going to eat their way through my stomach and up my throat. I can't just sit here, watching them read while we wait for lunch.

Curling up on the couch in the living room, I pull out my phone, lazily scrolling through my Twitter feed. News, news, the world is on fire, news . . . and then I'm stalled at a photo of Calvin standing next to a beautiful brunette on a red carpet. It's not even on his Twitter account, or the Levin-Gladstone social media feed.

It's on *Entertainment Weekly.*

It's like swallowing ice—everything in my throat seizes up. In the preview image, he has his arm around her waist. He's wearing my favorite smile.

I shouldn't. I really shouldn't—but how can I not? I click the link to the article.

For the second time in a month, Broadway guitarist and heartthrob Calvin McLoughlin steps out with indie actress Natalie Nguyen, this time for the New York premiere of the political thriller *EXECUTE*, starring his bromance better half and *It Possessed Him* star Ramón Martín.

The easy-on-the-eyes duo has been spotted twice in New York City, with—

Abruptly, I drop my phone facedown on the coffee table. There is a storm inside me named Hurricane Natalie.

Hey you! Checking in to see if you're free?

Calvin seems a tiny bit more alive these last couple weeks.

I lift a throw pillow to my face and scream.

"Holland, this is exquisite!" Robert yells from the table, misunderstanding my meltdown.

The pillow gets hurled across the room. "Does Calvin have a fucking girlfriend?"

Two sets of footsteps pad across the floor, coming to a stop behind the couch.

"Does Calvin have a girlfriend?" Robert repeats. "Not that I know of . . . but I haven't really seen him outside of performances."

Jeff gingerly retrieves my phone from the table, looking at the article still up on the screen. "Oh! She's the woman from . . ." He snaps his fingers. "What was that film with Josh Magellan, about the tour group that went to—"

"Right, right," Robert jumps in, "to Nova Scotia." He taps his mouth while he tries to remember. "What's her name? She was fabulous in it."

"Her name is Natalie Nguyen." I punch the pillow. "Can we skip the part where you tell me she's an amazing talent, and get to the part where my husband has his arm around her tiny waist on the red carpet?"

twenty-eight

It's probably no surprise that I bail on dinner.

Jeff and Robert insist that I don't know the true story, and that rumors like this happen all the time. No matter how much they want me to think otherwise, Jeff and Robert have to understand that Calvin dating Natalie isn't ludicrous. It's likely.

I give them a copy of the essay for Calvin to read and approve, and then I meet Lulu for drinks at Lillie's, telling her we're going to celebrate my *New Yorker* victory. Maybe if I focus on the positive, I won't melt into a Holland-shaped puddle of regret.

I think I want to get drunk, but only one glass of wine in, I text Calvin.

> I think it's probably best if we skip dinner. I'll have Robert give you a copy of the essay tomorrow.

Best for whom?

My heart sags. I'm positive that getting drunk will only result in me calling him later and sobbing into the phone. It might not be fair, but I'm furious with him for moving on so quickly. Just over a month! When I get angry, I cry. It's like the two wires cross in my emotional brain.

I haven't said anything to Lulu yet about Calvin and Natalie, but in her tiny pauses to draw breath outside of the Lulu Bubble—babbling about whether or not to break up with Gene, and getting Botox next week, and the new shoes she can't afford but is going to buy anyway—she seems to pick up that something is wrong.

"I thought we were celebrating the essay," she says, and pushes my wine closer to me. "You just got your thing published in the place you were super excited about. Why do you look like such a sad sack when I'm describing a pair of Valentinos?"

I stab a fry into a tiny ceramic cup of truffle sauce. Now, with her question, I'm defensive *and* sad. Why does Lulu always make it seem as though my feelings are an inconvenient distraction from hers?

"I'm a 'sad sack,'" I say irritably, "because I think Calvin is dating Natalie Nguyen."

She nods, popping one of my fries into her mouth. "I saw that the other day."

I feel like I've been punched.

I count to ten, and then give myself only one second to glare up at her. Something inside me is on fire. "Thanks for the heads-up."

"What did you want me to say? 'Good luck competing with that'?" She eats another fry. "Wouldn't that be worse?"

This moment, right here, is where my friendship with Lulu dies.

- - - -

"How are you?" Davis asks, and in the background I hear neither the television nor any sort of food preparation. The silence tells me that my brother is genuinely worried about me.

"I vacillate between excited about the essay and sad about the boy." Sad is an understatement. In the week since I saw the photo, and then had drinks with Lulu, I've spent a disproportionate amount of time sobbing into my pillow.

Davis, wisely, does not make a comment about how hot Natalie Nguyen is, or how I should have seen all of this coming. "I'm sorry, Holls. Have you talked to him?"

"No." I don't mention that he's called me twice this week. Both voicemails were simple and unsentimental—*Holland, it's me. Please call*—and although Calvin (the real one, not the past version who sexted me lines to show in an interview) is far more likely to be emotional in person than over voicemail, I also know him well enough to be able to read distance there.

I probably should woman up and have the conversation about initiating our annulment, but although Jeff and Robert still insist I might be wrong, even if there is a five percent chance that Calvin and Natalie aren't a thing, I'm not sure I'm prepared for the ninety-five percent chance of confirmation that they are.

"And Jeff said something about you having a split with Lulu, too?"

I groan in confirmation, but less out of heartbreak and more out of a surprising relief that the stress of that friendship is past me. With the mention of Lulu, though—and the reminder of her dismal display of tender emotions—I remember that I refuse to be a self-absorbed brat, and there *is* an actual reason why I called my brother. "I have good news, though. It's about Robert."

We found out yesterday that Robert has won the Drama Desk Award for *Possessed*, a huge Broadway honor. Jeff—who is over the moon about it—is planning a fiftieth birthday party/ award celebration. Of course I have to be there . . . and of course Calvin will be, too.

No way am I going solo. I need major reinforcements, and nobody makes me laugh harder than Davis.

"I know where this is going," he says once I've explained the situation. He lets out a long sigh. "Does this mean I need to get a plane ticket and rent a tux?"

"Well yeah, because I want my date to look hot."

"That is some *Flowers in the Attic* stuff, Holls. Don't be weird."

— — — —

"You ready for Saturday?" Jeff asks, putting an arm around me as we maneuver through the world's most expensive grocery store.

"I'm nervous," I admit.

"Have you picked out a dress?"

"No." I loathe shopping. "I have a nice black one I can wear."

My *proper* dress.

"We should get you something new. This is a big deal." Jeff pauses to inspect some produce, and doesn't notice my horror as he seems to seriously consider purchasing a tiny bag of cherries for twelve dollars. "I'm glad Davis is coming out. I haven't seen him in nearly a year."

Despite my mopey heart, I have to admit that good things are happening. The essay, Robert's award, Davis's visit. I know Jeff is right, and over time I'll feel incrementally better about this whole Calvin thing. I'm just not there yet.

So when Jeff puts the cherries down and turns to face me fully, wearing an expression of grim resignation, I know he's preparing to say something that will eviscerate me.

"What?" I ask, my voice low and predatory.

He laughs at this, but his eyes remain tight. "I think you know already that Ramón hasn't signed on for an extended run."

"Robert mentioned it a few months ago, but I wasn't sure whether that had changed with Calvin and Ramón's popularity."

"It has and it hasn't." Jeff looks down and picks up a pear—I'm sure as an obvious distraction from looking at my anxious expression. "Ramón's run is up at the end of this year. He and his fiancée are based in L.A. Two days ago, Robert was asked to open the L.A. run of *Possessed.*"

He turns back, watches me, and I feel my heart squeeze too tight—in joy and panic. *Robert is moving to L.A.?*

"He hasn't accepted yet, but is strongly leaning that way."

As much as I try, my "That's amazing!" comes out a little flat.

"It is," Jeff says carefully, putting the fruit down. "They would do a special performance of the soundtrack at the Staples Center before moving into the Pantages Theatre."

My eyes widen. The Staples Center is enormous. The Pantages is beautiful—it's where Robert and Jeff took me to see *Wicked* for my twenty-first birthday. Having a show begin to travel is an unquestionable sign of success. "Is Robert losing his mind?"

Jeff smiles, and it's the smile he saves only for his husband, the one that makes me ache with how happy they are. He looks younger, more carefree. "He is. He wanted to tell you about the offer, but I asked to speak to you first."

"Is there any particular reason why, or—" I stop, putting the pieces together myself. My stomach drops like a brick from the sky. "*Oh.*"

Jeff licks his lips nervously. "Right. If Robert and Ramón go to open the show there, Calvin has agreed to go, too."

Well, I guess I know now why Calvin called me this week. We'd better rush this annulment along; it's already June. The clock's a-ticking.

"Are *you* going to L.A.?" I ask.

"I'll go out as much as I can . . ." He smiles a little helplessly, and I'm sure he's as torn as I am about this. "I can't exactly work from the West Coast. It should only be ten months or so."

There's an odd consolation in that, at least. "And are you . . . asking my permission?"

"I wouldn't say that, but we did both think you should be consulted. You're the reason it was possible in the first place."

I hold up my hands in front of me. "I don't have any say in this, and even if I did, I'd tell them they're both crazy if they pass this up." It's amazing that I sound so calm because it feels like a fault line has just cracked my chest in two. "Tell Bobert I'll be at the opening show, and I'll be the loudest one cheering."

- - - -

"I can't believe that's what you're wearing." Davis looks at me, and then returns to his perusal of the minibar on his side of the car. My brother's beard is at Full Lumberjack, though he does look pretty great in his tux.

I smooth down the delicate black lace of my skirt. "Jeff picked it out. He said I have to look better for this party than I've ever looked in my life."

Our eyes meet again, and Davis gives a skeptical little shrug. "That's asking a lot out of a dress."

"Ha. Ha." I move my wineglass away when he attempts to refill it. Jeff sent a car to pick us up and I'm so nervous that if I don't slow down on the sauce, the chances of Appalland making an appearance tonight will be one hundred percent.

Sitting back in his seat, Davis cracks open a Red Bull from the minibar and pins me with a confused look. "Doesn't that mean something, though? You didn't spend two hours blow-drying and curling your hair because you hate him."

"Of course I don't hate him, but I don't want to look terrible when he shows up with his new girlfriend. I need to even the playing field a little. Rack up the team or whatever it is."

Davis swallows a long gulp, and then belches. "You are never allowed to use a sports analogy again."

"What I mean," I say, "is that I'm in a good place, and I don't want to forget all the awesome things that are happening just because I'm so sad that my fake marriage ended."

He looks up from the sleeve of cookies he's currently inhaling and raises a fist in solidarity. "This is your fight song."

"Excuse you, I'm simply being *positive*." We both look up as the car slows to a stop. I look out the window and see that we're in front of the restaurant. "Is it too late to turn around? I don't want to do this."

"Be positive, remember?" Davis slides across the leather seat and steps out once the door is open, reaching to take my hand. "You look beautiful. Shut up."

I smile up at him just as a camera goes off, one of many behind a velvet rope on either side of the entrance. A blue carpet leads the way to the door and I can hear the music before we've even stepped inside, the familiar notes of Calvin's guitar immortalized on the cast recording and filtering out of the ballroom.

It's the cocktail hour Jeff has planned before the big L.A. announcement, and the restaurant is a hive of chatter and movement. A chandelier hangs like a constellation in the center of the room; waitstaff wind their way through a sea of people in black tie.

It's telling that my eyes don't immediately search out the two people who should be my lifelines here—Robert and Jeff—but land directly on Calvin.

Our eyes meet, and a heavy weight falls from my chest to the ground. Half of his mouth turns up in a tentative smile before it straightens again, unsure.

"That's him?" Davis asks in my ear.

"That's him."

"I expected red hair."

"Shut *up*, Davis."

"Maybe a green top hat."

I elbow him roughly in the side. "If you embarrass me, I will cut your balls off and bury them."

My brother snickers in my ear. Nearly everyone here tonight knows the history between me and Calvin—the cast and crew are mingling everywhere, and I caught a quick glimpse of Brian when I first walked in; I am positive he's eating this up like cake. There are countless people in this room who have been obviously salivating for this awkward public reunion; it feels like the force of a hundred invisible hands is pressing on my lower back, urging me over to talk to my soon-to-be ex-husband.

Davis, suave as ever, presses a cold glass of something into my hand and then smacks my butt so hard I jump. "Go on," he says. "I'm right behind you."

I smooth the skirt back down over my ass, glaring at my brother. I'm aware that Calvin is watching all this from across the room. With one more tug at the hem of my dress, I make my way over to him and his slow-growing smile.

Sweet Christ on a cupcake, he looks good. He needs a haircut—but I like the wild russet thickness of it falling over his forehead. His skin is tanner from the early-summer sun, and his smile nudges awake a little flutter in my stomach.

I can imagine the hard curve of his shoulder beneath his suit, the way his stomach feels against my palm and how it spasms when I slide lower, taking the perfect heat of him in my hand.

Wow. How quickly my brain brands myself all over him, the minute I see him.

Mine, it says. *Reclaim.*

"Holland." Calvin steps closer, pressing his lips to my cheek. "Hey."

"Hi." My heart is vaulting up into my throat, kicking wildly.

He gives me another long once-over. "You look . . . *beautiful.*"

"Thanks. So do you."

He laughs through a full, openmouthed smile. "Why, thank you."

Two months without seeing each other and a good opener might be "Congratulations on the L.A. move," or something as simple as "How are you?"

Perhaps I could even introduce him to my brother, standing at my side.

But what do I actually do? I look around us, and ask indelicately, "Where's Natalie?"

Calvin's smile fades, and confusion replaces the sweet happiness that had been there. His dark brows pull in. "What?"

"I thought she'd be here with you tonight," I say, shifting on my feet, looking around us again briefly.

Davis groans, forgoing the introduction for now and immediately peeling away to the left.

Calvin studies me for a quiet breath. "Sorry." He blinks up at Davis's disappearing form and then back to me. "I don't understand. You thought I'd bring *Natalie* tonight?"

"Well . . . yeah."

Is he confused because he doesn't realize I saw the photo of them together? Or is he aware how awkward it would have been to have her here, and bewildered why I'd think he'd put us all in that situation?

He squints as if he's trying to puzzle this out. "I thought we talked about this," he says quietly. "I didn't realize Natalie was still an issue for you. I assumed we—"

"I saw the photos of you together," I explain quickly. I don't want to make him explain any more than he has to—I don't want details. But I owe it to myself to be honest with him, too. "I was sort of gutted when I saw them just before we were going to have dinner. I wish you'd told me."

"*Told* you? I don't . . ." Calvin's frown deepens and he shakes his head once. "What photos?"

"Calvin." I close my eyes, suddenly feeling sick and wishing we hadn't tried to clear this up tonight. "Don't."

He steps closer, wrapping a warm hand around my upper arm. "Holland, I don't know what photos you're talking about."

When I look up, I can tell from his face that he's being sincere, and of course he hasn't seen them. He's never on Twitter, he never reads gossip sites. I pull out my phone, finding it easily, where it's still open in my browser.

I am excellent at torturing myself.

Calvin reaches for my phone, but the microphone squawks jarringly from the front of the room and Jeff leans in, letting out a blasting "Is this thing on?"

Around us, everyone laughs at the volume and Jeff's comical reaction, and the tension between Calvin and me is sliced down the middle. At his side, I carefully shift back, stepping away and out of his line of sight. I look for Davis, but he's all the way on the other side of the room, standing with one of Robert's old friends from Des Moines whom Jeff flew out for the party.

"I'm sure everyone in this room knows Robert, but many of you may not know me," Jeff begins.

There are a few shouts of loving protest at this, but Jeff smiles, leaning in. "I'm Jeff, Robert Okai's husband."

Cheers erupt, and I clap limply along, feeling numb. I want to revel in all this adulation for Robert, but the moment has such a strange flatness to it, as if I'm watching it from a distance.

"I want to thank you all for coming tonight to celebrate Robert's birthday, to celebrate his award, and to celebrate the news that we have to share." Jeff looks across the room at his husband. "I am the luckiest man to have the life that I do, and I couldn't do any of it without you, honey."

Robert comes forward to thundering applause, kissing Jeff before taking the microphone. "Writing *Possessed* was a bit like *being* possessed," he begins, and people laugh knowingly. The story of Robert virtually not sleeping for a month while he composed it is legendary. "But the story of the present incarnation of *Possessed* is really something. Nearly everyone knows this by now, but several months ago, we were down a lead musician, facing the incoming brilliance of Ramón Martín, and I was struggling to figure out what direction to take this production. I worried I was too close to it, worried that it would somehow grow stale over time." He looks up and finds me, almost immediately. "My niece Holland dragged me to the subway station, where a young, Juilliard-trained guitarist was performing."

The party erupts again, and Calvin turns to meet my eyes. His are tight and searching, but they're quickly torn from my face when Robert says, "Come on up here, Calvin."

The tightness gives way to a reluctant smile as people make room for him to move to the front and join Robert. I feel swallowed by the crowd as it closes back in, hiding the path on the floor connecting me to Calvin.

Robert continues, recounting how Calvin came in, how he blew them away. He skips over the immigration issue and moves directly to the moment Ramón and Calvin played together, bringing Ramón to the front of the room, too. Robert talks about their first performance, and how very soon a high-pitched mania would greet them outside the theater after each show.

He's launching into his announcement about opening the L.A. performance with the two of them when I feel someone step up beside me.

"I'm sure this is hard for you."

I look over at Brian as he lifts his chin toward Calvin, and feel my cheeks heat. He's staring straight ahead, jaw tight. We've knocked heads so many times and it all just feels pointless now.

"Are you seriously choosing this moment to rub my nose in it?"

He meets my eyes, and a weird discomfort works its way

through me. I've never held eye contact with him for so long; I realize what strangers we are that I wouldn't have been able to name his eye color until now. "I'm not making a dig," he says quietly. "I'm sure it sucks that Robert is moving to L.A., and I'm sure it sucks to see Calvin with someone else."

I stare at him, confused.

"You did something for the production—it was ungodly stupid, of course, but you did it for the right reasons." His eyebrows pull down. "And now you're here hurting. I'm just saying, human to human, I'm sorry."

"Excuse me," I mumble, turning because I'm worried I'm going to start crying. I push carefully through the crowd and find a side door into an empty hallway connecting the banquet rooms. The floor is marble; my heels click quickly down to the end, where I lean against a door to the stairwell, breathing in and out.

I want to escape to my apartment, but Davis has my coat check ticket, and Calvin is still holding my phone.

Back down the hall, the side door opens again. The sound of surprised voices and riotous applause spills out; I assume Robert has just mentioned L.A.

But the cacophony dims back to a lull when the door closes with a heavy click.

Footsteps approach, steady and measured, and a quiet Irish accent comes from behind me. "Holland."

"Go back in there," I tell him, working to sound steady. I don't want to do this on a night that is supposed to be about Robert. "They aren't done with the announcement yet."

"They've just finished." He pauses, and I hear his heavy

exhale. "I saw you leave, and it's just . . . I'm confused about what happened back there."

Unable to face him yet, I swallow, trying to clear the thickness from my throat. "Which part?"

"The part where you saw me photographed with Natalie?" From behind me, his voice is gentle: "Did you look at it?"

What? "Of course I did. Obsessively."

"Are you sure?"

Finally, I turn around, confused. His expression softens when he sees that I'm a crying mess, and he reaches up, carefully moving his thumb across my cheek.

"Look again."

Sniffing, I do what he says, entering my passcode and looking at the photo I've already seen a hundred times now.

He bites his lip, waiting for me to understand before letting out a small laugh. "Natalie Nguyen." Calvin taps the screen, and now his eyes are smiling. "You think I'm dating Natalie *Nguyen?*"

"*Everyone* thinks that. You . . . have been seen together a couple times and you have your arm around her." I lick my lips, anxious that I'm missing something here. "That's what *Entertainment Weekly* said."

"I've seen her at a few theater events. This photo was at Ramón's premiere, right?" I nod. He points to the edge of the photo, where I can now make out a sliver of a sleeve. "I think this photo cropped out Ramón so it looks like it's just me and Natalie. Do you know how many photos I took that night?"

I wipe my nose. "No."

"Probably five thousand." He zooms in on the picture to an

extreme close-up of his hand before giving it back to me. It's my least favorite part of the photo—Calvin's hand is wrapped fully around her waist—and it takes me a second to realize what he's showing me: the glint of a ring on his finger.

My eyes fly down to his hand at his side, here in front of me. He's still wearing it.

"Natalie *Edgerton* is a friend of Mark's," he explains, and my stomach drops out in realization. "He set us up months ago, but then I got married, and fell in love—admittedly in that order. I never replied to her text from that day, by the way."

I groan into my hands. "Oh, my God."

"Natalie *Nguyen* is an actress with a small role in Ramón's film." Calvin pries my hands away and holds them in his. "Even if I was at all interested in seeing other women—which I'm not—do you really think she's the one who was calling an unemployed street musician for a date all those months ago?"

All motion has come to a halt in my brain. I want to throw myself against the wall repeatedly, until I'm unconscious and can forget this ever happened. "Maybe not."

He reaches up with one hand to wipe beneath my eye. "I don't have a girlfriend, Holland. I've got a *wife*, in case you've forgotten."

"I know, but—"

"Though she hasn't texted, hasn't rung me back, and hasn't wanted to see me."

At his tone, I glance up to his face, for the first time hearing past my own anxiety and hurt. In the stark hallway light, he looks devastated.

"You told me you loved me," he reminds me. "And I told

you I'd wait. But it's been painful wondering more and more frequently whether you'll ever ask me to come home." He ducks a little to hold my gaze. "We were going to have dinner, and you canceled last minute."

"I was working on myself, and getting past Amanda, and all of the uncertainty that started building between us," I admit. "And when I thought I was ready to see you . . . I saw the photo."

"So why not call?" he asks. "Just to ask me about it? Or yell at me? Anything. If I did have a girlfriend that would still be something to discuss, logistically, given that we're *married*, wouldn't it?"

I press my hands to my face, mumbling, "I don't know" from behind them.

Calvin gently pries my hands away again. "If I went off with someone else, wouldn't you be angry?"

"Yes. Furious."

"As would I. I would be homicidal if you were with another bloke. So why not let me have it? I could have saved you so many days of worrying about this."

I look up at him. "I wasn't actually sure a conversation about it would go that way."

"You mean, you weren't sure I still loved you after only two months apart? What kind of heart do you think lives inside here?" He presses our joined hands to his chest. "I *miss* you."

It feels like a fist curls around my lungs when he says this in present tense. "It made more sense in some ways to think you were playing along."

"That I—?" He blinks away, scowling. "Did you not read

your own essay? You act as though all this time you were simply going along with something. What you did for me was astounding, and who you are—calm, and assured, and sexy, and carefully creative . . . I am absolutely *smashed* in love with you."

I bite my lower lip savagely, looking back and forth at his eyes, trying to find the act. He has no reason to lie anymore. His hands come up, framing my face, and my heart pushes painfully against my breastbone, clawing toward him.

A breath away from me, and his eyes are still open. "So? Can I kiss my bride?"

- - - -

A hallway kiss turns into a full-on hallway makeout session, and I consider it a small miracle that no one finds us out here, with me pressed to the wall, one leg around Calvin's hips. In his touch, I can tell that he was telling the truth about our time apart being painful: against me, he's shaking, nearly frantic.

We go back into the party hand in hand. He gets me a wine, gets himself a beer, and we dance, pressed so close together I can feel what it does to him. When he apologizes with a quiet laugh, I look up, and we grin in unison at the shared, unspoken promise of the insane sex we are going to have later tonight.

I'm hoping neither of us can walk straight tomorrow.

My thoughts clean up a little when I introduce Calvin to Davis. Jeff and I watch in awe as the two men seem to strike up an immediate bromance centered on home-brewed beer and rugby.

With the two of them bent together, frantically discussing the Milwaukee microbrewery scene, Jeff pulls me aside, proudly spinning me around the room to some Sinatra.

Calvin breaks in a few minutes later, smiling in thanks to Jeff and pulling me close again.

"You disappeared."

"You and Davis were lost to beer. I was standing nearby like a floor lamp."

He laughs, pressing his lips to my jaw. When my hands slip up the back of his neck and into his hair, he groans quietly. "You feel so good against me. I'm so relieved, I could fall over."

"I think one more hour, then we can justify leaving."

He smiles down at me. "I took the liberty of telling Davis he was staying at the uncles' tonight."

I close my eyes and imagine being alone with him later, undressing him and kissing every bit of smooth, exposed skin. I imagine the feel of the mattress at my back, the view of him falling over me, moving down my body, mouth open and wet.

I can practically feel the electricity of his first kiss between my legs, the clamp of his hands around my thighs, and the weight of him when he moves back up over me.

"What are you thinking about?" His lips move against my earlobe.

"Being home with you later."

"You're thinking about fucking me right now?"

I look up at him, with a joke on the tip of my tongue, but it dissolves away at the fever in his gaze. "Yeah." I stretch, kissing him in a slow slide of my mouth over his. "Specifically about your mouth and how it feels to have you on top of me."

"You're not sleeping," he warns, and I laugh until a wave of relief hits me, so enormous that I wrap my arms around his neck, pressing my cheek to his.

When the song ends, he leads me back over to my brother and the bar. I know people are watching us, but I no longer feel like they're wondering what Calvin is doing with me. With his octopus hands all over me, and the way Davis is making us both double over in laughter, I feel for the first time like our love looks as easy and genuine from the outside as it feels from the inside.

In tiny stolen moments, my husband pulls me into dark corners for a kiss, or down onto his lap on a couch. Between sips of our drinks and conversation with people around us, we volley a hundred questions back and forth.

Should we have another wedding? A real one?

When should we go visit my family?

Are we both moving temporarily to L.A.?

And most important: I won the meat bet, so . . . when is he officially taking my last name?

We can debate that one for a while. Thankfully, we're not cramming to convince anyone else anymore. We have time.

acknowledgments

After our beloved feminist manifesto-romp of *Dating You / Hating You*, and the tender heartswell of *Autoboyography*, writing *Roomies* was pure, shameless *fun*. Holland and Calvin's story was a much enjoyed return to our romance roots, and we love nothing more than a story set in NYC!

So thank you, Adam Wilson, for saying yes when a new story idea rolls out of our collective imagination, and for always helping us turn the first draft of madness into an actual book. Our agent, Holly Root, is a star, and without her we would be blind (and contractless). To our ever-supportive publisher, thank you: Carolyn Reidy, Louise Burke (happy retirement!), Jen Bergstrom, and Paul O'Halloran, and the hardest-working sales team in publishing. Publicity badass report: Kristin "Precious" Dwyer is the calm to our crazy, the Nutella to our waffle, the punctuation to our sentence; and Teresa Dooley is the kind of stellar-on-the-ball that things are done before we even think to ask about them. Thank you, too, to the Gallery marketing group: Liz Psaltis, Diana Velasquez, Abby Zidle, and Mackenzie Hickey. Our covers are always phenomenal—thank you, Lisa and John of the Mustache.

Our prereader editorial lifesavers are Erin Service and Marion Archer. Without you, this book would still not have an ending. Thanks, as ever, for the honest critique and constant support! Thank you, Blane Mall for Irish'ing up our Irishman, and to Jonathan Root for help with the Broadway details; any mistakes are ours alone.

And to all of our readers out there, thank you for coming along for each one of these adventures. We love you all more than we can possibly say.

xoxo

Christina & Lo